UNSTOLEN

Wendy Jean lives on the west coast of
Canada with her British partner. She holds
a Bachelor of Arts degree in English, has
worked as a journalist and taught English
as a second language in Asia.
This is her first novel.

WENDY JEAN
UNSTOLEN

PAN BOOKS

First published 2006 by Pan Books
an imprint of Pan Macmillan Ltd
Pan Macmillan, 20 New Wharf Road, London N1 9RR
Basingstoke and Oxford
Associated companies throughout the world
www.macmillan.com

ISBN-13: 978-0-330-44518-4
ISBN-10: 0-330-44518-9

Copyright © Wendy Jean 2006

The right of Wendy Jean to be identified as the
author of this work has been asserted by her in accordance
with the Copyright, Designs and Patents Act 1988.

All rights reserved. No part of this publication may be
reproduced, stored in or introduced into a retrieval system, or
transmitted, in any form, or by any means (electronic, mechanical,
photocopying, recording or otherwise) without the prior written
permission of the publisher. Any person who does any unauthorized
act in relation to this publication may be liable to criminal
prosecution and civil claims for damages.

9 8 7 6 5 4 3 2

A CIP catalogue record for this book is available from
the British Library.

Typeset by SetSystems Ltd, Saffron Waldon, Essex
Printed and bound in Great Britain by
Mackays of Chatham, Chatham, Kent

This book is sold subject to the condition that it shall not,
by way of trade or otherwise, be lent, re-sold, hired out,
or otherwise circulated without the publisher's prior consent
in any form of binding or cover other than that in which
it is published and without a similar condition including this
condition being imposed on the subsequent purchaser.

Acknowledgements

There are many people to thank, the first of whom is Maria Rejt for her outstanding encouragement, kindness and belief in *Unstolen*

To the people of Macmillan who have offered their expertise and hard work

My children for their love and inspiration

Henry for teaching me to dream big

Sheri for being proud of me and bravely committing to the duties of best friend

Jean for being the kind of mother who allowed me to find my own way

Catherine and family for generously offering up one of your most precious memories while giving me a place to be

Tova for always being there

Finally, Caleb for pointing me in the right direction, and without whom I would truly be lost.

PART 1

Chapter One

2002

On Tuesday, October 15th, somewhere around five-thirty p.m., my mother struck Thomas Randal Freeman across the back of the head with an iron fire poker as he sat on a bar stool at his kitchen counter watching a rerun of *Seinfeld* on his fourteen-inch colour TV.

A blaring tube, a mouth full of peanut-butter-jelly toast, and ginger hairs clinging to his sticky fingers revealed that Mama must have had a clear first shot. Absorbed in his show, mindlessly champing, stroking the tabby on his lap, nothing less than a screaming bout of intuition would have prompted her victim to sense Mama advancing from behind.

TRF had been to Prince's Grocer forty minutes before the blow that sent him crashing to his kitchen floor. There he bought three tins of Nine Lives prime grill with beef, two packs of Marlboro 100s, one quart of low-fat milk and a twenty-five-foot roll of duct tape.

Mama was also in Prince's Grocer at the time. She had left my townhouse ten minutes previously to pick up some milk for the scalloped potatoes we were to eat for dinner that night. That was the problem with being a working single parent, especially now that my son, Ryan, was four. I could pack his mid-morning snack, dress us both, deliver him to nursery and myself to work on time, squeeze in three calls home during the day, race to the bank on my lunch hour to pay a few bills – and then forget to buy milk on the way home.

Though I had offered to drive, Mama insisted on walking to the store. The walk would do her good, she told me. She said by the time I had Ryan dressed and buckled up in his car seat she'd be there.

She had a good point. The temperature had dropped to the low fifties for the last couple of nights and Ryan would have needed socks, shoes, sweater and jacket just to get him out of the door. I would have had to stop peeling potatoes. Put dinner on hold. Besides, when I poked my head into the living room where I had left Ryan watching *Monsters, Inc.* he was sound asleep in his burgundy bean-bag chair, head tilted upwards, mouth gaping. And it's not like it was dark. I didn't feel bad sending Mama three short blocks to the store. She had been to Prince's plenty of times before with Ryan on the occasions she bussed down from Dartmouth, a 153-mile cross-state journey to my home in Helena, Montana, to visit.

The thing is that Lizzy Potter, a dime-eyed tubby redhead who has worked the evening shift at Prince's from three p.m. to nine p.m. four days a week for the last three years, said it wasn't Thomas Randal Freeman who was acting strange that afternoon. She said it was Mama.

According to Lizzy's testimony Mama had approached the checkout counter, slump-jawed, berry-cheeked, pucker-browed, clutching a two-gallon plastic jug of milk. After Lizzy rang Mama's purchase into the till and asked for $2.19 Mama shook her head and left the store empty-handed in somewhat of a daze.

'At first I thought she just didn't have enough money to pay,' Lizzy told the police. 'But the strange thing was she didn't even look in her purse. Not once, like she had no intention of buying the milk. Just kept looking at the door the whole time.'

Mama had made an impression on Lizzy, to be sure. So much so that Lizzy described her perfectly from the waves in her shoulder-length sandy-grey hair to the tan leather loafers on her feet. TRF, on the other hand, had slipped by as so utterly unremarkable that all Lizzy could recall besides his average build and bland Caucasian face was the fact that his purchases had included the tape. When the police asked Lizzy if she thought it was a bit strange that he had bought duct tape her voice raised a defensive octave as though they were accusing her of something.

'Of course not,' she reported. 'A lot of people buy duct tape, especially now after 9/11. Why, we've had so many people buying duct tape we've had to make a few special orders.'

Unfortunately she was right about that. It had become a household staple since President Bush suggested we all have plenty on hand to secure us against terror attacks.

So Mama was the weirdo. Mama was the one acting strange that late afternoon at the store, not psychotic serial child-killer Thomas Randal Freeman. He was every Caucasian male who had ever walked through the doors of Prince's, so utterly normal as to be deemed unmemorable, his appearance wielding the power of a smudge on a grimy wall.

The question was how did Mama know for certain, certain enough to strike later with fatal accuracy, the man she saw reaching into the refrigerator possibly at the exact moment she did? (Did their fingers brush? Did their eyes meet?)

A picture; that's how.

Not a photograph or a video clip, but an artist's rendering. I worked as a police artist and I had drawn a picture from the coaxed memory of five-year-old Amy Wetherall. It was a drawing Mama had seen the night before the incident. It was a drawing I hadn't yet released to the police, had left carelessly on a chest in the spare bedroom in a manila envelope. The bedroom Mama slept in when she stayed with us.

It hadn't been released due to my uncertainty, my lack of trust in the memory. It was a drawing that might well not have been released at all but, as it turned out, was accurate enough to convince my mother one hundred per cent that the man she saw in the store was the same man who had taken Amy's brother, Aaron. Accurate enough to have her follow TRF from Prince's Grocer five blocks west to Fairbourne Street in the middle-class Waylane district. To watch him from a side window, enter his home through an unlocked front door fifteen minutes later and bludgeon him to death with his own iron poker.

All of this was not particularly farfetched or insane behaviour on Mama's part. Given her certainty of the identity of the suspect, the time allotted to make the decision to follow him, the fact that she spotted an opportunity to take action, it almost made sense, although she could have made other choices at that point. She knew where he lived, was sure it was the right man. She could have walked away, called 911, called me. But what she did next was understandable, inevitable even, given Mama's past. How she crept stealthily into his house while his TV volume button was turned too high for him to hear her. How she picked up the fire poker to protect herself, how she approached him from behind while he stroked his cat, bit into his toast, possibly chuckled at the antics of Kramer. None of this was what you'd call unimaginable. What was, however, off-the-charts-incredible, give-your-head-a-rattle behaviour was that Mama didn't stop at the first or second or even the third blow to TRF's skull. That Mama, entering into some trance-like state, managed to turn his head into so much blender mush, stopping only when the adrenaline pumping through her veins failed to keep enough strength in her arms to enable her to lift the poker any longer.

It was explained to me by one of the young officers at the scene. Namely that the strength required to accomplish the extent of damage done to TRF's head would have challenged a top bodybuilder. Mama, a 55 year old weighing in at just over one hundred pounds who has never lifted a dumbbell in her life, was invincible during those moments. She had become the mother of legend who lifts the school bus single-handedly to save her child who is crushed under it.

How many blows were there? Over fifty to be sure. Not only to the head, but to the neck, back and buttocks although the skull weathered the worst. And she had then forgotten everything because her actions were to her as incomprehensible as her strength.

While Mama didn't remember anything about the incident she had enough awareness once her energy was depleted to walk over the blood-speckled floor and reach a trembling hand to a white push-button wall phone, to press the numbers 9-1-1 and recite to the receiving operator the exact address and a brief description of the pulverized body at her feet. When poice officers arrived Mama was facing the living-room door perched motionless on the very bar stool she had knocked TRF from, legs crossed, fingers tightly laced, eyes staring blankly into the space ahead of her. She didn't seem to hear the loud thud at the door, the raised voices calling her. What appeared to have start-led Mama awake was the sight of four stupefied police officers standing directly over the shattered corpse.

Sometimes being a single parent feels like I'm on an aeroplane and just as I begin to get involved in the on-flight movie I'm jolted back into reality.

So Mama's visits were more than appreciated these days. They felt necessary. She consistently hinted that Ryan belonged in Dartmouth with her, at least until I was married, until Will and I could both get it together with our careers, until Ryan was in school full time or all of the above. But I wanted Ryan home with me now. It had been heartbreaking during college, too hard without him. I was able to do most of my criminal justice degree online, but in my last year hands-on experience was necessary, so off I went to Carroll College. I recall those unbearable weekend visits home, travelling two-and-a-half hours from Helena to Dart-mouth, when he would either hide or ignore me, pretend he didn't know me at all. Mama said it was a natural reaction and would be forgotten once we settled down together in Helena, and she was right – about Ryan that is. I'm the one who will never forget. I'm the one scarred for life.

It was a complete surprise when Mama's partner, Richard, came up with a job for me immediately after graduation: a good job with decent pay and room to grow. I had been thinking I could relax for a year, be with Ryan, Mama and Richard. Be a family again. It was all happening so soon, but how could I say no to the exact job I'd been schooled for? Victim aide police sketch artist, to be precise. It was everything Mama had dreamed for me, and besides, Will was in Helena living on campus at the University of Montana doing his first year of an undergrad degree in business technology. I could see my boyfriend as much as I liked, rent a townhouse with a small yard, enrol Ryan in preschool, buy myself that Toyota Corolla I'd always wanted. I was the oldest, most grown-up nineteen year old on the planet . . .

This whole thing might not have happened at all had Ryan not conked out in his bean-bag chair during the *Monsters, Inc.* video. Had he been awake he would surely not have allowed my mother even to think about going to the store without him, and she, who has never denied him a thing in his whole life, would surely have been delighted to have his company. Mama might not have even been in the store at the same time as TRF had Ryan accompanied her. Walking anywhere with Ryan always took twice as long as when you were alone. Even if she had made it to the corner grocery store in time, even if my mother had noticed TRF, recognized him from the drawing, it would have been too risky to follow him home with Ryan chattering and singing the whole way there. And if she was really desperate and she did follow him with Ryan, my mother would then have scurried to the nearest phone to report the address, no more.

But Ryan did fall asleep during *Monsters, Inc.* because he'd been awake since six a.m. and I wanted him out of the kitchen so that Mama and I could plan dinner. And it was only after Mama and I had peeled a few potatoes that I realized there was only enough milk in the carton for a cup of coffee. So Mama did go to the store alone, she did recognize TRF, she did follow him home and she did enter his house and proceed to smash the devil back to hell.

Chapter Two

1989

We are a family with a hole blown through it, its edges tattered and flapping. It is a hole that must remain gaping lest my brother surface, the act of him walking through the only means of closure. My childhood memories consist of my mother preparing and waiting patiently next to that hole while my father and I tread different paths around it.

I am slipping down the wooden stairs that lead to the kitchen. It is early morning and I have just climbed out of bed. I am six years old. I know this because today is my brother Michael's tenth birthday.

I also know our house is old because everything creaks: stairs, floors, cupboards, doors, particularly now at the beginning of summer. Pipes gurgle like mumbled voices. I can hear my parents' words through the heating vent in my upstairs bedroom when they are all the way downstairs in the living room. I love our house. Its sounds are as comforting as a bedtime story.

I am wearing pyjamas: the kind with the feet in them that have tacky material on the bottom to save me from falling down the steps. They are pink, furry and a little too warm.

From the middle step I can see a block of golden-pink light on the floor that juts into the hall from the adjoining laundry-room window. When I reach the bottom step balloons appear, taped by their knotted necks along the door's frame that leads to the kitchen. They are baby blue and white and wave hypnotically in some enchanting drift of air. There are matching blue and white streamers: long thin ribbons that curl like my ringlets.

When I peek into the kitchen a gentle wave of warm sweetness rolls over me, impels me forwards. I feel like a cartoon cat floating dreamily, a stream of aroma lifting my body, stretching my nose forwards. Angel-food cake. My brother's favourite.

Mama is at the counter with a glass mixing bowl brimming with snowy hills of icing sugar. I watch from the doorway as she drenches and flattens the mounds with droplets of milk from a measuring cup. Next she cranks a metal beater into a buzzing, powdery flurry of action. It rattles and clanks against the glass. She sees me as I enter, and smiles.

'Morning, hon.' She sings her usual greeting over the knocking, whirring din.

Across the kitchen table there is wrapping paper spread wide from its tube weighted by unbreakable glasses on its corners. I was with Mama when she bought these tumblers from the hardware store downtown. There was a handsome man in the kitchenware department demonstrating their durability by using them to hammer thin nails into a plank of wood. Mama bought a whole set after she saw that, but it turns out they are breakable after all; when Mama accidentally dropped one on the cement floor of her work room it broke into a million pieces. I didn't know something could break like that. The pieces weren't even sharp. The glass transformed into tiny crystal marbles. Mama let me hold some because they wouldn't cut my skin. They were so beautiful, glistening like gems in my palm, that Mama kept them. She says she'll use them some day for her furniture creations. They now sit on one of her work-room shelves in a bright yellow margarine container.

Mama's cheeks are pink from the oven heat and the exertion of vigorous whipping. I climb onto a stool and watch the powdery sugar miraculously transform into gooey snow-capped peaks. I wait with bone-to-dog anticipation knowing the creamy blades of the beater will soon be mine to lick.

My tacit expectancy is interrupted by a sudden series of raps. Mama and I can see the round, grinning face of our neighbour Mrs Brown peering through the small square of glass at the back door. I am closest so I run to open it. Mrs Brown is wearing the same delicately flowered summer dress I've seen her wear dozens of times since the weather warmed up. At first she seems surprised, then delighted, as her eyes spring from me to our kitchen of sweetness.

'Happy birthday, Bethany!' she squeals, brushing my shoulder warmly. I smile up at her.

'Oh it's not my birthday, Mrs Brown. It's Michael's.'

You'd think I'd kicked her right in the privates by the way her face changes, turns into a scowling stone. She leans down into my face and hisses. 'That's not funny, little missy.'

I turn to look for Mama, whose silence has become conspicuous. I see her stunned face, a deer caught in the glare of headlights, a clear wordless admission of shame.

Mama releases the beater in the bowl of icing then quickly leaves the room and I am stranded with Mrs Brown. I notice the cloaked basket in her hand for the first time. She passes it to me and I lift the square of white linen to investigate. There are cookies of various shapes nestling in a check cloth.

'Are these for Michael's party, too?' I ask. But she doesn't answer. Mrs Brown just pats the top of my head and walks away.

Chapter Three

2002

Lesson number one at the Helena Police Department: it was practically impossible to get an all-male veteran staff to take seriously anything a nineteen-year-old female grad had to say.

This I understood to be as much a part of the law as stopping at red lights. I appreciated I had a long way to go before earning their respect, but I also knew that about this particular point I was right. So I whined and pleaded and screamed and cried and hid the photo book and was eventually called into Police Chief Harrison Wathy's office.

'What in the devil is going on, Miss Fisher? I've been told the photo book has been misplaced.' The chief was leaning into his desk, both elbows pressing down against a clutter of loose papers. His ruddy, angular face was wearily serious, eyebrows like tepees.

'Yes, sir,' I said, standing before him like a child in the principal's office ready to justify my rebellious actions.

'Do you know where the photos are, Miss Fisher?'

'Yes, sir,' I repeated. Neither his nor my sober expression changed.

'Well, would you mind putting them back?'

'Yes, sir,' I said again. 'I would.'

'You would what?'

'I'd mind putting them back, sir.'

'Miss Fisher.' The chief moaned. 'Do you like your job here at HPD?'

'Oh yes, sir. I love my job here very much, which is why I would mind putting those photos back and showing them to victims of crime before their own memories have had a chance to surface. With all due respect, sir, you might as well show the victims clown shots.'

The chief leaned into his winged office chair, and released an exasperated sigh.

'Miss Fisher, we here at HPD have been using that very system of photo aides, successfully I might add, to jog the memory of victims of crime from a time before you were born.'

'That's exactly my point. Sir, if I may tell you a story.'

The chief had four kids of his own – all boys – so I took advantage of his soft spot for girls whenever possible.

'A story? You think I have time for a . . .'

'There was this little girl, see, and she watched her mother cook a rump roast.'

This soft spot of his went deeper than gender. None of his grown boys had followed in his footsteps. They seemed to have leaned as far away from police business as possible.

'Miss Fisher, I am not in the mood for an anecdotal—'

'And she asked her mother why she always cut the end of the rump roast off before she put it in the roasting pan.'

His eldest came out last year to announce his love of herbs and root vegetables and men. His youngest is an apprenticed carpenter, his middle two in college studying the arts.

'Miss Fisher, I have a lot of work to do.'

'And the mother said, "I don't know, honey. That's the way my mother did it. Maybe you should ask your grandmother."'

Not that the chief had confided any of this in me. He was much too professional for that, but these well-known facts had made their way around the station like an unpleasant smell.

'Can you please just find the missing photo book?'

'So the next time the girl saw her grandmother she asked her why she cut the end of the rump roast off before putting it into the roasting pan. And do you know what the grandmother said?'

So not only was I the daughter he never had, but I was doing the work he'd dreamed of for his boys.

'I couldn't begin to guess.'

'She said she didn't know, that her mother used to do it that way.'

'Please return the book to the exact place you found it.'

'So one day the girl visited the nursing home where her great-grandmother lived and she asked her, "Why do you cut the end of the rump roast off before you put it in the roasting pan?" And the great-grandmother said, "Oh, sweetie, I cut it off because my roasting pan was too small." '

Then I turned and walked out of the police chief's door, went directly to my office, pulled the photo book out from the bottom drawer of my desk and returned it to its original cupboard in full view of the chief and day staff. After lunch the chief called police officers and front-line workers together into the staff room to go over a few vitals.

'Don't forget to put your quarter in the tin if you drink coffee so Angela here can buy some more.'

The receptionist's forty-something face produced a knowing sparkle behind thick glasses.

'And I don't want to hear any more public complaints about police officers parking in pick-up zones while they run into Baked to Perfection for their morning muffin.' Abashed snickers all around.

'Oh and one more thing, let's give the Fisher kid a one-month try-out without the book. All crime victims will go directly to her without prior aid. We will continue or not based on results.' He directed his gaze

at me. 'And we'll see if the rump roast fits, so to speak.'
I couldn't help but beam.

Amy Wetherall came to me, hair like curly fries, a
tabula rasa, her icy traumatized stare transfixed on me.
Positioned directly in front of her I could tell the five
year old didn't see me, could tell she didn't see anything
but the blank screen she'd pulled down over her mind.
It was my job to ensure the images that eventually
flickered across it were accurately represented. She
came to me untainted, came to me first before the dicks
got hold of her, before they implanted a thousand
photographic images in her pristine memory. She was
the experiment to see if the rump roast fitted.

In the beginning Amy and I talked about everything. Anything but the man who walked into her
room in the middle of the night and took her brother
Aaron from the lower mattress of the bunk bed they
shared. During the first two weeks we played Scrabble,
drew pictures or made puzzles in my office. In the
following weeks I went to her house.

The Wetheralls lived in a three-bedroomed rancher
on the west side of the city not far from my town
home. Her young mother, Sharon, a grown-up version
of her daughter, looked on with a kind of silent hope
as Amy and I played with Barbies on the living-room
floor, talked about her favourite videos, smeared Cheese
Whiz over Ritz Crackers together in the kitchen. Finally
Amy invited me into her room, a place her mother had
told me she wasn't able to sleep in since the incident. I

asked her if we could play a card game on the bottom bunk but she refused, said it was her brother's bed. When I asked her if we could ask her brother if we could play on his bed, she snapped, 'He's not here.'

'Where is he?' I asked.

'He got tooken.'

'Tooken? By who? Who took your brother?'

'The fat man.'

'The fat man?'

'Yes, the ugly fat man.'

I doubted the ugly fat man was real. Anyone who took her brother was going to be ugly in her mind. The man who abducted her brother might have changed into an ugly fat man in her dreams. It was suspicious, but it was a start.

In the days to follow she changed her mind, told me her brother wouldn't mind us playing on his bed.

'How do you know?'

'Because he's not here so he won't mind.'

'What about the ugly fat man? Do you think he would mind?'

I didn't want to scare her but I did want her to start thinking and talking about him again.

'No,' she said.

'Why wouldn't he mind?' I asked.

'Because he's not here either. He's with my brother.'

'Where do you think they went?' I asked.

'I dunno,' she shrugged.

'Do you think he'll bring your brother back?'

'I dunno.'

This was all about Amy's time, however long it took, whenever the right trigger would pull bits out of her brain, synapses click into place, when it was safe to come out. But it was also about what this five year old could express and how much knowledge she had.

That's where preparation came in. I pulled out my bag of tricks, which included hundreds of wooden facial-feature shaped blocks to place on a face frame.

Amy learned the shape names including almond, oblong, rosebud, clover, crescent to complement the ones she knew already: square, circle, triangle, rect-angle. In essence we were building sophisticated Mr Potato Heads.

Amy and I played *What shape is it?* I'd hold up an almond shape then, after accolades to her for the right answer, I'd ask her if my eyes were almond shaped. We'd do the same for all my features and hers using a mirror. Never did I ask her about the ugly fat man. It would be she who would introduce him into the mix when she was ready.

Amy did not disappoint me. On an ordinary day while we were hunched over a game of *Go Fish* on her bedroom floor she began to unravel the mysteries of TRF's features. They came to her unsmudged, as clearly as if her small eyes had projected his image onto a wall . . .

Chapter Four

1990

Mama's in her favourite chair, the one in the living room next to the window that overlooks our front yard. It is a brightly flowered rocker with thick fanning arms. She's crocheting an afghan in various shades of blue. A yarn basket abloom with a jumble of blue balls is stationed at her feet. The circles of thread bobble and jerk every few seconds as she tugs for slack. The metre-and-a-half of finished product blankets her lower body. Her face is content and yet there is something in the wash of morning light that fades her. She hums as her fingers work. If you couldn't see her moving hands she could be a photograph, greying and dated.

I am cross-legged on the carpet near her socked feet. I am sorting my collection of stamps. Not the kind you lick and attach to envelopes but the kind you press into inkpads and display on paper. I have three inkpads: red, black and royal blue. I have twenty-six rubber stamps, some with simple shapes (a star, a heart), some with messages (*kiss me, my love*), but my best are the collection of penguins: cute, fat penguins all different but clearly of the same clan.

They do different things: dance, skate, swim. I have a singing penguin floating in a circle of musical notes, but my favourite is doing something quite un-extraordinary. She is reading. I imagine which book it is every time I see her. I can hear the words to *Cat in the Hat*, *Snow White*, or *Gulliver's Travels* in my head.

'I'm not crazy, you know,' says Mama.

If Daddy were here I would think she was address-ing him, but he's in the garage, where he goes to fiddle with the engine of our Volvo. No, it's just Mama and me here in the living room and this cool statement afloat between us. I look up. I see her face now gone serious like she's told me to clean up my room or some-thing. Her hands are motionless.

'I know,' I finally say. It seems like a long time ago that she said it.

'They'll try to tell you different,' she states.

'Who will, Mama?'

'The kids.'

My face contorts. Despite my efforts to understand she might as well be speaking Swahili.

'At school,' she says with an edge of impatience. 'Tomorrow at school. The first day is always the worst and you'll hear all sorts of things.'

'Like what?'

'Untrue things. Hurtful things.'

'I won't let them,' I say.

'They'll say your Mama's crazy.'

'I'll tell them you're not.'

'And they'll say Michael's not coming home.' Mama leans down closer to me, layers of crocheted blanket crinkling against the floor.

'But don't you believe any of it.' Her voice transforms into a harsh whisper as though she is confiding a dangerous truth. 'They don't know anything. Only we know the truth. Detective Adams says every day is a day closer to finding Michael. You must always remember that, and when he does come home, in our hearts and in our heads and in every way, we will be ready.'

I know this is true. I know that if Michael comes home at Christmas or on his birthday or at Easter then we will be ready. That there will be gifts and cake and chocolate bunnies for him and I know if he comes home on an ordinary day he will receive all those things he's missed out on.

Mama sits back in her armchair, resumes knotting lengths of yarn into Michael's blanket. Yes, if Michael walks in the door this very minute, we will be ready.

Chapter Five

Mother Murders Monster

My mother.

A monster murderer.

She had done nothing less in the eyes of the media than slay a dragon. Because of my mother public safety went up a hundred notches. In the span of twenty-four hours, the time it took for the daily headlines to hit the streets, the TV airwaves to reach the people, Mama's status went from murderess to heroine. Of course, it wasn't quite that simple. There was still the nasty little business of this ordinary woman smashing TRF's skull, grey matter stuck to walls thirteen feet away from the head it belonged inside, and let's not forget the inescapable fact that something inside her shut down and decided to deny it all.

After Mama was escorted from the scene into a squad car in handcuffs, what the police found in TRF's utility closet was a starved, bound (wrists, mouth, ankles), anally ravaged, four-year-old boy. Breathing. Alive.

He looked nothing like the plump, smiling Aaron Wetherall whose twinkling eyes reached out to the public on missing-children posters displayed on store windows and telephone poles throughout the city. He was a skeletal, ashen, pygmy version of himself when he was rushed to the emergency ward, where he would remain for five months and ascend steadily up the medical ladder from critical to steady to the miracle of good.

Because of Mama Aaron Wetherall would live, his broken body repaired, his crippled spirit revived through the glorious workings of love. Mama wasn't able to save the seven children whose bones and skulls were carefully unearthed from under TRF's basement floor and reassembled like some abominable jigsaw puzzle. Missing children dating back over a span of ten years. But what Mama did do was solve the mystery of their disappearance, close the door of hope for their families. Create resolution.

Richard and I watched through the two-way glass as officers McDowel and Dunny questioned Mama. She had been fingerprinted, photographed, stripped, medically examined and given an oversized navy prisoner's uniform to wear. By now Mama had to know something was very wrong; yet she didn't appear confused or frightened. She seemed serene, could have been sitting on a park bench, watching children play. Safely.

Freely. Maybe that's exactly where she was in her mind, watching children from a distance, knowing somewhere deep down that it was she who had saved them. Freed them.

Mama may not have remembered the details of what she'd done, but it was clear to me that she knew exactly what had taken place. She had murdered a monster, slain a dragon, demolished her own demons.

Her hands were clamped between her crossed legs, something I thought nothing of until she reached for the cup of water officer Dunny had offered her. She brought it to her lips, the liquid sloshing over the sides of the Styrofoam cup leaving dark streaks across the front of her Helena police issued garb. The actions of a drug addict in the stages of withdrawal.

'I'm sorry, I'm sorry,' she repeated, returning the half-empty cup to the table. 'My arms are so sore, so weak.'

It was I who had called Richard at home with the news of Mama's arrest from my place of employ after the chief had called me at home. The chief had asked me if Doris Fisher was my mother, reassured me she was OK, unharmed, but that I had better get down here, get a sitter for Ryan (thank God for Vivian next door) and talk to no one.

Awaiting Mama's return, I had already worried myself sick, had worked myself up into a complete tizzy, as Mama would say, because by the time the phone rang she'd been gone for over three hours. Three hours to walk three blocks to the store and buy some milk. I was visibly trembling by the time I arrived at the station, was brought into one of the interviewing rooms where I had questioned so many victims. Now it was me sitting there on the wrong side of the table listening to the chief explain the scene officers had walked into less than three hours ago: the blood, the slaughter, the discovery of the little boy alive and Mama sitting there on that bar stool, waiting.

I called Richard before I called Daddy. I knew Richard would know what to say, know what to do. I knew even though it was his wife we were talking about that his detective instincts would override his emotional reaction temporarily; that his concern would be for Mama and me first.

Richard had always been there in the background of my life, a safety net for Mama and me even when Daddy was there, even when his own wife was alive, because Richard had always been our link to Michael. He was like a piece of Mama's furniture waiting to be fully appreciated, waiting out his time, never asking for more. Big gentle Detective Adams, my step-dad even before my real dad left . . .

Richard told me to wait at the station with Mama, arrange for Ryan to stay the night with Vivian. He said he'd be there as soon as he could, as long as it would take for him to hang up, jump in his pick-up, go to my father's house then get to Helena. If I thought the fifteen-minute drive from home to the station unaware of the truth was stressful, Richard's two-and-a-half-hour jaunt from Dartmouth to Helena knowing the details must have been horrific.

I was glad I had waited to tell Daddy, glad I'd talked to Richard first. I was thankful I'd listened to some sort of voice of reason before I was subjected to Daddy's *Oh, my God*s, listened to him repeat the unfolding of events to Lori followed by an onslaught of tears and *Are you OK*s.

I explained to Daddy that Richard would be there any moment. That they could come up with him if they wanted to, but that they didn't have to, that there wasn't much they could do anyway, that I was OK, that we'd get to the bottom of this, that I'd keep them posted. Lori had picked up the extension by this time and it was she, not Daddy, who said she'd come up with Richard. She said that she'd take care of Ryan, that Daddy would come up at the weekend because things were crazy for him at work right now.

I heard their doorbell ring through the phone line before I hung up, felt secure Richard would see them through. I was relieved too that Richard would have someone to talk to on the drive up.

Next I called Lucy, who was also ready to drop everything and come up to the city with Richard and Lori, but I insisted she stay at home until she had a break from school. My best friend was in the first-year culinary arts programme at Dartmouth College and to leave now would mean missing vital presentations.

I saved the most difficult call for last, the one I

knew I couldn't be strong for, the one I knew would break me apart. Will. I was bawling before he had a chance to say, 'What's going on?'

He listened to me blubber out the story. Told me he'd come down right away. Fifteen minutes later he was there, his arms spread for me to fall into, his heart swollen with compassion. We huddled in a sort of rocking embrace until Richard arrived. Richard had dropped Lori off at my place, where she relieved Vivian from Ryan duty. Will left, and Richard and I, as police staffers, were allowed to watch Mama's interrogation through the two-way.

'Why do you think your arms are aching?' asked Dunny almost lovingly. The undercover detective, thin, nose like a hosepipe, sat next to Mama while McDowel paced and contemplated behind them. I was grateful Dunny was gentle with her.

Mama considered the question, her eyes drawing up to the left in her head.

'I just don't know,' she shrugged, baffled by her own inability to recall. She thought about it again, hesitated, shook her head and repeated, 'I just don't know.'

'Mrs Fisher,' interrupted McDowel. His gruff voice and towering advantage made him seem less patient than his colleague. 'Can you tell us exactly what you *do* remember about the events of this evening?'

Mama's eyes flipped upwards and danced around like she was having a waking REM experience. She cleared her throat then spoke so softly and elegantly you'd think she was sitting among friends sharing her day.

'Bethany was making scalloped potatoes for dinner. Ryan really likes scalloped potatoes. He always finishes his little plate whenever his mom makes them. She got the recipe from me, but I actually think I like hers better.'

'OK Mrs Fisher, how's about we try to stay focused on the events,' Dunny said. 'What happened next?'

'Well, we ran out of milk, I remember. You certainly can't make scalloped potatoes without milk so Bethany asked me to check in with her neighbour Vivian. Sweet thing. Been widowed now about five years but you'd never think it. She has such a happy disposition. I was so glad to see that Bethany had such a lovely lady looking out for her and she adores Ryan. She's there for Bethany no matter—'

'Did she have any milk, Mrs Fisher?' interrupted Dunny.

'No, that was the thing, she was all out too. So I told Bethany I'd take Ryan for a walk to the store, but when I went to ask him if he'd like to come with Grandma he had completely flaked out in his little chair. It was so cute, you should have seen him.'

'Did you go to the store on your own?'

'Yes, I did.' Mama stopped talking, seemed to be trying to recall what came next.

'How far is the store from your daughter's apartment?' Dunny asked, but Mama had left the planet. Her face had gone blank, her head cocked to the left, staring into space like the crazy woman she'd denied being all these years. There was a weightlessness to her face as though her actions had given her the power to defy gravity, had smoothed away a decade's tension headache and the lines it had produced. My mother the monster murderer looked younger than I had ever seen her looking before.

Finally Mama muttered, 'The store. He was there. I saw him.' She was talking to herself.

'Who did you see, Mrs Fisher?' urged McDowel.

'He was standing right there in the dairy section. Just standing there.' Mama was still mumbling in a daze but using her hands now, reaching out to the invisible ogre, her mouth warped into some kind of loop.

'Yes, yes, there he is, Doris,' indulged Dunny. 'What did you do when you saw him?'

'Just standing there. Right there for everyone to see,' said Mama.

'What did you do, Doris?' repeated Dunny. 'What did you do when you saw him?'

'Right there in plain sight.'

And so it went. Mama was rooted there in that store, in the dairy department of Prince's Grocer, staring and recognizing TRF, and then someone else took over Mama's body, mind and soul. What came after were the actions of the beast that had been growing inside Mama since July 16th, 1983, the day of the Dartmouth Jamboree. The day Michael disappeared.

Chapter Six

Mama is driving me to school in the Volvo. I want to take the school bus that stops just down the street from our house, but she says *no* and that is that.

From the window of the front seat I can see children walking with their backpacks and new fall jackets. My jacket is old, but my turquoise and white dress underneath is brand new, bought at K-mart just last week when Mama and I shopped for school supplies and new clothes. Michael and I both got backpacks. Mine has Tenderheart Care Bear on it because we couldn't find a penguin and Michael's has Alf. Mama said she knew Michael would love the furry alien as soon as she saw the TV programme.

My backpack is on the seat next to me. Inside are fresh notebooks, shiny new crayons, unused felt tips and a hard plastic pencil case bulging with pencils, pens and erasers. I feel exhilarated. I don't have to look at Mama to recognize her fretfulness. I keep my eyes focused on the road.

The school is all the way across town, much too far to walk. Mama veers into the parking lot. I've never seen so many kids gathered in one place. Gaggles of giggling girls, bunches of bounding boys, fidgeting, flailing, fanning children of all shapes and sizes, hair squeezed, spiralled, spiked, swished, a blur of crisp clothing weighted with heaving packs. I wonder which among them are the horrible kids.

Mama parks and shuts off the ignition. The car interior fills with a sudden ringing silence then slowly reloads with muted outside squeals and the busy chattering of a hundred small voices. Instead of getting out, Mama sighs then turns to me in warning. 'Remember what I said. Nobody knows our business.'

'Yes, Mama,' I say.

I wait for her nod of approval then unbuckle my belt, and release the door catch. Mama clutches my hand all the way into the building and all the way down the long hallway towards the main office. Her grip is finger-bunching firm and I can barely keep up with her purposeful pace.

In the office Mama signs some papers and then we join the mass of children slouched cross-legged over the gym floor, a stretching blanket of squiggling squirrels. It's noisy and exciting like crackling fire. Everyone seems to know each other.

My name is called and I'm assigned to Miss Robart's class. Mama escorts me in a long line of children and their mothers to my new classroom. Once we arrive at the doorway Mama hunches down and whispers, 'I'll meet you here after class.'

I choose a desk far left with a view of the courtyard. Miss Robart introduces herself and tells us to remove our books and supplies from our packs and place them on top of our desks so we can label them. She is pretty with long blonde hair, a soft smile and a short skirt.

After printing our initials on all our supplies, Miss Robart wants us to introduce ourselves and say something about our lives. I listen while kids stand and recite.

'My name is Kevin Moore,' says a kid with buck teeth and hair the colour of a basketball. 'I have two sisters and a dog named Spike.'

'I am Charlene Lovit,' says Charlene as though it's obvious. 'My dad is a lawyer and my mom is a librarian.'

When it's my turn I remember what Mama said. I remember those horrible kids out there somewhere waiting for their chance to say something untrue and hurtful. My face flares with a rush of heat when I stand.

'I'm Michael Fisher's sister. My brother was stolen when I was a baby, but he will come home soon.'

I slink into my desk relieved it's over. Then Miss Robart says, 'You didn't tell us what your name is.'

I resume standing position.

'I'm Bethany, the unstolen one.'

Chapter Seven

It didn't take the media long to come sniffing around for information, for the details of our lives. While Richard and I were watching Mama attempt to answer McDowel and Dunny's questions, then giving our own statements through the night and into the morning, reporters from all sources were calling my home. Lori answered every ring, laboured over orderly, precise messages, revealed nothing to their barrage of questions.

'Why didn't you just disconnect the phone?' I asked her in my kitchen, scanning the lengthy list of newspapers, TV and radio stations who'd tried their luck. Even *People* magazine had called.

'I wanted to leave the phone line open in case you called,' said my frazzled, freckled, father's wife. Things had to be pretty bad to fray Lori's imperturbable nerves.

Ryan was hanging on my leg, whining to be picked

up. I'd almost forgotten to give him a kiss and a hug, almost forgotten I'd been gone nineteen hours. My tiny kitchen gleamed with morning light yet I could barely keep my eyes open. Lori suggested I get some sleep and when I saw myself in the bathroom mirror I understood why. Dishevelled hair, drug-addict eyes. Lori was right. I was exhausted but my head was swollen with images of TRF's smashed skull, little Aaron's skeletal body, Mama's bizarre serenity. I knew I couldn't sleep without finding a way to relax. I flicked my wretched image away to survey the medicine cabinet behind the mirror. All I had was some children's night-time medicine from when Ryan had the flu. I guzzled the remaining half bottle of sickly sweet brown liquid and eventually passed out on my bed.

I knew when I awoke in a fitful jerk to Will's soft nudge that the day had ended. He had already finished school and what I remembered of daylight had turned into October's early night sky. The townhouse complex lights had been triggered, their blue-white glare beaming through my window frosting Will's hovering head.

'God, I'm sorry. I didn't mean to sleep this long. Where's Ryan?' Energy streamed through me as memories returned at a vengeful pace.

'Shhh,' Will soothed, a finger to my lips. 'He's fine. He's with Richard and Lori in the living room. It's good that you slept.'

'I have to see him. I have to . . .' I tried to get up

but Will climbed in next to me on the bed and pulled me into him.

'Just stay here with me a minute. Just for a minute,' he said, his arms twisting around me, but I couldn't stay. Not even for a minute. I had to check on the world that had fallen apart.

Richard, Lori and Ryan were constructing some kind of Lego fortress on the living-room floor when Will and I emerged. Tiny, brightly coloured blocks spread out along the carpet like spilled candy. Ryan spun dizzily from us to his architectural masterpiece, his loyalties suddenly divided between his building commitment and his mother's untimely resurrection.

'Mommy, Will, lookit, lookit,' he squealed, dragging us forwards to peer into the reaching walls of his tower. I produced motherly utterances of adoration.

'Wanna play with us?' asked Ryan, resuming his building position on the floor. I noticed the clock on the wall for the first time: seven thirty-five p.m.

'I think it's bath time, mister.'

The sleeping arrangements saw Richard in the guest room where Mama had been. I would sleep with Ryan in my bed and Lori would take Ryan's Captain's bed. A bathed, squeaky-clean Ryan was excited to sleep in his mommy's big bed when I tucked him in, despite the unsettling mayhem that had descended over his life in the last twenty-four hours. Will came in, gave Ryan a squeeze and goodnight kiss. When we were alone again

I told Ryan I would join him shortly, the beginning of an assortment of cushioned lies I would soon be telling my son.

When I returned to the adults the scattered Lego pieces had found their way back to their box, and the castle had taken up residence near Ryan's bean-bag chair. Richard and Lori were curled into opposite corners of the sofa, bookends of in-laws. I joined Will on the floor, our legs stretching outwards, our backs leaning against the television cabinet. Here we discussed the unfolding of events.

'She'd just had enough.' Richard was the first to speak, his massive hands forming bowls displaying the weight Mama had carried throughout her life. 'Ultimately took matters into her own hands.'

'The elements of circumstance met with your mother's experience in a fluke of coincidence,' added Will as though Mama's actions could be broken down mathematically.

'There are no coincidences,' replied Lori in her enlightened, crinkle-nosed manner.

'All I know is that the world is a better place because of Doris,' said Richard. 'She rid the world of an insane beast.'

'Yes,' I agreed. 'We are all happy to be rid of TRF but it's the way Mama did it.'

We pondered, hypothesized, deliberated, made endless assumptions, yet felt no closer to the complexities of Mama's truth. We aimed and scraped for clues in vain for the small comfort our own words brought us, as there were no more answers as to what provoked Mama on the early evening of October 15th, 2002 than there were to what took place on a grassy field way back on July 16th, 1983. And so it went until my yellowed lamp-lit living room glowed gloomily with the ghostly dead blue of dawn and bloodless, over-tired faces turned bed-wards. When I finally kissed Will goodbye at the door the hall clock read six o-five a.m.

Somewhere over the course of the evening we decided we'd reveal nothing to the media. They could get the story from the police, they could do their own digging. It wasn't exactly top-secret information that Michael had been abducted years ago. They'd find out soon enough and put it all together, make a goddamn made-for-TV movie out of it, determine their own connections, seek out their own professionals to sur-mise why it all played out the way it did. We didn't have to help them. We'd talk when we were good and ready and we'd do it our own way, tell the right people. We had enough to worry about. We had Mama to think about now.

Chapter Eight

At recess a band of boys play dodge ball in the court-yard. I am leaning against one of the metal posts in the covered area observing. A large rubber ball, the colour of a brick, flies through the air. It wallops a running boy leaving a dusty splatter on the back of his royal blue T-shirt. He releases a shriek, chases the ball, retrieves it and hurls it back, missing his victim. The ball rolls out of the cement court towards me. I move forwards to kick it back into play when some voice hidden in the jumble of faces shouts. 'Don't touch it. We don't want your germs.'

Everyone laughs. I hear another voice, this time attached to the freckled-faced boy approaching to retrieve the ball.

'Did you forget your name, Miss Unstolen?' he jeers, scooping the ball up then booting it back into the halted crowd of waiting boys.

I can feel the tears welling behind my eyes. My nose

prickles and stings like when I eat sour pickles as my tormentor jogs away to join his playmates. Next I hear a small, timid voice behind me.

'I'm Lucy.'

I turn. There stands a dark-haired girl in a denim pinafore holding a jumble of silver jacks and a miniature version of the ball in action on the court.

'Wanna play?'

Mama is here to pick me up right outside the classroom door like she said when the bell rings. Because it's the first day of school we only have to stay until lunchtime. I wave goodbye to Lucy as Mama takes my hand. She waits until we're in the car to ask, 'How was it?'

'Fine.'

'Do you like your teacher?'

'Yes.'

'Did you make any friends?'

'Yes. Lucy.'

She starts the car, leading me to believe falsely the questions are over. I click my seat belt into place then adjust my dress.

'Did anyone tease you?' she asks, dropping the gearshift into reverse. When I don't answer she moves the stick into park once again.

'Did they?' she repeats.

I know I cannot lie to Mama. She can always tell.

'A little,' I say.

'What did they say?'

Reluctantly I relay the words and jeers of the

horrible kids in the courtyard. Mama's face turns to a brick of hardness and colour. Her lips form an ugly tight line. The keys jingle in her hand as she snaps them out of the ignition. She gets out of the car, closes her door with a firm thud. It seems like forever before she opens my door, reaches to unclasp my seat belt.

'Where are we going?' I plead but she is deaf.

We are marching down the same long hallway. We're in the main office once again. Mama is demanding to speak to someone. Her face sputters with fury.

I am told to wait on a chair behind the receptionist's desk while Mama goes into an office marked *Vice Principal* to talk to a man in a black suit. I can see her distorted figure through a series of glass-block rectangles. I can hear her strained voice behind the closed door. She is the only one talking but I can't make out what she is saying, like when the TV is turned a little too low.

I watch the second hand of the large wall clock above me glide silently past the numbers. I listen to the sound of clicking typewriter keys and ringing telephones. I swing my legs under the chair. If I slouch the way Mama hates when I do it at the dinner table I can touch the floor with the tips of my white leather shoes. The foghorn tone of the pre-programmed buzzer tells me lunch is over. By the time Mama reappears the big hand on the clock has clicked off forty-two minutes. But I don't mind because now those furious eyes are smiling and she is shaking the suited man's hand.

She holds her arm out to me. I take hold of her

hand and we return to the car. There, once buckled and idling, she announces that those mean children won't bother me any more. Mama says I can go to school tomorrow and the next day and for a few weeks maybe but that she has ordered a home-school programme and eventually I will stay at home with her.

I think about Lucy and Miss Robart. My new turquoise and white dress and my Care Bear backpack but I don't make a fuss. It seems to me that Mama is on my side. I decide I will always be on hers too.

I'm in bed, my door half open to allow the hall light in. I can hear Mama and Daddy speaking, their angry language twisting up through the vent taking hold of my breath.

'They're my hopes. I can get them up as high as I like,' shouts Mama.

'It's just a bloody sighting. How many of those have we had?' says Daddy.

'We only need one. The right one,' Mama rebuts.

'How many times do we have to go down this road? That damn detective keeps feeding you these crappy leads and you continue to eat them up.'

'And I will not stop until—'

'Until what! Until you've driven everyone away including your own husband and child?'

'Stop it! That's enough,' says Mama and I hear a bang like something hard has hit the wall. Then everything stops and I can't decide which is worse: the yelling or the silence. I wait for whatever comes next. My ears are hot. They feel like they've grown six times their original size. Super ears that can detect even the smallest, weakest, muffled cry. Yes, there it is. Mama's sobs.

I hear the downstairs bathroom door close, the water run, the toilet flush, the awful silence and then someone is coming up the stairs. I see Mama's figure silhouetted in the hall light at my door. I realize I am sitting straight up.

'OK hon, it's OK. Everything is fine,' says Mama, taking a seat on my bed. Her voice is normal again like nothing's happened. She strokes my hair, tucks me back in, swaddling me tightly in my blankets until I feel like a living mummy. I think about the words I heard them use.

'What's a sighting, Mama?' I ask.

'Shh now, time for sleep. Did you say your prayers?'

'Yes, Mama. Do you think God hears my prayers?' I say.

'Of course he hears them,' says Mama.

'Does God hear Michael's prayers?'

'Yes. He hears everyone's prayers.'

'Then could I tell God to tell Michael something?'

'You could try that. It might work. What do you want to tell Michael?'

'That it's OK, he can come home.'

'I'm sure he would if he could, honey.'

Mama stands to leave.

'Mama?'

'Yes,' she says, hunched over my bed.

'Why doesn't God give Michael back?'

Chapter Nine

One of the uniformed police officers who had been first
at the scene asked me if I'd noticed anything unnatural
in Mama's behaviour in the time leading up to the
event. I invited the two officers who'd come to interview me into the living room of my townhouse, where
Richard and Lori were watching TV, but they said they
preferred to stand in the twin-bed-sized patch of space
that was my foyer. I was grateful they had come in the
evening after Ryan was asleep. He'd witnessed enough
insanity over the last day and a half. His mother
rushing off to spend the night at the police station, the
sudden appearance of Richard and Lori, the ceaselessly
ringing telephone and our constant and unconvincing
reassurance that everything was OK.

The officer asking the question was the younger of
the two, a stocky Asian man with tea-stained skin. He
held a small notepad and pen in his hands. The older
officer, a thin, towering contrast, a face grooved like

clawed sand, surveyed the inside of my small end unit with attentive eyes.

I couldn't think of a single thing that was out of order as I replayed the events, the Asian officer scribbling notes. Even when Mama found the half-inserted drawing in the manila envelope the night before and asked me who it was, she didn't seem emotional in any way – unless curiosity could be deemed an unnatural behaviour.

'What did you tell her?' asked the officer. There was no hint of an eastern accent to his words. I had to think hard to remember.

'I told her that we didn't have a name yet, but that it was a drawing Amy Wetherall had described as the man who took her brother.'

'And what did your mother say to that?' he asked.

I felt sorry for him, sorry that he had to witness the aftermath of such brutality. I imagined it was the first corpse he'd ever seen other than the clean stiffs at the morgue they bring out for training exercises. But this was no rehearsal. This was as real and bloody a corpse as this young officer would probably ever see in his career.

'I'm not sure what she said. I think my son called me. Yes, yes he did, I remember now because I was running him a bath and I had just ducked out for a minute to grab some fresh towels, which were stacked in the laundry basket in the guest room.'

Even as I was explaining it all I wondered what exactly my mother's reaction had been. What was she doing while I was soaping Ryan's little body and he was sinking Scooby-Doo figures into the bubbly water? Was she studying that pencilled face? Was she committing every stroke to memory? Was she already damning him, smashing him, killing him in her mind?

'And where is the drawing now?' asked the older cop. I remembered his face now from the station. I was sure I'd seen him before, somewhere in the tangle of uniforms that move through the halls.

I looked first in the guest room where Mama had been staying. I opened the drawer next to her bed and there it was on top of the envelope, there *he* was, the lead-grey version of TRF's face staring up at me. I felt my heart leap as though it was attempting to jump out of my body away from those evil leaden eyes. What had Mama been doing? Studying that face all night? Enticing the devil to move off the page into her world?

I slid the drawing back into its envelope and brought it to the waiting officers. The young officer gasped when I handed it to him as though he'd received a tiny electric shock. He looked carefully at the picture for a moment then slowly handed it to his partner without taking his eyes off it.

'When did you draw this?' he asked.

'Well, let's see, maybe a week ago. No, last Friday, six days ago,' I said.

'Had you seen a photo of the suspect?'

'No.' I told him I'd drawn it from the descriptions given to me by Aaron Wetherall's sister Amy. 'Why?' I asked.

The older cop looked to his partner, nodded some kind of signal. The young cop then reached into the inner breast pocket of his uniform and retrieved a mug shot.

'This was pulled from police files last night once we had the suspect's name. He was kept for questioning a year ago after being spotted hanging around several schoolyards. No criminal charges were laid.'

He handed me the photo. Now it was me who gasped.

I could see the three events lining up like balls on a billiard table. Amy had that memory stored. It was inside her awaiting retrieval.

Ball one.

Once she envisioned it and offered it to me I too had memory awaiting retrieval, the memory of art, the memory of how to draw her memory.

Ball two.

As for Mama, she had a memory that we all have and don't ever want to retrieve. Mama's memory was the memory of a fire-breathing demon that fits into a thimble where it awaits somewhere between the heart and guts. Most of us never get to meet our demon. In most of us it slumbers forever. Unfortunately for TRF Mama's demon awoke.

Ball three.

Bing-bang-boom.

Daddy came at the weekend as arranged and seemed to want to go through the whole thing again and again, his fretful, dimpled face trying to piece it all together. Finally I had to tell him to stop asking questions, to help us figure out what to do next. When Sunday night rolled around and Daddy had to get back to Dartmouth, back to work, I convinced Lori to go with him. She wanted to stay another week, help out with Ryan, be there for me, but I had enough support with Richard and Will and Vivian next door and besides, I told her, I wouldn't be returning to work for a while. The chief had given me an undetermined amount of time off with full pay. I wanted her to go home. I loved Lori and was grateful she came all this way at a moment's notice but there was just too much going on. Too many people in my house, reporters growing like mushrooms outside the townhouse complex and too few moments to clear my head, to figure out what I could do to help Mama.

Mama's memory remained a closed door after six consecutive sessions of interrogation, each one more intense than the last, the detectives becoming more and more frustrated with her inability to remember. It was the chief who signed the order for Mama to be moved to State Hill hospital for the mentally ill. It would provide maximum security and, more importantly, daily sessions with a psychologist whose job it would be to retrieve what lay buried so deeply in the forbidden part of Mama's brain. It also meant I could visit, talk to her for the first time since she left my kitchen so innocently in search of milk six days earlier.

Chapter Ten

It always begins the same way. I feel a cool breeze playing in my hair. Someone else might not think twice about it but I know better. I know what's coming. This is no ordinary breeze. This is a warning.

I can see my house. Not the way it really looks with other houses around it, part of a neighbourhood, but small and alone in the distance. I know I must get to it and I had better hurry because the wind is already picking up. The harder I try to run the stronger the wind becomes until it is a torrent of pressure and it feels like I'm running under water. Just when I think I'll be whipped away, a stop sign appears and I grasp the metal pole it's attached to with both hands. My hands are too little, my fingers barely reach halfway around it and the wind tugs at my body tornado strong. Papers, dirt and other debris race by me. Tiny pebbles bounce off my face. My nose is full of dust. My fingers are slipping. The wind lifts my body until I am horizontal, waving like a flag. My arms are tired and weak. I want to let go but I know if I do I will be flung away and never find my way back home. A final gust tears my grip from the pole and I am flying.

Grandma and Grandpa Wallace are here for a visit all the way from Florida. Mama, Daddy and I are at the kitchen table listening to them explain how their trip was. Florida is very far and Grandma and Grandpa had to take an aeroplane for seven hours to get here. Mama showed me Florida on the map once. It sticks out into the ocean and looks like it could break off if there was an earthquake or something. When I asked Mama about it she said I shouldn't worry about things like that.

I am sitting on Grandpa's knee.

'How long are you staying?' I ask Grandpa while Mama and Grandma talk about the tomatoes in the garden at the back of the house and Daddy listens, sipping his coffee. Grandpa's whiskers scratch and tickle my face when he tells me in my ear that they will be here for two weeks.

'Can't you stay until next year because you missed my birthday?' I ask.

Grandpa laughs loudly but I think it's a reasonable request since Mama told me that Grandma and Grandpa stayed a whole year when I was a baby, after Michael was stolen.

'I don't think so,' says Grandpa. 'But maybe we'll come back for it next year.'

I remember the seven dollars they sent me in a card this year and I tell Grandpa I will buy more penguin stamps with it. They always send an amount of money to match my age. I figure when I turn one hundred I'll be rich.

Grandma has one big red suitcase and Grandpa has one small black one. Grandpa puts his shaving kit on the bathroom counter next to the sink. Grandma hangs her polka-dotted shower cap on the hook on the back of the bathroom door. Grandma brought me a T-shirt with the Florida sun on it. She says the sun in Florida is hotter than the sun in Dartmouth. They are allowed to sleep in Michael's room.

In the morning Grandpa is slurping coffee and reading the newspaper at the kitchen table when I get up. Grandma is frying bacon. Its savoury smell came all the way up to my bedroom to wake me. Next Grandma fries eggs in the bacon grease, toasts and butters an ongoing stack of white bread. More coffee is percolating on the stove. I like watching the brown liquid gurgle up the glass bubble in the lid of the percolator. I like the smell of coffee but not the taste. Mama let me try hers once and it left a sticky, bitter taste in my mouth.

I've almost finished my breakfast when Mama and Daddy surface together. It's unusual to see them enter a room at the same time. Daddy is usually long gone to work on weekdays or if it's the weekend already in the garage by the time Mama gets up.

Daddy sits in his spot at the head of the table. Mama pours coffee. Grandma makes up plates of breakfast for them and soon we are all at the table eating.

Everything about this moment feels delicious, the salty flavour of bacon in my mouth, the rich smell of coffee, the warmth of so many bodies in the same space. This is my family: Mama, Daddy, Grandma, Grandpa and me.

Daddy's parents passed away before I was born. I've seen black and white pictures of them. They look old like they should be in a history book alongside President Lincoln. Daddy's older brother lives up in Canada with his wife and kids. My cousins are already grown up and go to college. Daddy says I met them when I was two years old. He says we took a trip up to Toronto in the Volvo, but I don't remember.

Everything feels so good this morning that I almost forget there is something missing. Almost but never quite forgotten is the gap that is my absent brother. He resides in Mama's vacant eyes, in the silence between Mama and Daddy. He is as subtle as a blink but he is here. To forget Michael is to deny Mama's existence. When I'm happy the memory of my brother always comes to me with a jolt like I've caught myself from falling.

'Today is a special day, Girly,' announces Grandpa. 'Because we missed your birthday Grandma and I are taking you to the movies and then for ice-cream.'

'Oh boy,' I say and look to Mama for approval. Nothing is real until I get the nod.

The Dartmouth theatre is a single movie house that smells of stale seats and fresh popcorn. They play matinées on the weekends and R-rated movies at night.

Today it seems like every kid in Dartmouth has come out for *The Muppet Movie*. The theatre is brimming and bubbling with kids of all ages. After we buy a large bucket of popcorn and three colas we have to budge our way past a line of wiggling legs to get to three empty seats in the middle row. I sit between Grandma and Grandpa, the popcorn on my lap for us to share.

I like the movie. Grandpa eats the most popcorn and laughs louder than anyone in the theatre. At the diner he asks me in his new voice, 'Hello, Kermit the Frog here, would you like strawberry, chocolate or vanilla?' when a young, pigtailed waitress in a white uniform comes to take our order. Grandma rolls her eyes and the waitress smiles.

'Strawberry,' I say but Grandpa wants me to be Miss Piggy, so I raise my voice and play along.

'Oh, Kermie,' I swoon and everyone laughs.

By the time we turn into the walkway that leads to our house Grandpa and I have perfected our skits.

I am ready to give Mama and Daddy a demonstration of our great talents, but when we open the front door to our house a wave of heaviness douses our humour. The house is silent. Daddy is gone. Mama is sitting in her chair by the window, in a suffocating dark pillow of a mood. It looks like someone took a fine paintbrush and outlined her eyes in pink. She sways hypnotically, one hand tucked up inside her shirt, fingers moving mindlessly under the top button. Grandpa whispers that we'll do more Kermit–Miss Piggy later and asks me quietly if he can see the penguin stamps up in my room.

Chapter Eleven

'Hello, please do come in.' I'm outside the office of Mama's state-issued psychologist. The chief had briefed me on Dr Kenneth Ashley, said he was one of the best in the business. Twenty-seven years in this country hadn't done much to affect Dr Ashley's Liverpool accent. For some reason it soothed me, peeled the edge off realism. Made me feel like I was chatting with Ringo Starr.

He wore a banal charcoal suit emblazoned with a shocking periwinkle tie. For an old guy he was well built, his thick frame towering over me. His features, basset-hound eyes, a twisted peanut shell of a nose, made him appear both cranky and sad, but when he grinned all that changed. His smile did for his face what his tie did for his suit.

'Have a seat then, my dear,' he said graciously, unfolding his left hand to indicate the armless black leather seat across from the massive wooden swivelled chair he settled into. Between us a narrow, mirror-polished oak desk displayed a silent but blinking telephone, a stack of papers and a picture frame, its photo turned towards him. The walls featured a large Native American print of a lone winged figure and his framed credentials, showing years of study split between Britain and America.

'You a soccer player?' I asked surveying the shelves, full of textbooks and sports trophies. His face transformed into a beacon again.

'Rugby, my dear, rugby. The unprotected version of your football I suppose. Played for years right up to the day I came here. Traded in my cleats for an American beauty,' he said and flipped the photo around for me to see. She was a beauty indeed, long, straight, jet-black hair, almond cat eyes, mocha complexion. Dr Ashley explained that his wife was a member of the Crow Nation, a south-eastern Montana tribe. It was either an old picture or she was at least twenty years his junior.

'It looks like you made the right choice,' I said, wondering when we were going to get to the point, get to Mama, the bludgeoning of TRF. I knew from a professional point of view that Dr Ashley had to establish some sort of rapport with me first, but I had scant patience for it.

'Yes, indeed. Two grown children back in the UK from my first marriage but none in this one and none intended. My wife is an orthodontist and has shown no desire yet for the role of parenting. Well then,' he said indulgently, either reading my mind or my fidgety body. 'Shall we come to the purpose at hand?'

'Yes, please.'

'I've had the opportunity to speak with your mother for a wee bit, and as you know she's unable to recall the incident, is experiencing what we like to call localized amnesia. My job therefore is to try through therapy to help her recover that memory so that she is fit to stand trial. Now, Miss Fisher, I understand that you and I have this in common professionally. Aiding in the recovery of buried memory.'

'Yes indeed, sir,' I said.

'So you understand very well that the memory is certainly there. It's just a matter of time and the right triggers to bring it to light.'

I knew exactly what was involved, knew the process could take anywhere from weeks to years, depending on the stubbornness of the subconscious, the readiness of the emotions, the gravity of the trauma.

'When can I see her?' I asked. That was the reason I was here, wasn't it? To get an update and the OK for visits.

'That's what I wanted to talk to you about. Not only to arrange a schedule of visits, but to try to assess how you can help with the outcome.'

'The outcome?'

'Yes, coaxing the memory back.'

'What can I do?'

'Your help may be invaluable. Now, looking at the rather unmistakable link between the abduction of your brother, Michael, and the act of killing a child abductor, what you can do is to help fill in the blanks. You must have some very interesting observations growing up in a house with a missing brother, things that your mother wouldn't necessarily think to mention. It's my understanding that neither you nor your mother had any therapy concerning the disappearance of your brother. Is that correct?'

'We couldn't afford it,' I said defensively. 'Besides, my mother would never have sought help in dealing with Michael's disappearance because she always believed he was coming home. And, although we haven't spoken about it for some time, she probably still does.'

Dr Ashley scribbled something in a notebook that seemed to be part of a file, Mama's file. He looked up at me and smiled, displaying the teeth his wife had probably perfected.

'The thing is,' he said, 'what we ultimately have to figure out is if your mother killed Thomas Freeman in self-defence. That is for the trial, and ultimately the jury to decide, but what's really important here is to find out how and why your mother was capable of such an action.'

'That's the part that has stunned everyone,' I said. 'My mother is meek enough to inherit the earth. She's never done so much as raise her voice to me. She's never struck me or anyone before.' The moment it was out of my mouth I knew it wasn't true. It wasn't so much the single time in my life that my mother had smacked me that I remembered but what she had said after-wards.

'Those are the ones to watch for. The quiet ones with a belly full of rage. Maybe your mother had no outlet for all that anger.'

'She has dedicated her life to finding my brother. She has never lost hope. Never given up.'

'And that's exactly where you come in, where you can help. Are you willing to help?'

'Of course. Any way I can.'

'That's what I needed to hear.'

'But how? What do you want me to do?'

'Firstly, there's something I don't want you to do. I don't want you to talk to your mother about the incident. I want you to keep the visits light-hearted. Tell her about things you've been doing lately and I don't mean worrying sick about her and what has transpired. I mean daily activities, things you do around the house, with your son, an interesting TV show you've watched. Talk about anything except the matter in hand. Then what you can do is listen to her, anything she wants to talk about without passing judgement or opinion, just listen. If she does independently divulge anything concerning the incident I want you to report it to me.'

'Yes, I can do all that. No problem.'

'Now what I do want from you is information. After every therapy session I have with your mother I will want to talk to you. You can confirm, deny or expand on anything your mother and I have talked about. In other words, I'll need to see you twice a week for at least an hour each visit. Is that possible?'

I conducted a mental run through of my weekly activities; at least I had Vivian and Richard on hand to watch Ryan.

'Yeah, that would be OK,' I said. 'Whatever you need. Whatever it takes.'

Dr Ashley grinned and told me I could visit my mother as soon as this afternoon. He lifted the receiver of his desk phone, made a quick call to State Hill hospital and I was slotted in for a one-hour visit at two forty-five p.m.

'Thanks. But I have one last question for you,' I said.

'Go on.'

'What if it wasn't self-defence? What if my mother just walked into this guy's house and started beating the life out of him?'

Dr Ashley thought about this for a moment. 'There is more than one way to defend oneself. Sometimes the threat doesn't come from external actions. Sometimes it comes from a much more powerful internal source. That's what we have to find out to save her.'

Chapter Twelve

It's Sunday morning. I'm in bed and Detective Adams is in the kitchen talking to Mama in low murmurs. I know it's him because before I heard the rumble of his voice I was woken by the unmistakable roar of his motorcycle throttling up the street. I know they're talking about Michael. That's the reason Detective Adams comes here.

I know too that Detective Adams will give Mama a new computer-enhanced photo of Michael and that she will hang it alongside the others. We have watched Michael grow up on his bedroom wall.

I also know that after Detective Adams leaves Mama will be inflated, filled up as if from a revelation-filled sermon, full of hope and faith.

I am in my bedroom stroking my new stuffed penguin. It is a gift from Daddy because he is leaving us.

He's leaving not because he doesn't love me or

because of anything I've done. He's leaving because he and Mama can't *see eye to eye* any more, but that's OK because he'll be living in a town home just up the street and starting next month I will visit him twice a week, Wednesdays and Sundays. Those are his days off from the paper mill.

We will do things together like go skating or swimming or I will read to him. I can call him any time. I've already memorized his new phone number. I can call if I need him to fix my bike or to make me a house for my penguin. Daddy's good at fixing things. Mama calls him a regular handyman. He built the high wooden fence around our house, added on the garage that never used to be there, put metal bars on all our windows and installed our household alarm system all by himself.

He says that even if I don't need anything I can call just to chat. I think I should feel sad but I don't. I'll be here with Mama just the same and instead of being in the garage Daddy will be just up the street, just a phone call away.

Hugging my new penguin I climb down the stairs and join Mama and the detective in the kitchen. I am right about the computerized photo, which is between them on the counter, but I am wrong about Mama's mood. Instead of hope I see something closer to sadness. The detective releases an odd rendition of his normal laugh when he sees me, as if I've caught him at something he shouldn't be doing.

'There she is, little Bethany,' he says.

I sit at the kitchen table and Mama asks if I want cereal and fruit and I say just cereal, but when she prepares it she gives me both anyway, but I don't mind because it's blueberries on my Shreddies and milk with lots of sugar.

'Have you heard from Michael?' I ask the detective as though he talks to him every other week.

'Not yet, little sunshine,' he says.

I like Detective Adams. Mama says he has a heart of gold and I know what she means. His voice is scratchy like something Mama could clean her pots with. Still, it is slow and quiet. He seems too gentle to have hands as big as baseball gloves and too thoughtful to ride the thundering, sputtering motorcycle that wakes me if he visits after bedtime, or like this morning, before wake-time. Mama says he's a motorcycle cop like the ones on *Chips* reruns, but his bike looks like it could spit fire and take flight. And he looks more like a member of the Hell's Angels with his grey-brown moustache frowning shaggily over his top lip.

'How's your crappy lead?' I say, and I like using Daddy's words because they make me feel powerful and wise though I'm not positive what they mean.

Detective Adams glances at Mama and she answers for him.

'It fell through, Bethany. It was a dead lead.'

I don't like Mama using that word and I start to cry.

PART 2

Chapter Thirteen

The thing about being the unstolen one is that you'd better be strong, you'd better stay safe, you'd better not rock any boats or surely they will sink. People depend on you, people who can't take any more stress in their lives, and you'd better count yourself lucky because, after all, you weren't taken, you're still here and you'd better be grateful for all that's been given to you because your brother sure didn't get anything.

On the drive over to State Hill my stomach muscles were doing cartwheels and somersaults, gymnastics of Olympic proportions.

I hadn't seen Mama for six days, hadn't spoken to her since she'd walked out of my door to go to the store. What did she look like now that she'd been questioned and re-questioned, moved from a jail cell to a nut-house? Killed someone? Did they let her do her hair the way she liked, curled with a hot iron then smoothed into soft waves, collected up into a loose bun? Would she be wearing an olive-coloured hospital gown with her butt sticking out? Or even a straitjacket? Did she wonder where she was? Where I was? What if she didn't recognize me? What if I was part of her memory loss? Mama had snapped, that was certain, but would she snap back once she'd realized what she'd done?

The hospital was a four-storey cement building with tiny rectangular barred windows and sprawling lawns. I pulled into the allotted visitor parking area and drew in a few deep breaths of crisp autumn air before heading towards the side entrance.

I signed in at the front desk, left a piece of ID and proceeded through security, where I was asked by a humourless bald staffer for my bag and jacket, which were run through an X-ray machine. I was stick-searched with a metal detector by a businesslike young woman, just like at the airport. If only my next move was to board a flight to anywhere but here.

I followed a black male intern in white hospital garb through a set of doors that buzzed then locked behind us, where he passed me on to the next guard as though I was a relay wand, an Olympic torch. The walls changed from olive to steel blue: the colour of a miserable day. My final escort, a large woman with stringy hair, brought me to another desk of warders and computers. Once again I signed in.

Mama's ward was made up of a common area

where patients watched a blaring TV. *Bob Barker and the Price is Right. Come on down.* There was a hallway with rows of shut doors disturbingly locked from the outside, and a visiting area where I was directed to wait for Mama by yet another uniformed escort. Tables and chairs were set up in clusters. The smell of disinfectant and foot sweat permeated the area. Thankfully I was alone in the large room. I wasn't sure my fragile nerves could cope with nightmarish scenes of wailing, ranting, raving lunatics.

I took the furthest seat under one of the barred windows I had seen from the street. At close range the bars formed a bold grid of bird-poop-speckled black iron. Shiny, dark lenses peered inconspicuously from each corner of the ceiling. All-seeing eyes ready to witness and record any unusual behaviour. Whatever constituted unusual around here.

When Mama arrived she looked old and small, diminished. She wasn't wearing the pathetic backless hospital gown that I'd imagined. She was in light pink pants, smock shirt and white knitted slippers, two exhausted pom-poms flopping to her steps. I stood as she approached, the chair I had occupied dragging and echoing in the empty space. Mama wasn't a tactile person but when she wrapped her arms around me she didn't let go for what seemed a very long time. When finally she released her hold she held my face, hands like tiny cushions against my cheeks.

'It's good to see you, honey,' she said. We sat down.

'I would have come sooner, Mama, but . . .'

'I know, I know, it's OK, they told me.' She waved a dismissive hand. 'Policy. So many policies, procedures, rules. Anyway, how are you?'

'I'm OK but how are they treating you?'

'As well as expected.' Mama sighed. 'The food is terrible. Everything's mashed. Baby food. Guess they don't want you to choke on something.'

'I'll see if I can bring you some real food. A casserole, maybe some cake.'

'Sounds good, honey.' Mama looked longingly out of the barred window. 'What I'd really like, though,' she began, but trailed off and started mumbling.

'What, Mama? What is it?'

'What I did must have been pretty bad for me to end up in here. Was it bad, Bethany? What I did? Was it really bad? Please tell me that. Just tell me that. Was it really bad?'

Dr Ashley's words were in my head.

Talk about anything except the matter in hand.

'Please, Bethany,' Mama pleaded. 'Just tell me.'

'I can't, Mama. You know I can't.'

'Bethany, I know I've done something wrong.' Mama leaned into me, and lowered her voice to a hush. 'But no one will tell me what it is. What have I done? Why don't *you* tell me? Please, Bethany. Tell me why I'm here.'

'I can't, Mama. I can't do that and you know it. You have to remember for yourself. That's why you're here.' I struggled to be firm.

'Maybe if you explain.' Her voice rose pleadingly

then she glanced up at the ceiling eyes, caught herself, resumed her whisper. 'If you just tell me then I'll remember.'

'It doesn't work like that, Mama.'

She sat back in her chair, deflated. 'Why can't I remember?' she asked herself. 'Why?'

I took her hands in mine, squeezed them tightly.

'You will, Mama, in your own time. When you're ready.' I lowered my head. I, too, felt like the air had been sucked out of me.

Mama flipped her eyes to the ceiling again. Fluorescent lights hung like beaming suspended benches above us. She shook her head. 'Not you, Bethany. Not you. I can take almost anything but that. I need you on my side.'

'Of course I'm on your side, Mama. Of course I am, we all are, Richard, Daddy, Lori, Will, the Zinglers. We're all here for you.' Desperation dictated a call for reinforcements. But my inadequate words washed over her unabsorbed.

'OK, Mama, listen. It was bad, OK,' I confided, breaching my promise to Dr Ashley. 'But it was also good. You'll understand when you remember. That's all I can say, Mama. Now come on, let's talk about something else. Anything I can do for you?'

'I've already told the people who work here that if they insist on keeping me cooped up in this place then the least they could do is let me knit or crochet, something to pass the time, but of course there's a policy about knitting needles. What do they think I'm going to do? Go around poking people's eyes out with them? Can you imagine?' Mama's eyes rolled around in her head.

The thing was, I *could* imagine. I could now imagine Mama doing things that six days ago would have seemed plain crazy.

Chapter Fourteen

Mama was right about those mean children not bothering me any more. It's not that they suddenly changed into good children or miraculously disappeared. It's more that Miss Robart said that for the next little while Lucy and I could play inside classroom 201 at recess and lunch hour with the Grade Five lunch monitors and crosswalk patrols. I know Mama set this up, but I don't care. Lucy and I are thrilled we don't have to feel the damp cold nor worry about dodging balls and hurtful comments.

Lucy and I have butted two desks together in the back of the classroom. First we play jacks, which she proves to be much better at than I am. After we've eaten the sandwiches and both tossed away the apples in our bagged lunches I show her my stamp collection.

'This is dancing penguin. She likes rock and roll,' I say. Lucy presses the stamp into royal blue ink and watches as the outline reveals itself on a sheet of white paper.

'What does singing penguin like?' she asks.

'She sings only country and western music like Tammy Wynette,' I answer. 'Swimming penguin can swim across the whole ocean,' I continue. 'Roller-skating penguin is the skate champion of the world.'

'What about reading penguin?' asks Lucy, pressing the stamp down into red ink.

'She reads everything. She has a library as big as the one at school and she knows about everything. She knows how to cook Chinese style and how to fix a car and how to speak Japanese.'

'If she knows everything she'd have to have a library as big as the one in New York City.'

'OK,' I say. 'Her library is as big as the one in New York City.'

'My mom speaks French,' Lucy announces.

I'm not sure I believe her.

'Can you?'

'Just a little. *Bonjour, Bethany. Comment ça va?*' she says.

'Wow.' I am truly impressed.

After school Mama is there at the classroom door to pick me up. I beg her to let Lucy come over and play. I know she would never let me go to Lucy's.

'Pleeasse,' I screech.

'No, Bethany, I'm sorry. I have too much work to

do. Mrs Marshall is expecting her chair by morning,'
says Mama.

'We'll be quiet. We'll play in my room, I promise.'

'The answer is no,' says Mama and smiles at Lucy,
who is standing by wondering whether to go out to the
school bus or come to the office where Mama can call
her mom. 'Maybe some other time.'

I deposit that promise in my memory bank.

Mama does work on Mrs Marshall's chair but not
until after dinner and I can't figure out how Lucy
would have been such a bother. But I do as I'm told
and follow Mama into the pre-heated garage where
half of her workspace is taken up with wooden furniture stacked to the ceiling, which in the garage is twice
as high as in the house. Daddy has strung up a protec-
tive green net to hold them all in place in case there
is an avalanche of chairs, ottomans, loveseats. Mama
says that's her pile of diamonds in the rough, pieces
that she found, bought secondhand, or was given, that
she will one day refurbish better than new.

The project she works on now is a giant's rocking
chair with flowers carved in the shiny maple wood. All
she has to do, she explains, is attach the cushioned
seat.

'See, Bethany, better than new,' she says, letting me
touch the richly textured material. She tips the massive
chair first on its side then upside down. If I hadn't met
the Marshalls I would think they were eight feet tall.

Mama says I am to read to her while she taps thin nails into the cushion's frame. I open *Cat in the Hat* and slowly begin to form the words. Mama starts to tap and I lose my place.

'Why is the chair so big?' I ask.

'Because rich people either have very big furniture or very small furniture,' she says. 'Not like us normal people, honey.' But I don't think we're normal at all.

Chapter Fifteen

I had been strong for Mama, had smiled courteously at each warden in turn and retrieved my ID from the main desk graciously, gratefully, as if to return what belonged to me was a magnanimous deed. I had walked through the olive green halls of State Hill as though visiting your mother in an asylum for the insane was the most natural thing in the world. I smiled goodbye outside in the fresh air of the parking lot, but when I got to my car and slid into the driver's seat there was no one left to be courteous to, to nod or smile at, to be strong for, and I let go of it all. Things I didn't even know I was hanging on to.

I grabbed the steering wheel, rested my head on its cool padded cover and bawled: the kind of crying that has you heaving, gasping, gulping air in rapid fire. The kind of punch-in-the-gut crying that twists your stomach muscles like a towel in a wringer washer, that buckles you in half, has you whining, sputtering, singing your grief.

I let it out, all of it, until I was shaking and exhausted. White knuckles locked around the steering wheel, splotches of tears and snot darkening my jeans.

I lifted my head, reached to the glove compartment for a tissue and what I saw at the hood of my car caught me like a cornered animal, open-mouthed and frozen. There stood a woman in a burgundy leather jacket aiming a lens the size of a telescope through the windshield. It took me a moment to realize that lens was aimed at me, that my red and swollen face stretched into some kind of Silly Putty monster was the unspoken subject of a roll of film, a contact sheet, a magazine article, a local newspaper headliner, the front page of a sleazy tabloid.

Plastered.

Blown up.

Syndicated.

Panicking, I rummaged through my bag for keys (please God where are my keys?) and sparked the ignition. Now this same reporter was at my window, knuckle rapping against the glass, calling out my full name, *Bethany Anne Fisher*, pelting out a storm of questions.

'Is your mother OK, how's her health, will she be able to stand trial, does she know she's a hero?'

Her muffled words faded as I screeched away.

Chapter Sixteen

It is Friday at recess. Lucy and I play in our assigned classroom pretending my stuffed penguin is at first dancing penguin, and then finally singing penguin.

'D-I-V-O-R-C-E,' I spell out to the tune of the Tammy Wynette song I've heard Mama play.

'What does that spell?' asks Lucy.

'Divorce,' I say as though it's obvious.

'What's dicorse?' asks Lucy.

'Divorce!' I correct, feigning exasperation. 'It means your mommy and daddy don't live together any more.'

'My mommy and daddy don't live together any more,' states Lucy.

'Are they divorced?' I ask.

'I don't know, maybe. My daddy's dead.'

I've never known anyone who had a dead daddy. I'm amazed.

'Why'd he die?'

'Car crash,' she says, wiggling dancing penguin. 'When I was a baby.'

This thought is disturbing. Lucy is right here, so close I could touch her, and her daddy is dead.

'My brother was stolen when I was a baby,' I say as though we're competing in some kind of morbid one-upmanship.

'I know, you told me,' she says. 'My younger brother has CP.'

'What's that?'

'I don't know. It means he's in a wheelchair. But my older brother is normal. He's in Grade Five.'

Dancing penguin has become swimming penguin and she's diving into imaginary water.

'Who takes care of your younger brother with CP?'

'My mom.'

'Doesn't she work?'

'No. Yes. Not really.'

'Not really?'

'She works from home but its OK because Daddy left us lots of money.'

When Mama comes to pick me up I know this is the last day of the week, but more than that it is the last day I will go to public school. I withdraw her promise and use it like a weapon.

'You said some day.' I pout. 'Please can Lucy come to play?'

'Not today, Bethany. I've got too much to do and I'm expecting Mr Adams.'

I start to cry, but my tears are ignored. I wave goodbye to Lucy as Mama tugs me towards the car. The tear-blurry image of Lucy waving in the hall recedes until she is a distant figure, like I'm looking at my best friend through the wrong end of a pair of binoculars. I think I'll never see her again.

Mama shows no sympathy as I continue to sob on the drive home. When we stop at the second red light before turning onto our street Mama strikes out, wordlessly cuffs the back of my head with the precision of a martial artist.

'That is quite enough, young lady. You are trying my nerves.'

I feel like crying harder, but am so shocked by the smack to the back of my head, its sting an almost visible reverberation in the space between us, that I just stare up at her dumbly.

'Life is full of small and large cruelties and this is neither,' she says. 'You remember that and stop such blubbering. You save those tears for something worth crying over.'

We are at the kitchen table, which between the hours of nine and three becomes my school desk. My home-school textbooks and all the supplies that were in Miss Robart's classroom desk just a short time ago are now on the two small shelves above the table that Daddy came over to build at the weekend. Pencils and pens are leaning against each other in a tin can marked

Bethany's Pens. Felt tips and pencil crayons lie next to each other in their plastic covers.

'Everything should have a home,' Mama said when she prepared the area for study.

She shows me again on the map where we live. It is a blown-up map of Montana on which our town takes centre importance.

'What country do we live in?' Mama grills.

'USA,' I say. Mama frowns.

'United States of America,' I clarify.

'Good. What state do we live in?'

'Montana.' It feels good to know I am right.

'Where is Dartmouth?'

'It is in the north-east of the state.'

'Why is it called Dartmouth?'

'Because it is at the mouth of the Dart River.'

I know this like I know my birthday is March 2nd or Michael's stolen day is July 16th. I know the Dart River snakes north to rest in Bear Lake another fifty miles away on the Canadian border. I know the railway that runs through Dartmouth carries people south to the larger towns of Fleebeck and Warmish and eventually the big city of Helena.

As we study the map I know Mama and I are pondering the same thing. We are thinking that whoever took Michael might have followed the northern path of our river into Canada or they might have followed the railway route south to the big cities and beyond, to Mexico.

'And what are these?' Mama is pointing, fingers

trembling, to the Rocky Mountains. My cue. She knows I know the answer.

'Tell me the story again,' I say and I know in a moment Mama will oblige. I can tell by the way she stares up at the ceiling, the gauzy agony that takes hold of her face.

I can feel the ominous breeze, taste the dust in the air before she begins. The story of my brother is like an old eight-track tape Mama plays again and again, a loop she can neither rewind nor erase. No matter how many times she tells it, it comes out the same. Vivid. Raw. Relived. Mama's version is the only one I will ever believe.

'It was the annual Dartmouth Jamboree. People came from miles around to enter their pies, their jams and jellies. It was the first time I'd entered my black-berry jam.'

In my lifetime, I'd never known Mama to make this infamous jam.

'I only did it because your father suggested I ought to. He said it was the best damn jam around.'

I know those are Daddy's words. Mama never curses.

'You were just a baby, four months old. You practically slept through the whole thing, all bundled up in your stroller.'

I love this part, the part about me. I was there on this historic day.

'I was setting up my table, spooning jam into

tasting bowls. You were asleep. Michael was playing
with someone's dog under the table. Your father was
off somewhere. Socializing.'

I am now fully engulfed in Mama's trance-like state.

'The breeze started to pick up. The tablecloth was
lifting and the overhead tarp flapped. The competitor
next to me, Marcy Day, asked if I would help her
secure the ties around the poles. Just as we pulled the
tarp tight a wicked gust upended all the plastic bowls
lining the table. Jam spilled out staining the cloth.
Plastic bowls rolled over the grass. We all fanned out,
collecting bowls, removing the cloth.

'I stacked jam-dabbed bowls in my hand and when
I looked around for a trash can I noticed the dog, the
small dog that Michael had been playing with. It was
far away in the field, a little brown dot. It was then I
began to look around for Michael. The wind came in
stronger than ever now. The crowd on the fairgrounds
was running in all directions. A plastic bag flew into
my face. Tarps rattled like sheet metal. You began to
cry. Michael was nowhere to be seen.'

As Mama tells the story in the raw mid-afternoon
light I can see my brother in her face, the places where
she holds him, in the creases around her eyes, the
tightness of her lips, the drooping folds of her forehead.
Her agony keeps my brother in place like a fixture.

Chapter Seventeen

The media presence was multiplying. I had temporarily taken Ryan out of preschool. I wasn't going to subject him to the wolves, have some slimeball corner my son between the boy's washroom and the water fountain. You never knew where the line was with the media. It kept shifting.

When demolition crews flattened TRF's bungalow and found those seven small, dismembered bodies under the rubble there was no longer the option of dodging the press. We waited for them to confirm the names, confirm my brother's bones were not among them. Somewhere out there seven sets of parents felt something of both relief and grief at the knowledge of their missing child's death. Mama's public status rose from heroine to saint.

By now reporters had done their homework, got hold of the raw footage of Mama's cross-country tour, resurrected the *Newsline* and Oprah interviews. They strung the pieces together with commentary and visuals, today's and yesterday's. The viewer saw Mama as a vigilante heroine who'd spent her whole life awaiting the opportunity to crush life from a person like TRF. Maybe it wasn't that far from the truth. Maybe Mama had spent her life dreaming of ways to murder Michael's abductor, had already killed him over and over again in her dreams.

In the eyes of parents and protest groups Mama had acted on behalf of the people, restored public safety. They could be seen pacing the parking lot of State Hill with placards. *Free Doris, Hero to the People, An eye for an eye, Justice for all.* A river of questions. A flood of cameras.

Richard said they weren't going to go away any time soon and if I wanted any semblance of the normal life I was leading prior to Mama whacking TRF's brains across his three-bedroomed bungalow then maybe I should consider an interview. On my terms. On our terms, Richard and me. We were a team now.

We agreed on local news presenter Lindsey Sanders. Richard and I planned our action into the night. What we wanted to say, what we didn't want revealed, questions anticipated, our answers to them all. We would do it together. We would be a united force just as he and Mama had been through the Michael interviews. But this was different. Instead of welcoming the exposure in hopes of finding my brother, Richard and

I were simply putting ourselves out there, necks fully stretched under the guillotine, opening ourselves to every kind of criticism as we attempted to protect Mama, throw them off her scent, make ourselves the target.

We would try to present her in the light of a normal woman who, under extraordinary circumstances, short-circuited. Armed with our debut answers we set the interview for the next day in my townhouse. Vivian would watch Ryan. We couldn't explain Mama's actions, but we could try to make people understand how something like this could happen to anyone who'd been through what my mother had suffered with her only son.

Chapter Eighteen

You wouldn't think there'd be much call for a furniture refinisher in a town the size of Dartmouth but you'd be surprised. That's what Mama says. She explained to me that because she is the only one around within a one-hundred-mile radius who possesses this talent (and she always stresses that it is indeed a talent, not merely a skill), people seek her out again and again. Not just your average Joe Blows, she would say, with a split seam here or a toddler's gauge there, although she'd had plenty of those, but Mama says her reputation is built on the expectation of her exquisite craftsmanship competed over by the occupants of Mansion Mountain.

Mansion Mountain consists of approximately 150 fine six- to ten-bedroomed homes encircling Dartmouth mid mountain like a half halo. At night their yellow windows sparkle like jewels in a tiara and manage somehow to portray both untouchable beauty and a sense of unabated safety like the mountains themselves.

Mama says the original Mansions (about twenty in total, long bought and paid for) were built by hard-working minor royalty seeking refuge from the war. Later Mansions added to the horseshoe were built with cheap labour to those lucky in the stock market, real estate or the lottery.

The Mansion people don't come down from the mountain often. Their servants can be seen in town buying up great quantities of food and alcohol. Occasionally their children attend our schools, unmistakable with their tended hair and clothes, but only the children of late Mansion owners: never the originals – those children are schooled by the best tutors and instructors Dartmouth and surrounding towns have to offer. Mama says they even have their own lake up there. She says there is no public access, that it is protected by the original houses. She says you'd have to go tromping right through one of the properties to get to it. But Mama's seen it. She's seen it because the authorities dragged the lake after Michael was stolen and Mama was there every day, watching, for a week. She says they finally gave up because the lake was too deep in some spots and in the middle it possessed some kind of dangerous vacuum. Mama also says it's the most beautiful place on Earth.

So Mama has relations with the Mansion people, relations that began when my brother was stolen. She says the Mansion people were instrumental in organizing a speedy search. She says she received something of comfort every day for a year after Michael went missing, and it wasn't long before they started visiting her in person with condolences and a respect for her services.

Sometimes I imagine my brother living up there in one of those twinkling diamonds, home-schooled like me, oblivious that his roots reach this far down.

Mama drives the van up the winding hill once a week to drop off finished pieces, pick up new projects. I've been with her on two of those trips. Once to the Marshalls, whose house is so big it's no wonder they need a chair that would seat Big Bird comfortably. The next time I met the Coopers, who have three children, seven-year-old identical twin boys, William and Henry, and nine-year-old Victoria: names like their house, roomy and important, names they will have to grow into.

Mama says hers is the kind of work that has instant rewards. She has before-and-after pictures of all her major projects and has accumulated an impressive portfolio, one that speaks for itself. Mama claims refinishing furniture is soulful work.

'No wonder Jesus was a carpenter,' she says.

Mama explains that she could never find that kind of joy working in an office. She says the in-tray looks exactly the same at three p.m. as it did at nine a.m. She should know. She worked at McGregor's Realty before I was born, before my brother was stolen, at which point furniture refinishing was just a hobby.

She says my brother used to help her hammer small

nails into chair seats or sit on cushions until the glue took hold. Mama might still be at McGregor's Realty had Michael not been stolen. Who knows?

For certain, our lives would be different; normal, I suppose. Normal like the Cooper children with their royal names or the Marshalls with their big chair, who haven't known any hardship to affect their normal minds, their safe futures. Their lives are like my mother's projects upon completion. Perfect. Ours are like before. I suppose, too, that's why I like Lucy. With a dead father and brother with CP, she's more like me. Un-normal.

Today is another day I get to go with Mama up to the Mansions. Now that I'm being home-schooled it will probably be one of many days and I am happy.

Today we are not going to the Marshalls' or the Coopers' house but to the Bennetts', where Mama will pick up four high-backed, winged dining-room chairs for refurbishing.

'Do they really have wings?' I ask in the van. I am strapped into the front seat and can barely see out of the windshield.

'No, Bethany, they just look like wings. You'll see,' says Mama as she struggles to insert the long floor stick into hill-climbing gear.

I boing my stuffed penguin up and down on my lap.

'Why don't penguins have wings?' I ask.

'They do. Look.' Mama reaches over and flaps what I always thought was a fin. 'But they can't fly because their fat little bodies are too heavy. There are lots of birds that can't fly,' she says. 'We'll get a book at the library.'

Birds that can't fly, I ponder. Then why do bats have wings when they are really rodents? The idea seems ridiculous, unfair. I examine chubby penguin looking more like a fish than a bird. I wonder if penguins want to fly or even know they can't. Maybe they used to have big eagle wings growing out of their backs and some wicked master rat stole them. I imagine colonies of ancient penguins coming together to devise a plan to find their wings.

'Are there fish that can't swim?'

Mama snickers. 'I don't think so, honey, but there are mammals that can swim, whales and such.' Mama sighs. 'We'll get a book.'

'What about horses? Are there horses that can't run?' I ask. I am truly interested.

'No, Bethany, there are no horses that can't run. That's enough now. We'll get a book.'

'But there are people who can't walk,' I say. 'Like Lucy's brother. He has TP.'

'You mean CP. Did Lucy tell you that?'

'Yes. And her daddy's dead and her mom speaks French and so does Lucy. What's CP anyway?' I ask.

'That's just terrible,' says Mama. 'CP is something you're born with, a sickness. It's short for cerebral palsy.'

I try to say it but it comes out *cereal pauly*. I look out of the side window at what has become a view of the whole town below. If Mama were to suddenly turn right we'd fly straight off the cliff. Below are tiny clusters of white Lego houses amid patches of green. I can see the river from here too. It is a grey-brown snake.

'Are there snakes that don't—?'

'Bethany! Enough.'

Finally the road levels out and we are surrounded by big, beautiful houses. Front yards as long as the soccer field at the school. The trees are big up here too, ancient evergreens, trunks thick as Dart River aqueducts. I wonder if there are trees without leaves, but I don't dare ask.

Chapter Nineteen

The crew arrived an hour before Lindsey Sanders. Two cameras were screwed into tripods, one facing the chairs Richard and I would sit in, one directed at the chair across from us that Lindsey would grace. There was even a make-up person, a tiny man aflutter in colourful clothes, ignited with fitful energy, who insistently smeared Richard and me with a frighteningly vivid orange foundation, and distributed a soft pink sheen over my lips.

Lindsey arrived with a tall, athletic male assistant who looked like he had walked out of *GQ* magazine, dark sorrowful eyes in a face of dazzling symmetry. He took notes on paper attached to a clipboard, referred to them frequently and spoke only to Lindsey.

It was hard not to be a little star-struck at the sight of a famous celebrity in my living room. She was taller than I expected, well-tended blonde hair swooping down in pointed curves under her chin, so elegant and poised, warm as a family member.

She sat us down in our allotted seats and told us what to expect with the help of her gorgeous aide.

'If at any time you feel uncomfortable with the questions, just tell us you'd like to take a break. If it's OK, Bethany, I was hoping you would take us through the kitchen where you were the last moments before your mother left.'

I looked at Richard, who shrugged. He seemed to be taking the ruckus in his stride. He was no stranger to media mayhem.

'I guess that'd be OK,' I said.

'All introductions will be done in studio so I'll go right into the questions.'

'OK,' I said again and inhaled deeply.

'Any time you're ready,' said Lindsey.

I glanced at Richard, his face a powdery terracotta, then at the camera pointed at me, the resplendent assistant frozen mid jot. It felt like a dream I couldn't wake from, the surrealism of this icon reporter sitting across from me like a concerned aunt I hadn't seen in years. I felt the bubble rise between my ribs but I couldn't stop it from turning into a teary church giggle. The more everyone stared at me in disbelief the more I laughed until I had to excuse myself, go into the washroom, look at my own pumpkin face in the mirror and completely crack up.

It took twenty minutes for me to collect myself, for

the make-up man to repair the damage, for me to give a sympathetic Lindsey the nod.

'Can you describe for me what it was like growing up in a household where your brother had been abducted?'

Richard and I knew she'd ask this, had refined our answer down to TV size.

'Well, as you know, I never knew my brother because he was stolen when I was a baby. But of course I came to know him through pictures and stories as I grew up. Sometimes I felt sad he was gone, thought it would be nice to have an older brother and other times I would feel anger towards him for getting all the attention. Mostly, though, it felt normal, I mean I never knew any other life so why would I think it was strange? It was just another fact like my name is Bethany Fisher, like I live in Dartmouth. My brother was stolen.'

'That's an unusual term that you use. Stolen. Instead of abducted. Why do you use that word?'

This question I hadn't expected. Heat rose in my face. I turned to Richard, but knew he couldn't help me find an answer.

'I don't know,' I finally said, shrugging off my discomfort. 'It's how I think of it, I guess – or did when I was a kid. Like someone took something that belonged to us.'

Lindsey seemed satisfied and moved on.

'Growing up, what was your mother's behaviour like? How did she react to Michael's disappearance?'

'Like I said, I didn't know what was normal behaviour and what wasn't. My mother always believed Michael would come home one day, would be returned to us, so she just got on with the business of finding him and preparing for his return.'

'What do you mean by "preparing for his return"?'

I felt defensive. This woman was over-analysing everything.

'I just mean she expected him to come home. There were no other possibilities in her mind, so she wasn't about to change his bedroom into a sewing room or move away to forget him.'

I hoped that would satisfy her, hoped she wouldn't harp on about Mama's behaviour, hoped I wouldn't say something that would make Mama sound crazy.

'Did you believe he was coming home?'

'Of course,' I snapped. 'Children believe what they are told.'

'And you were told your brother was coming home?'

'It was more what Mama did than what she said that made me believe my brother would return. It was simply a belief in our house, a given like faith in God.'

'What about now? Does your mother still believe Michael will be found?'

'I don't know, maybe. I don't think she'll ever give up hope. Mama's never been too concerned about time. When it's time he'll come home.'

'And do you believe that still?'

'There's always hope. Nobody believed Aaron

Wetherall would be found and he was. Many missing children have been returned over the years. Maybe Michael doesn't even know he's missing, doesn't even know he's Michael. There are still too many possibilities left unexplored to give up.'

These were Mama's words coming out of my mouth. I felt that Mama, in making herself unavailable, had passed them on to me to carry on with her work like an exhausted inventor who almost had the formula but was too tired to continue the research. Lindsey shifted in her chair, referred to her notes.

'What about anger? Did your mother display feelings of anger towards the abductor?'

'Never.'

'Did she ever strike anyone?'

'Never,' I insisted.

'What kind of person is she?'

'My mother is a strong but gentle person. She never yells, she never swears, she never strikes out and she rarely shows emotion. What she does do is pray and take action. Those are the qualities that make her strong and have pulled her through the trauma.'

'So when you learned what your mother had done did it come as a complete shock to you?'

'Of course. It was, and still is, unbelievable. The fact that she doesn't have any recollection of the incident tells me that she herself can't believe she was capable of such an action. Something happened to her, something took over at that moment and what that something was is for the professionals to figure out at this point.'

'What do you say to those supporters out there who are hailing your mother as a hero?' Lindsey's voice was as warm and soft as rolls from the oven.

'I don't know what to say to them,' I said. 'My mother did what she thought she had to do at that awful moment, I suppose.'

Seemingly satisfied, Lindsey turned her attention to Richard. She paraphrased his intro as the detective who has always been on the scene – at first professionally then personally.

'Why did you stick to the case long after it had been deemed unsolvable and put in a file?'

'As Bethany was saying, her mother never gave up, and she was such an inspiration. How could I turn my back on a woman who was doing so much to find her own son? I just helped any way I could.'

I tried to listen, to stay focused, as Richard explained how he and my mother became more than work partners, more than friends, but against my will I was drifting back to a place where Mama hadn't always been perfect.

Chapter Twenty

Mama's downstairs on the telephone. I can hear her voice and I know she's talking to Detective Adams by the way she laughs a lot. I'm at the top of the stairs, but instead of turning right in the direction of my room I turn left into hers. Maybe it's the way the light is streaming across the salmon carpet in golden bars or maybe it's Mama's voice murmuring at a safe distance. I don't know but I must go in.

I smell the faint odour of lilac carpet powder. Her room is so tidy, so taboo. There are deep vacuum tracks underfoot as I stealthily commit myself to the crime of entrance. Mama's bed is made hospital perfect. I circle the room with my eyes, spot bottles of perfume on her dresser, move towards them.

Mama's tall wooden jewellery box dominates the dresser, holds the important position of exact centre and dwarfs everything around it, her perfumes in elegant tear-drop bottles atop delicate white doilies, various shades of gold liquid almost reaching the top of their containers. It seems strange to me that she has all this perfume, has made an effort to organize the bottles in a half-moon shape around the jewellery box, dusts them regularly so they always twinkle in the window light. And yet she never smells like anything but cookie dough or chicken broth.

I don't recall her wearing jewellery either, yet the times she has allowed me to open the jewellery box lid and peek inside I have seen a great array of colourful gems: diamonds, emeralds, sapphires. She says they are mostly heirlooms from her mother and she will hand them down to me when I am older. The things she does use are placed in a drawer on the left side of the dresser: a brush, comb, a few tubes of pale peach lipstick.

On either side of her jewellery box are gold-framed pictures of Michael and me. The picture of Michael is one of the last snapshots taken of him blown up to an eight-by-ten. He's outside in the back yard, has just picked up an acorn then turned to show Mama, smiling and proud of his treasure at the time of the click.

He was always finding things.

My photo on the other side of the dresser is a studio picture taken at Sears last year, stiff and grinning in a frilly yellow dress I hate.

I can see myself and the neat room behind me in Mama's domed mirror. My hair is a swarm of choc-olate worms, not the sculpted ringlets of my photo-graph. I reach for a perfume bottle with a glass swan for a stopper, pull its plastic cork with effort. It releases with a pop and the wild stinging fragrance is an invasion to my nose. I continue my aromatic investigation lifting stoppers, spilling droplets of White Velvet, Oscar de la Renta, Wild Musk on myself and the doilies.

In the kitchen Mama doesn't yell when she sees me, or sniff the air between us. She doesn't send me to my room. She just bunches her lips, a squashed raspberry of a frown, stares me into silence, shakes her head slowly, widely, and tells me to change my clothes.

That's all Mama has to do. Frown. My guts wrench. How could I upset Mama after all she's been through? She relies on me. I'm all she has. I'm all that's left.

We are going to Lucy's house and I am so excited I feel like laughing and crying at the same time. I don't know what to do first, put my shoes on, gather my penguin stamps, shove stuffed penguin into my backpack. I'm scared if I do anything wrong between now and when we leave Mama will change her mind.

Mama tells me we are going after my studies, but I have to wait an hour until Lucy is home from school. Mama says she'd like to meet Lucy's family and I don't know if it's because of her dead daddy or her brother with CP but I don't care about the reason. I get to play with Lucy.

I am surprised how close Lucy's house is to ours.

We are only in the Volvo for a couple of minutes before we turn into a driveway a few streets away.

Lucy and her mom answer the door together. When Lucy sees me she jumps up and down and pulls me inside while my mom and Lucy's mom introduce themselves by their first names.

'I'm Doris,' says Mama.

'Nice to meet you. I'm Sylvie,' says Lucy's mom and they shake hands.

My jacket, shoes and backpack are already off by the time Mama enters the living room.

'Bethany. This is Mrs Zingler,' says Mama, and Lucy's mom bends down and says, 'Bonjour, Bethany.' In a thick French accent, she tells me it's nice to meet me. She has Lucy's dark brown hair and a wide, gum-filled smile.

'Oh, hi, yeah, you too,' I say, but I am mostly thinking about lining my stamps up in a straight row. Mrs Zingler tells Lucy to say hi to Mrs Fisher.

Mama watches Lucy and me from a smoke-coloured sofa, her arms and legs twisted like yarn, while we arrange the stamps and Mrs Zingler produces a tray of coffee, juice and cookies from the kitchen. Lucy and I pause to snatch an Oreo as she places the tray on the coffee table.

Mrs Zingler sits next to Mama then raises her voice in the direction of a long adjoining hallway. 'Mon cheri, come and meet our visitors,' she commands.

A moment later a door swings open at the end of

the hall and at first I see two feet that crash into the wall. The feet are attached to a shrunken boy with the same dark hair as Lucy. He is spinning the wheels of a large chair with his hands, gliding effortlessly down the wide hallway's shiny wooden floor. I can see thin, dull, rubber-tyre marks that run up and down the path to his room. When his wheels meet the shag carpet he slows to a stop.

'Hi.' He says it the way my daddy might after he's had a few beers, a little too loudly and a bit slurred. His head is twisted towards his left shoulder.

'This is Daniel,' says Mrs Zingler. 'Daniel, meet Mrs Fisher and Bethany.'

'Penguin,' Daniel says, pointing a thin, crooked finger at my stuffed toy.

'Yeah,' I say. 'Wanna see?'

I bring it to him and place it in his lap. He laughs in large gurgles as he touches the fuzzy black and white material. His mouth is wet with saliva. I notice his bony legs and crunched toes for the first time.

'He can't fly but he can swim,' I say. I am on my best behaviour for everyone.

Lucy springs up behind Daniel's chair, where there are two plastic hooked handles, and pushes him closer to us on the carpet. He watches as we resume play.

Mama and Mrs Zingler are talking grown-up talk about how long they've been in Dartmouth. Lucy disappears down the hallway then reappears with a bouquet of Barbies. Daniel seems content watching with penguin though he does occasionally jerk for no apparent reason the way I do sometimes when I'm falling asleep. I am absorbed in play until I hear what sounds like a plan involving me being made.

'How many times a week were you thinking?' asks Mrs Zingler.

'Just twice,' says Mama.

'We could tag it onto the end of a day and that way she'd be here when Lucy gets home from school. If you don't mind, that is.'

'No, that sounds wonderful. If *you* don't mind,' says Mama and the two women chuckle politely.

'Bethany?' says Mrs Zingler.

'Yes.'

'Would you like me to teach you French?'

I can hardly contain my excitement. 'Yes. Oh yes. Can I, Mama?' I ask even as I realize it was Mama's idea in the first place.

I hear a noise at the back of the house, a door open and shut, shuffling. All heads turn in the direction of the kitchen and wait in silence until a tall fifth grader appears in the entrance between the two rooms.

'This is my other son Benjamin. Say hello, Ben,' says his mother.

'Hey,' says Ben. His hair is the colour of sand and makes him look like he belongs to another family. When Mama doesn't say anything I look up at her. She is smiling in a way you would if you were trying to smile but were really scared and her face has bloomed strange patches of red. Then it occurs to me. I know why. Benjamin is exactly the same age as Michael,

probably the same height and weight too and with that
sandy hair . . .

Mama clears her throat.

'We should get going, Bethany,' she says in an odd
low tone and I immediately begin to collect my stamps.

Lucy protests. 'Can she stay for dinner, Ma'ma?'
but before Mrs Zingler can answer I say, 'It's OK,
Lucy. I'm coming back soon for my French lesson.'

We get into the Volvo. Mama's eyes bulge and mist.
The radio blasts out a deep DJ's voice when Mama
turns the ignition key and her hand darts out like a
frog's tongue to silence it. I wave timidly at Lucy and
her mom in the doorway. I sit in the front seat listening
to the hum of the engine with a kind of dread, not for
what Mama will say but for what she won't. For the
gap she will leave for me to fill.

Chapter Twenty-One

You never knew who was going to be on the other end of the phone when it rang. It could be the police with more questions, Dr Ashley with a schedule change, but more than likely it would be some reporter trying for a new spin on an already whirling story. So when Richard called to me from the hall phone to report it was Lucy on the line I was both relieved and delighted.

After my quick call to her from the police station I'd put her out of my mind. She was the kind of friend you could do that to. Not talk for months or talk every day, it made no difference. If there was anyone I could rely on outside my immediate family it was Lucy. Our friendship was a given and Ryan adored her.

'Hey you, what's up?' she said. I had unplugged the hall phone, reconnected it in my bedroom for a little privacy. At eight p.m. Ryan was already asleep. Richard was stationed in front of the TV mindlessly listening to some over-dramatized reality programme as he pored over motorcycle magazines. I had just surfaced from the bathroom in my nightgown after a hot, drawn-out shower, scrubbing the last of the TV make-up off my face when he'd called me to the phone.

'Lindsey Sanders was here today,' I said, drawing out the *awe* sound in her last name to emphasize her royal status.

'Oh my. You've hit the big time. When do you air, darling?' Lucy asked, playing along. I missed her humour. Life was so dark and bleak with everything that had happened, but less than two minutes on the phone with Lucy and life was a sitcom.

'Next week, I guess. Thursday,' I said.

'I'll be sure to tune in, sweetie. I always knew you'd make it one day. Don't forget about the little people now.'

'It was a collaborated effort really. I couldn't have done it without Thomas Freeman and, of course, my mother.'

'Oh, now you're just being modest. Good to see it all hasn't gone to your head. How is she?' asked Lucy still in character, but I knew the question was sincere.

'Yeah, good, I guess. Still no memory of the event. Everything else she remembers just fine but not the . . .'

'It'll come,' reassured Lucy.

'Yeah, it's what we're all looking forward to.'

'Speaking of the little people, how's my little guy?'

'Yeah, Ryan's doing OK. Hanging in like the rest of us, I suppose. And how are you? Tell me something trite or ridiculous. Give me some fluff to sink my tongue into.'

'Well, if it's fluff you want I got fluff. My meringue got an A-plus at presentation with a soufflé coming in at A-minus.'

'Well done, Julia Child.'

'Yes, maybe one day I can cater one of your private galas with Lindsey and crew.'

'Of course, darling. You are first on my list. So when can you get away from your egg beaters and Dutch ovens?' I asked.

Lucy told me she had four weeks off at Christmas, that she'd come up to Helena then. I found myself hoping that I could wait that long.

Richard had fallen asleep where he sat on the sofa, motorcycle magazine in lap, the weather channel cooing out future forecasts. I snapped the TV off with the remote and the sudden silence roused him.

'Must be time for me to go to bed. Good night,' he called out with effort.

I took up Richard's spot on the sofa stretching into his warmth like a cat. I listened first to running water in the bathroom, then to the soft click of the guest room door and finally to silence. Blessed silence. No ringing phones, no four-year-old demands, no background TV, only quiet. It felt a bit like awaiting a tempest.

I thought I could feel a slight breeze play in my hair as I nodded off.

Chapter Twenty-Two

Mama flips to the section in an animal book entitled *Flightless Birds* and points to an ostrich. There are so many birds that can't fly, not only now but a long time ago too, like the dodo, which no longer exists.

'Does that mean penguins will become estinct too?' I ask Mama, sincerely worried.

'I don't know, Bethany,' she replies. 'They might, but it won't be for a very long time. It took hundreds of years for the dodo to disappear.'

I imagine a world where all the flightless birds live together, even the dodo. A place for the ostrich and penguin, emu and rhea, a place that nobody knows about except those whom evolution has cheated. It is a world that has trees with no leaves and fish that can't swim, horses that can't run, snakes that can't slither.

'Did you hear me? Pay attention, Bethany. I asked you a question. What's this?'

'Huh?'

Mama is pointing to another extinct bird.

'It's a dinornis,' I say. 'From New Zealand.'

'That's right. OK, I can see you're getting tired so we'll take a break and then change to astronomy.'

After a tub of strawberry yogurt Mama pulls a broad, hard-covered book from the shelf called *The Planets*. Mama starts to read it to me pointing at the pictures.

'Hey look, Mama. This one's called Pluto like Goofy's dog.'

'That's right, it is. Pluto is the furthest planet from the sun so it's the coldest planet.'

'How cold?' I ask and Mama refers to the index to find Pluto. Once she's located the information she relays it to me.

'Pluto can reach temperatures of minus four hundred degrees Fahrenheit.'

I imagine my penguin world is Pluto, but it is attached to our planet like a small pebble attached to a soccer ball. It is in the middle of the ocean and the bottom of the planet has grown through the earth almost to the other side. You can't go there by aeroplane or boat because the air above and the water around it move as quickly as a tornado and if you came near it you would get sucked in, break apart into tiny pieces and get spat back out again. It is the place just beyond my windy dreams.

I wave at Mrs Brown who is looking out of a small curtained window as we pass. Mama doesn't wave when Mrs Brown returns my gesture. Mama isn't even looking in her direction, but I know she sees her because she tugs me harder and more quickly along the street.

I don't realize how much I miss him until I see him standing in the doorway of his new townhouse. When I'm with Mama I hardly think about Daddy but now that I am here, clutching his leg with my penguin-free arm, the woodsy, nose-itchy odour of sawdust on his jeans, Mama and Michael are far away.

'I'll be back at three,' says Mama to Daddy and I walk into his new living room featuring a few of Mama's unfinished pieces of furniture. I suddenly feel sorry for Daddy living all alone in a townhouse with old, battered chairs and tables.

It is Sunday, my first visit to Daddy's. I've been waiting until he got *set up* and I can see now that he has. He's even set up a room for me down the hall with a bed and everything in case I sleep over sometimes.

'And look what I have for you, honey bunny,' he says, his identical set of dimples forming tiny caves in his mountainous cheeks: caves I used to poke my fingers into when I was a toddler. If not for the large gift-wrapped box on top of my new cover-less single bed the room would be completely empty.

I move towards it, lift it up. It is deceptively light.

'Open it,' says Daddy.

I rip through the paper and remove the top of a floppy white box to reveal a Rainbow Brite character.

'White Sprite,' I say, examining the snowy, fuzzy creature with dangling rainbow legs.

'Now Miss Penguin has a friend,' says Daddy. I realize I will have to either continue to call her Miss Penguin or come up with an actual name. I hug my daddy.

'Thank you.'

Daddy slides a box of leftover pizza from the fridge and warms it in the oven for our lunch. It is bacon and pineapple, my absolute favourite, although it could be squid and spinach and I'd like it just the same because eating pizza with Daddy is the treat. I drink milk from a rinsed-out glass and Daddy drinks beer from a short brown bottle. There are dirty dishes piled in the sink and spread out across the counter.

After lunch Daddy clears the glass kitchen table that I've never seen before and sets up the Scrabble board. Miss Penguin and White Sprite are watching in the seat beside mine. We don't play *for real* because I don't know many words but Daddy asks what I want to spell and he puts the words on the board. We play a game to see how many words we can make out of one word.

'Look, Bethany, if you mix up the letters of *chicken* you can make *chick, hen* . . .'

'And *in*,' I shout.

'Yes, very good, sweetie. Now let's try another word. How about—'

'Penguin,' I insist.

'Oh yes, of course, penguin.'

Daddy starts to find the right letters on the tiles laid out in the box lid, but before he can finish, he only has GENPU, we hear a knock at the door. We look up at the clock above the table then at each other like we've just been caught eating ice-cream before dinner.

Mama.

Mrs Zingler is not only teaching me French but she's telling me about Canada where she's from. I like the way she stirs French into English sentences so that I can hear the French but still understand what she means.

Mrs Zingler is movie-star pretty. She smiles all the time.

'OK Bethany, what's your name?'

'Je m'appelle Bethany,' I say with slow accuracy. I am picking it up easily because Mrs Zingler plays fun word games, like if I can name all the fruit in the basket she gives me a lemon drop. I like coming here but I don't know why Mama has to sit in the living room and wait for us. The first two times Mama just sat there doing nothing, but today she brought her yarn and knitting needles. She finished Michael's blanket weeks ago and is now working on a pair of burgundy and white slippers for herself.

When Lucy comes home Mama visits with Mrs Zingler and talks about my *speaking abilities* and *listening skills* while Lucy and I draw and colour penguins in the world I've told her about. Lucy's

Cabbage Patch kids Sophie and Olivia keep Miss Penguin and White Sprite company on the back of the sofa. It's easy to draw them when they pose.

I am grateful for this time because Benjamin could stroll through the door at any moment. I know Mama's taking a chance for me.

At bedtime I'm very tired. I lie in the glow of the hall light. Miss Penguin is in my arms while White Sprite lies next to us on my pillow. I tuck Miss Penguin into the blankets and turn to her, nose to beak.

'Goodnight, Miss Penguin, I love you.'

Suddenly I imagine the letters that Daddy gathered in the Scrabble holder just before Mama arrived.

'How about a proper name for you? Genpu?'

'I like it. Genpu it is. Hey, do you want to go somewhere with me?'

'Like where?'

'Like where I come from. My world.'

'OK, but isn't it really cold? I'll need my winter coat.'

'You will need more than that. If you come to my world as you are you will crack in two. You'll need the special shield. It's an invisible layer of skin that protects you from all the elements especially the cold. I will give it to you.'

'But how can you take me?'

'In your dreams, of course, just beyond the wind. We can do anything in your dreams.'

'But I'm not really dreaming. I'm still a bit awake.'

'That's OK, your mind is free. We have lots of visitors.'

'Are there other children like me?'

'Oh yes, lots, all the children who love their animals more than anything in the world. If you love something that much you become part of their world too.'

My eyes feel heavy. I squeeze Genpu and White Sprite together in my arms. I feel the wind coming, taste its dry grit. There's my house in the distance. I walk towards it. The wind gets stronger. There's the stop sign. I cling to it until I am a human flag but I don't wait for the wind to take me. This time I just let go.

I see the ice mountains in the distance, each coloured by rainbows like multicoloured snow cones. Tall, leaf-less ice trees grow in groves, their reaching branches intertwine like fingers to form ice fortresses where penguins play hide-and-seek. Rainbow fish bask in the sun on icebergs. Ostriches stand like headless statues, their stretching necks disappearing into snow heaps. Horses ice skate with dodos on their backs. Ice snakes swim in calm violet water. In the distance I hear singing, the voices of ice angels echoing behind the mountains.

Genpu guides me to the village where the other children are; so many children each with their own penguin. Some slide down the hills on sleds, others play outdoor Scrabble with large lettered ice blocks, which they slide into place. Some kids sit outside ice houses on ice benches slurping spirals of icy juice.

Genpu announces my arrival and everyone gathers around me laughing and tugging me forwards. They call for the winged chair and it flies in, scoops me up like a shovel scoops up a clump of snow and deposits me at the head of a long table. An ice princess, who Genpu tells me changes colour depending on the weather, glides forward with a transparent jelly cake. Inside is coloured fruit in the shape of big-bellied Buddhas. Two bongo players begin to rap on their instruments. The music causes the Buddha babies to dance, the cake to jiggle. The princess, a lovely peach colour, welcomes me to Icebowland.

It's Saturday and I am in classroom 105 at Dartmouth Elementary to write a test. I have to come here once a month as part of my home-schooling programme. Mama says my test gets marked then mailed to an education office and then it gets sent back to us.

The classroom looks strangely large with no children in it. I am sitting in some other first grader's desk in the front row. The letter M is carved in blue ink along the edge and lead smudges streak the surface of the light wood where pencil marks have been erased. I study the art taped to the wall on my left. There are dozens of pictures of fall leaves and trees, brilliant reds, yellows and oranges done in oily pastel crayon. Mama is at the window facing the parking lot.

'Are you ready for this, Bethany? Do you remember everything we went over last night?' She speaks without turning.

'Yes, Mama. I'm ready.'

A tall woman wearing a navy pantsuit walks into the classroom smiling and saves me from what will surely be more of Mama's questions.

'Hello, I'm Miss Rimby, one of the first-grade teachers here at Dartmouth Elementary. I will be giving you your test today, Bethany.'

She places the papers she was holding on the teacher's desk in front of me.

'You must be Bethany's mother,' she says and Mama nods.

'OK, when you are ready, Bethany, we can begin. Mrs Fisher, you can either sit in the back of the classroom or wait outside.'

Mama takes a seat in the back row. Miss Rimby hands me the first of five test sheets.

It takes two hours to finish exams in math, science, English and French. I'm very tired but I know I've done well.

Afterwards, Mama takes me for a strawberry milkshake. From our booth we can see Dartmouth Hardware and Supplies where Mama bought our breakable/unbreakable kitchen tumblers, Ed's Barber Shop where Daddy gets his hair cut and Betty's Boutique, a place I've never been in.

'It's important to do well, Bethany,' says Mama. I slurp and nod.

'Education is important to do well in your life. I never had the chance to go to college. Cost money to do that and we were much too poor. But I could have. I was smart enough,' says Mama. 'Michael knew all the presidents when he was four,' she adds.

I think about this.

'I did well,' I say, but Mama's not listening. She's looking out of the window, her eyes fixed somewhere above the hardware building.

'He knew how to read most of his books and he knew all the names of the dinosaurs.'

'Did he know about penguins, Mama?' I ask.

'Oh, yes,' she says but I can't hold her there. She's slipping into that place she goes.

'He could count up to over one hundred. He would count the strokes when I brushed his hair. He always said *don't stop*. He loved to have his hair brushed.'

Mama strokes the air with an invisible brush. It's like the brush is really here but I'm not.

Chapter Twenty-Three

'How's Mama?' I asked Dr Ashley the question before I sat down. He made me wait for an answer until we were both seated in our allotted chairs, until he had organized the fanning papers on his office desk.

'She appears to be fine.' He was wearing the same dark grey suit and a different tie, a strip of daffodil yellow today. 'Super, in fact. She's lively, animated in her gestures, answers all my questions, wonders when all this *hullabaloo* is going to be over with. And all this fine-ness is cause for concern.'

'What do you mean?'

Dr Ashley leaned back in his chair, formed a tepee with his index fingers.

'She is entrenched in a denial buried so deep I believe it will take much longer than the set four-month trial date to uproot. Unless your mother has some recollection, something to trigger a memory, a dream, a smell, a visual, the courts are going to keep her in State Hill until she does. If we aren't ready by the end of February it could be another six months to a year before another trial date is set. Temporary insanity is not temporary if she doesn't remember. But the good news is that it's early and that you can help.'

'I am helping, aren't I, by coming here? I told you, I'll do what I can.'

'Yes, good. Thanks, Bethany. Like I say, we need a trigger. I need to know what to ask her, what to show her. That's where you come in.'

'What can I do?'

Dr Ashley produced a puce file folder from his top right desk drawer, and quickly surveyed the pages inside.

'At this point we are assuming the rage against Thomas Freeman is related to the rage your mother has for whoever took your brother. With the assumption that this is the connection, I need to know more about your mother as you were growing up, what she was like, what activities she engaged in, things you remember her saying. Any time you remember something about your mother, her behaviour, something said that now as an adult seems a little odd or out of the ordinary I want you to make a note so we can discuss it. OK?'

Dr Ashley waited for me to respond. 'Yeah, I can do that,' I replied eventually, but I wanted to know more about his theory. 'So at this point you are assuming this all has to do with denied rage. I don't know if

I buy that, I mean I know my mother must have been plenty angry at the abductor but—'

'Careful now how you use the word denial,' he interrupted, a thick knobbly finger waggling. 'Denial doesn't mean you hide your anger from the person who provoked it. It means you hide it from yourself. Denial is a very necessary device used to control an anger that is too frightening to acknowledge. Imagine having a look inside at the murderous rage that is contained in the recesses of our innermost selves. To acknowledge that rage would be to admit ourselves murderers and yet we all have that capacity. The problem with people with pent-up emotions is usually not their inability to express them but their capacity to generate them. Your mother had years to proliferate her guilt. It grew inside her like a tumour until it was too big to control.'

Dr Ashley scanned more notes in Mama's file. He sorted through small bits of paper with hand-written scribbles. Mama's file was beginning to look like an afterthought, details thrown together like a suitcase packed in a hurry. Discovering something worthy of mention, Dr Ashley's eyes sparked then met with mine.

'Do you notice that when your mother talks about your brother she goes into a dream-like state and presents him to you on a pedestal as you would a king or saint?'

'She loves him,' I said, shifting in my chair. 'She has a deep attachment to him.'

'Yes, and the intensity of that attachment is used to

mitigate the guilt or exculpate the act. You see, the greatest rage over loss of love is occasioned when the love is more symbolic than real.'

'Her love for Michael *is* real,' I countered in disbelief. Who was this man to attach some textbook theory to my mother after knowing her only a few weeks?

'I'm not saying it's not real but over the years it has become something else, something other than what it once was. She has maintained a relationship for years with someone who is simply not there.'

'Sounds like you're making her out to be a common stalker in love with a photograph.' I squeezed a muscle twinge in the back of my neck. Dr Ashley's ideas were making me uncomfortable.

'There are similarities in the psychological process, yes,' he said. 'Basically what we are talking about here is distortion. I find it remarkable that your mother never had any therapy after the disappearance of her child, that she has coped with the loss by denying that it is indeed a loss, and by the activity of searching for your brother.'

'So how do you propose to get to this rage so that she both recalls the incident and never does it again?'

'Quite right, good question, Bethany. And there is the tender territory of how she will cope with the information once it is presented to her. Since it is unconscious rage that set your mother on a mission to destroy Thomas Freeman it is unconscious rage that we need to unleash again in the hope of recovering the memory. A tool I'd like to introduce, with your permission of course, is a punching bag and plastic bat. These episodes will be filmed and viewed via a two-way mirror.'

'Episodes?'

'I will interview your mother at the facility and encourage her to release any anger she feels during the course of our conversation into the said punching bag. It's a common and effective technique.'

I couldn't stop myself from laughing. The vision of my controlled and private mother walloping a punching bag with a plastic bat in full view of Dr Ashley and a two-way mirror took on a surreal quality in itself. I suddenly pictured Mama as the crazed Granny of a Sylvester and Tweety cartoon running about the house in her nightgown smashing a bat into lamps and walls. Splat. Boing.

'I'm sorry, I'm sorry,' I snorted as Dr Ashley looked on bewildered. Eventually I cleared my throat and searched for the note we left off on.

'Who watches the interviews?' I asked.

'There will be myself and the assistant director of the ward Dr Nancy Sloan and two interns ready to come into the room should your mother confront me.'

'You mean try to take your head off.' I giggled weakly, still teetering on the edge.

'Yes, that too,' he said.

'What about me? Can I watch?'

'I thought you might ask. I'll need clearance from Dr Sloan, but I don't think it will be a problem once I explain that we are working together and your help is essential in this case. Your job, should you choose to accept it as they say, would be to take notes and explain any behaviours that might come up.'

'What about Richard, Mama's husband?'

'What about him?'

'Can he view the sessions too?'

'Why do you feel that's important?'

'I want him there.' I suddenly felt desperate. I couldn't imagine doing this alone, listening to Mama reveal our lives from within a glass cage. I didn't know what to expect but I knew it would not be easy. 'I need him there,' I said.

Dr Ashley scribbled something in his notes.

'I'll check with Dr Sloan.'

'What did you mean when you said any behaviours that might come up?' I asked.

'For example, if while you're listening to our conversation and let's say your mother found something amusing or disturbing or refused to talk about a particular topic, maybe you could shed some light on the issue. It'll save time, too. Instead of me reporting back to you on what your mother said about something, having to set up weekly visits at my office. You can talk to me as soon as I have seen your mother and then visit her if you like. It's a more manageable option. I'm sure they'll go for it.'

'Well then, let's give it a try,' I said. It sounded reasonable enough. Dr Ashley drew a series of invisible esses with his finger down a page of notes, then stopped the movement somewhere in the middle of the paper.

'Your mother tells me you've written a series of children's books,' said Dr Ashley.

'Yes,' I said. 'They didn't start out that way. They were just stories I made up for English class. It wasn't my idea to get them published.'

'Whose idea was it?'

'Will's and his mother's,' I said.

'And what about your mother?'

'She agreed to it. That's all.'

'She raved on about your books to me,' said Dr Ashley.

'Yeah, sure she did.'

'What do you mean?' asked Dr Ashley.

'Nothing.' I tried to dismiss my original comment, my gut reaction. 'That's just not how I remember it, that's all.'

'How do you remember it, Bethany?'

I squirmed in my chair like a child in the principal's office who'd said too much, implicated a trusted friend in a crime.

'I really don't see what all this has to do with . . .'

'I'm just trying to work out any discrepancies. Trying to see the whole picture so that I might know where to begin to help your mother. But if it makes you uncomfortable.'

'She just wasn't that interested, that's all. Her focus was on getting me through school.'

Mama's words floated back to me.

I don't want you to get sidetracked with penguins and forget all about math and science.

'How about you, then? You must feel very proud.'

'It's no big deal. I just happened to know someone who happened to know a publisher. It's not like I'm some great novelist like J. K. Rowling or anything, not like I had to sacrifice much. They're just stories I made up. Anyone could do it.'

'Are those your words or your mother's words?'

I felt as though Dr Ashley was systematically pinning me to the wall. When I didn't answer he rephrased the question. Adopted a gentler tactic.

'Did you enjoy writing them or was it something you had to do?'

'No, I loved it. English was my favourite subject, that and art, so making the stories up and drawing the pictures to go with them was a source of fun for me. I could forget everything when I wrote.'

'Like what?'

'Like anything, whatever.'

'Do you mind if I read them?'

'Not at all. I'll bring them to the hospital next week for you.'

'Do you still write?'

'I haven't since university. Not that kind of writing anyway. Writing in university meant essays and reports. Then I got the job at the police department right away so I became too busy.'

'Do you miss it?' he asked.

I was getting annoyed with his line of questioning. What did my story books have to do with Mama's mental state?

'It's not something I think about. I told you, it's no big deal. Anyone could do it.'

'I beg to differ.' Dr Ashley laughed. 'I'm sure I couldn't write a decent children's book on my life. I don't think just anyone could write a children's book, and most of those people out there who could never will.'

'It wasn't like that,' I told him. 'It was just something that happened.'

'Just happened?'

'The publishing part. I knew someone who knew someone. It wasn't my idea.'

'I don't know much about the world of publishing but I would think it wasn't that easy.'

'Well, it was for me.'

'It seems to me you've accomplished quite a bit for a girl at the grand old age of nineteen.'

'I had a lot of help.'

'Mainly from your mother?'

'Yes. I owe everything to Mama.'

Dr Ashley referred to his notes once again. 'How is your son coping with all of this?' It was like I was in a vehicle with Dr Ashley, he the driver leading me over hills, through valleys, deciding when and where we would turn next.

'He seems OK,' I said, then added, 'He misses his grandmother.'

'Yes, I imagine he does. She raised him, did she not?'

'I had to finish college,' I countered defensively. 'I came home at weekends.'

'I see,' said Dr Ashley, nodding with interest. 'So your mother was the primary care giver for the years you were at school?'

'Just my last year,' I corrected him with urgency. 'I took courses over the Internet in the beginning.'

'And your mother cared for him while you studied?'

I didn't appreciate the underlying insinuation of my parental neglect.

'My mother was always there for Ryan,' I said flatly. 'That's why I felt it was important to move out here for the job at the police station. I felt it was time for Ryan and me to begin our lives together.'

It wasn't exactly the truth. I could have easily stayed in Dartmouth for another year or two.

'And how did Ryan feel about that?' asked Dr Ashley.

'My mother's grandchild wasn't happy at first,' I said carefully. I told Dr Ashley how he started to wet the bed when we first came to Helena but that with time and frequent visits from my mother he adjusted.

'He likes preschool now and seems to be happy. We are trying to play this whole Mama thing down for him. I think he'll be OK.'

'What about Ryan's father?'

'What about him?'

'Is he involved in raising Ryan?'

'He isn't uninvolved.'

'What do you mean?'

'I mean it's not like he's a stranger, he's always been there in the background. Now that we've moved to Helena Ryan sees his father when we go to Dartmouth. I mean he knows who he is and he spends time with him when he can.'

'Does he come to Helena to see Ryan?'

'He hasn't yet. I think with time he'll grow into fatherhood but his family is very supportive. Besides, it's not like Ryan doesn't have a father figure here. My boyfriend, Will, is very much involved.' I could feel my upper lip flare with heat. I felt like I'd been tricked into saying too much. 'Listen, I think we're getting a bit off topic,' I said.

'Just trying to see the big picture, Bethany,' said Dr Ashley, his voice suddenly stern. 'The more I know about you and the dynamics of your family the better equipped I'll be to help your mother. Your full co-operation in this regard is vital to the process. I don't need to tell you the sooner we find a way to stimulate your mother's memory the better. It may seem like a long way off now but court dates have a way of sneaking up on you. We don't want to miss that window of opportunity when it presents itself.'

It sounded like a threat although Dr Ashley grinned at me as if we'd been chatting about the weather.

'OK,' he said, eyeing the clock on his desk. 'Our time is coming to a close.' He folded the pages of the file together. 'Super. I look forward to reading your children's books.'

Chapter Twenty-Four

1992

Mama is Michael Fisher's mother. Daddy is Michael Fisher's father. I am Michael Fisher's sister.

Together we make up *that poor family*.

Poor with grief.

Poor with unanswered questions.

'Make a wish, Bethany.'

I focus on nine thin, flaming candles on top of mounds of strawberry icing, inhale loudly then scrunch my eyes tight.

Hold it. Hold it. Wish. And blow.

Smoke curls upwards to the applause of Mama, Lucy, Mrs Zingler, Daddy and Detective Adams.

I never know what to request when I'm pressured to make a wish. It's like I have to hurry up and think of something I've always wanted, but I can only think of little things like having a sleepover with Lucy or getting a new tape deck even though the one I got for Christmas works just fine. I end up wishing for the same thing I wish for every year. Not that it's a small thing. It's a very big thing to wish my brother would come home, but it just seems like a waste of a perfectly good wish because it never comes true.

'Birthday girl gets the biggest piece,' announces Daddy as he pushes a long, serrated knife through the icing. Inside is white cake with deep, red swirls. Lucy and I sit together at my kitchen table with our slices and Mama releases perfect balls of vanilla ice-cream onto our plates from an ice-cream scoop. Lucy devours hers, but I can't consume all that sweetness. When the plates are cleared, it's time for presents.

'Can I open the big one first, Mama?'

It's from Daddy, who is smiling in the back row of people watching me. I am the star of the show, the honoured guest. Mama clunks the gift on the table before me with effort.

'Goodness,' she says. 'What could it be? Feels like a pile of rocks.'

'Only one way to find out,' says Daddy and nods the go-ahead to open. The paper peels away easily revealing what looks like a doll's house made of tiny glass blocks.

'I made it for your penguins, honey,' says Daddy but he doesn't have to tell me it's for my penguins or that he made it because I know the minute I see it. It has four levels and a hinged panel that swings open doubling its size. I'm sure everyone can see from my elated face that I love it. Daddy zigzags through the jumble of bodies to reach in for a hug then carries my towering igloo up to my room.

After tearing through paper to reveal a bubble-bath and brush set from Lucy, a *National Geographic* penguin video from Detective Adams, nine dollars in a card from Grandma and Grandpa and ice-skates from Mama and Michael, Lucy and I climb the stairs to my room to get down to the business of setting up my icy fortress.

I have acquired eighteen miniature rubber penguins over the years, which stand in a cluster on a shelf above my desk. Lucy and I grab them in handfuls. They fit inside the castle perfectly as if Daddy came in the middle of the night while I was asleep and measured them. I have named all the penguins and they belong to the children of Icebowland whom I've also named.

Pen, the singer, belongs to Not, the boy who is in hospital with cancer.

Gin, the dancer, belongs to Dury, the girl whose parents died.

Nig, the skater, belongs to Lace, the girl in a wheelchair.

Peg, the artist, belongs to Vin, the boy whose mommy and daddy are never home.

Guen, the Tae Kwon Do master, belongs to Raly, the boy whose daddy hits him.

Nin, the swimmer, belongs to Fity, the girl who can't sleep because she's scared she'll wet the bed.

Mox, the horseback rider, belongs to Yam, the girl whose mommy yells all the time.

Pug, the cook, belongs to Gelan, the fat girl.

Bip, the boxer, belongs to Nek, the angry boy.

Genn, the photographer, belongs to Shine, the albino girl whom everyone laughs at.

Enu, the clothing designer, belongs to San, the burnt girl.

Egu, the mountain climber, belongs to Daw, the boy who was run over by a car.

Pegi, the knight, belongs to Lap, the boy whose uncle touches him in his privates.

Inp, the pianist, belongs to Stree, the girl who has nightmares.

Igu, the cyclist, belongs to Raine, the girl who has two broken legs.

Ipen, the teacher, belongs to Mase, the boy who has brain damage.

Ug, the gardener, belongs to Lib, the boy whose family moves a lot.

Upin, the fisher, belongs to Treb, the big-headed boy.

And, of course, Genpu and White Sprite, who watch from their permanent residence on the bed. Genpu reads and White Sprite writes. Mama says everyone is good at something.

*

Daddy has a new girlfriend and now his townhouse is always clean, the dishes always done. She doesn't live there but she's there every time I visit.

Daddy met Lori at the Traveller's Inn restaurant on the outskirts of Dartmouth, where she works as a waitress, where Daddy often eats dinner on his way home from work. She's so different from Mama you'd never think the two of them had a thing in common let alone a mutual partner. It's not just that Lori's younger than Mama or that she always wears long crinkled skirts that look like they've been held hostage for eons in a storage bin under a heavy weight. It's more the way Lori *goes with the flow*, as she calls it, veering this way or that depending on her mood or what's happening at the time. To change her mind, to deviate from set plans, to absorb and adapt to other suggestions or outside interference is all part of Lori's amiable, whimsical way, be it in relation to what she will eat for dinner or with whom she will spend the rest of her life.

Today she is not wearing her usual sweeping, rippling, wrinkled attire. Instead she swishes through Daddy's house in baggy blue jeans ripped and frayed along the ankles and knees, a thick rust-coloured braid winding across an oversized mustard sweater, because today we are going ice-skating. As Mama releases me into Daddy's care at the doorway she gives him a stern warning to keep an eye on me rather than on Lori. She says it loud enough for Lori, who is in the living room, to hear.

'Go get ready,' says Daddy and I gladly dash away from what has become a mean-spirited staring contest between my mother and father. I follow the hall to my room in search of gloves, hat and scarf. I have lots of clothes now in my bedroom closet at Daddy's town-house. There is a bright penguin comforter across my bed and matching curtains over the window. There are books on the shelves.

Lori helps me find my winter wear in a box at the bottom of my closet. We can't find a scarf so she lends me one of hers, a thickly knitted rainbow ribbon. Daddy, Lori and I pile into the front seat of his pick-up, my new skates with fluorescent orange blade guards slung over my shoulder. I'm scrunched in the middle butting shoulders with Daddy and Lori. Mama would be angry if she saw I wasn't wearing a seat belt.

The rink is a snow-swept patch of the Dart River that appears black until you are on it when it trans-forms into translucent mud-green. Daddy says this will be one of the last weekends we can skate on the river before it begins to thaw and break up. Already it glistens wetly in the sun. I can see frozen brown leaves under the ice, curled or flat at various levels from the surface. I wonder if the fish are also frozen down there waiting for the thaw to release them.

Daddy and Lori take my hands and we circle the gleaming ice patch unsteadily, gaining speed then slow-ing to turn. There are only four other people here, a knot of teenaged boys at the far end kicking a rock between them with the flat edge of their skates. Daddy catches most of my weight as I almost fall over a small ice mound. When we glide to the middle of the rink Daddy spins Lori and me in a circle like a whip until Lori, who is on the outside moving the fastest, screams 'Stop!' My nose begins to run. Bulbs of steam escape from my mouth.

I tear away from the two in an attempt at freedom but glide too fast, swing onto my backside at the first bump. I stand, wobbling, clap the dusting of frost from my mittens and hear, 'Hey, Bethany,' but it's not coming from Daddy or Lori. I look behind me to see Lucy's brother, Benjamin, in the midst of the rock kickers, his ears beaming red on his hatless head. I'm not sure what to do next. I certainly can't join them in their game, but going back to Daddy and Lori is like a baby running to its Mama. I wave a knitted hand and inch away in a neutral direction. Benjamin races up to me then stops suddenly, spraying the bottoms of my jeans with ice shavings. He reaches out and flips the rainbow ribbon in my face. 'Nice scarf,' he teases, then charges back to his gang with the ease of a professional hockey player. My face is on fire in the frosty air.

I can hear Mama praying in Michael's bedroom. I can almost make out every word because of the heat vent that connects our rooms. I imagine her standing in front of Michael's picture as she speaks: the latest computer-enhanced image, fourteen years old, Benjamin-cute.

'Mama is here, sweetheart, waiting for you. Come

home, baby. Please come home. This is where you belong, where you've always belonged. No matter where you are or what you've been through, just come back to me.'

I imagine my brother opening the front door and walking into our lives. Mama wouldn't be surprised, just delighted. Her face would light up like a lamp that's been snapped on, every wrinkle would disappear as in a flash photo. With her taut young face she would lean over my brother and kiss his cheek. He would look exactly like his photo. It's hard to imagine him any other way but slightly blurred, wearing that green and white striped polo shirt, that smirk across his lips like he's been in on this all along.

I imagine that if my brother came home today my mother wouldn't even ask questions. She would just start the mending process. Who cares where he'd been? What horrors he'd seen? He'd be home now and she would mend him with her love.

It's Saturday after a chicken and potato dinner and I'm leaning against the pillows on my bed, full and lethargic, doing my homework. I have a week to write a story for English before Mama and I go to Dartmouth Elementary so I can take my exams. The story is part of the exam too, but they are letting me do it at home then turn it in with the rest of my test papers.

The only story I can imagine is about penguins and Icebowland so that is what I'm writing. After endless description of rainbow-coloured ice mountains and leafless trees my story features Raine, the girl with two broken legs, and her penguin, Igu, the cyclist. I settle into the realm of periwinkle weather and spiralling ice towers that reach out-of-sight heights. In this world where pinecicles grow in ice fields and snow insects swarm and whirl overhead like tiny helicopters I am mighty and liberated.

'Bethany, bedtime soon,' says Mama. She is in my doorway, arms crossed against her chest.

'Yes, Mama, just doing my homework.'

'Your English project?'

'Yes, almost finished. Wanna hear?'

'You can read it to me tomorrow. Turn out the light soon.'

'Hey, Mama?'

'Uhhuh?'

'Does God know where Michael is?'

Mama is silent for a moment then says, 'What made you think of that?'

'Dunno,' I say. 'I thought I heard you . . .'

Mama moves into my room, sits on the edge of my bed. She looks directly into my eyes.

'I wasn't praying. I was talking to Michael.'

'Oh,' I say. 'Does he ever talk back?'

Mama considers her answer then nods. 'Sometimes,' she says. 'I hear his voice in the morning just before I wake up.'

I straighten my body.

'What does he say?'

'He just says I love you, or I miss you or sometimes he just says it's OK.'

'Does he ask about me?'

Mama smiles, cocks her head to the right.

'He thinks about you all the time,' she says. She reaches to tuck a strand of hair behind my ear.

'Maybe if I prayed,' I suggest.

'Yes, that might help.' Mama looks down into her lap. 'Can't hurt, I suppose.'

'Why doesn't God just give Michael back?'

'I don't know the answer, Bethany. He has his reasons, I suppose. Maybe it's not up to him. Maybe there is no . . .' Mama pauses, re-forms her words. 'Sometimes I wonder if I can believe in a God that would take Michael away.'

'Daddy says in times of trouble our faith should grow stronger.'

'Well, you can tell your Daddy . . .' But Mama stops herself, stretches her long fingers over her mouth to squash the toxic words that might sneak out.

Since Daddy met Lori my praying is done on Sunday in church. It's a united church where Daddy says anyone can come no matter what their religion or creed is.

I don't go into the basement area with the other children but stay with Daddy and Lori on the hard wooden pews to listen to the minister. Daddy shares a hymn book with me and moves his fingers under the words as we stand to sing.

'Glory be, Oh, glory be.'

I listen to the thinly moustached minister talk about how things don't seem as they appear, how a dirty clump of hard snow is soft and pure on the inside and quickly melts away when opened up. I like the image of the soft guts of a giant snowball spilling out. We bow our heads to pray and I can hear Mama's words, *can't hurt I suppose*, so I ask God to bring Michael back to her.

After church we go to Daddy's house and Lori makes us cheese and cucumber sandwiches. When Lori and I have cleared the table she asks if I want to draw. When I say that I do she brings out a large sketchbook and some charcoal pencils. I tell her I want to draw penguins so we set up the five birds I've brought with me in a row on the table.

Lori helps me with the lines and the shading. We sketch one after another until the entire page is filled with my flightless friends, Bip, Enu, Pegi, Guen and Igu, front view, side view, back view, just the head.

'Can we draw Igu on a bicycle with a girl on the back with two broken legs?' I ask, pulling Igu from the line-up, holding him up for Lori to examine.

'Can you be any more specific, Bethany?' Then she tosses her head back, laughing at my request, her long, milky neck stretching taut.

'Look what I drew,' I display the page for Mama at the door.

'Well done, Bethany. Let's go then.'

'Can I take it home with me?' I yell back into the kitchen where Lori has stayed at the table. She comes into the living room holding a charcoal pencil.

'Sure and you can take this with you too.' She hands me the drawing stick then returns to the kitchen without acknowledging Mama. I feel as if I've done something wrong.

Detective Adams's motorcycle is in the driveway when Mama and I pull up to our house. Before we get out of the Volvo she tells me she has invited him for dinner.

'We're just having chicken soup, nothing fancy. Detective Adams is alone these days. His wife is up at Dartmouth Memorial and she's very sick, so we want to make the detective feel welcome. He's done so much to help us over the years,' says Mama.

'What's wrong with her?' I ask.

'The doctors don't really know. She came to the hospital with a very high fever then slipped into a coma a few days later.'

'What's a coma?'

'It's like a sleep that lasts for a long, long time.'

'How long?'

'I don't know, Bethany, but don't you ask any questions of Mr Adams. We want him to forget his troubles tonight. OK?'

'OK, Mama.'

The towering bulk of Detective Adams is stooped over the stove stirring a steaming pot of soup when we arrive in the kitchen. The table is set. Thickly fanning slices of homemade bread are displayed deliciously on a centre plate. My mouth waters.

'Oh my,' says Mama. 'You didn't have to do all that. You go and sit down now.'

'Hey, squirt,' he says to me and ruffles my hair as I pass.

'Go wash up,' Mama says and I do as I'm told.

During dinner I am careful not to say anything about Mrs Detective Adams. I don't think I should say anything about church or God either or Daddy or Lori, or even Michael for that matter, because Mama looks so happy passing the bread and filling up the detective's bowl with ladles of meaty soup. Mama looks unusually pretty when she smiles. I eat quietly and listen politely to their grown-up talk about the expansion of the Dartmouth Public Library.

When I am excused I go to my room, retrieve the sketchbook and charcoal pencil from my bag and perfect the shaded drawing of Igu and Raine. I will include it with my story for exam day.

When I get my exams back Mama seems satisfied. I have passed every subject above 80 per cent, but my story is the best. She seats me at the kitchen table and reads the comments.

Great work, Bethany. Your story is well constructed with few grammar problems and perfect spelling.

'See,' Mama interrupts her own reading. 'All that double-checking paid off.'

She continues.

You have a fantastic imagination. Thank you for including the drawing. It was a nice addition to the story. I hope to read more Icebowland adventures in the future.

Then a PS. *If you don't mind I'd like to enter your story in the annual Dartmouth Elementary Short Story contest.*

'Can we, Mama?' I plead. 'Put my story in the contest?'

'We'll see,' says Mama. 'The prize for doing well in school is doing well in life, going to college, getting a good job. I don't want you to get sidetracked with penguins and forget all about math and science.'

'I won't, I won't.' I promise to work really hard, but she still doesn't answer my question.

A large red-inked A+ marks the front page of my story. Mama tacks it and my drawing to the refrigerator door with fruit magnets.

'They tell me our hard work has you working at a Grade Eight level,' she says. 'If you keep going at this rate you will finish high school when you're fourteen years old. After that we can study college courses.'

I don't care much about that. I'm just happy my story has made it to the refrigerator.

Chapter Twenty-Five

Mama wasn't the only one who was famous in the city of Helena. Once XYI TV aired our story with Lindsey Sanders, Richard and I couldn't move beyond the front walkway without being accosted by a fog of questions and unwelcome photographs. If I thought that going public with our story would quell the media's fierce demand for information I soon became acutely aware that you don't throw a steak to only one ravenous lion in the pit without the others coming around expecting their fair share.

Added to the braying knot of media on the front lines of my townhouse complex was a torrent of shouts and cheers, the visual assault of placards and banners from the concerned citizens of Helena. They had awoken to our story with the urgency of starving vultures, felt it was somehow their responsibility to show support for one of their own. Their pride for Mama's actions was almost palpable. She hadn't hunted down a Kennedy or a movie star in a crowd. She'd followed her gut, listened to every molecule in her body and followed through on a screaming hunch to fell a monster.

Of course it was the media's job to play devil's advocate, but I resented the questions and implications they barked at me through the glass of my car window every time I left the premises.

'How did your mother know it was TRF? What if it turned out to be someone else?'

What if I ran all you vermin over? I wanted to rebut from inside my car, but it really was a good question they posed. *What if?* It was a question the courts would eventually be asking too. How do you convince a judge it was her guts that knew?

Richard, Ryan and I became besieged hostages in my townhouse, which was becoming smaller by the day. We sent Vivian out for groceries and necessities. I felt terrible for asking after all she'd done for me, taking care of Ryan at a moment's notice. But Vivian, wonderful Viv, seemed truly happy to help as though she had been waiting for a reason to be vital. This little old lady moved confidently through the outdoor crowds with the innocent believability of a professional actress, lying straight-faced to anyone questioning her knowledge of my mother. The media soon lost interest in her and let her pass through their barricade of bodies on her way to fetch our staples of bread, bananas and coffee.

I was grateful, too, to the townhouse management; they warned they would not allow a single media member's toe to slide onto compound property without threat of a hefty lawsuit. Management presented each eager face with a written warning from their lawyers stating such action. It meant that while Richard and I could be spotted the moment we opened the front door we could easily slip out the back and be shielded from view by the square of attached homes surrounding the community courtyard. The centre of the courtyard housed a small playground, a swing set and monkey bars that Richard or I could take Ryan to. At least we could do that, sneak out into the prison courtyard for some fresh air.

Today it was Richard who was out there entertaining his grandson, pretending everything was normal. I watched the pair at play from my bedroom window, Ryan bundled in his bright red parka running his Hot Wheels over the cold ground, Richard in black leather pointing and smiling from a wooden bench. Ryan looked even smaller out there alone in the square of sand, his giant grandpa nearby.

Will was sitting cross-legged on the bed behind me hunched over the pages of Mama's police report, which Richard had insisted we be allowed to copy. The chief would do anything for Richard, their paths had crossed many times over the years. I was happy for this time with Will, a small blip in otherwise insane time schedules. Between his impending mid-term exams and me juggling Ryan, Dr Ashley, Mama and the media our moments together were beyond precious. They felt life-supporting. I turned to him, his hair like ice in the window light.

'Dr Ashley wants to read my children's books,' I announced. He looked up from the strewn pages.

'Why?'

'Not sure. I think he's convinced it will help Mama if he understands me better. But I feel like I'm the one in therapy.'

'Come here,' he said, his voice like the kind offering of an umbrella in the rain, his hand reaching for me. I moved from my watching post at the window, took up a small space on the edge of the bed. He pulled me into him, the rustle of papers crunching under us, spilling onto the floor. It felt like I hadn't seen him in eons, not really seen him. Not looked into those gorgeous pale blue eyes and remembered how much I loved him, how much he meant to me. It seemed forever since I'd run my fingers through those curls as soft and fine as my four year old's. We spread out on the comforter. Our legs tangled and I held his warm body against mine, felt the transfer of heat. I hadn't realized until now that I was cold, my hands icy against his skin. He jerked upwards, resting his head against his elbow, studied my face, smoothed my hair.

'You have to relax. Take a breather from all this for a while,' he said.

'Easier said than done,' I complained. He leaned in, kissed me, his lips baby soft, the gentle flick of his tongue against mine. As Will reached up under my T-shirt we heard the back door open, Ryan's busy chatter, the shuffling of boots and coats being removed. Relaxing would have to wait.

When Will and I caught up with Ryan and Richard they were in the kitchen, Richard slicing ready-made cookie dough onto a cutting board while Ryan gently lifted the perfect circles onto a tin sheet.

'Hi, Mommy, hi, Will,' Ryan squealed.

'Hey, monkey.' Will gave Ryan's hair a rustle.

I reached down, hugged my son until he squirmed for release.

'Mmmm, chocolate chip,' I said, surveying the platter. Will moved to the archway, smiling at the sweetly hectic scene.

'Yeah, Mommy, and know what it has?' A wide-eyed Ryan held up the package of white icing that came with the instant cookies.

'But we have to wait till they cool. Right, Papa?'

Richard grinned, nodded at my boy.

'Can we send some cookies to Grandma?' asked Ryan.

'Maybe we can,' I said.

I noticed fresh bagels and green bananas next to Richard on the counter. Somewhere over the course of the day Vivian had been shopping for us again.

'Thanks, Papa,' I said and gave Richard a little squeeze on my way to the refrigerator. Inside were more new items – a jug of iced tea, a jar of dill pickles, a carton of milk, strawberries the size of fists. I poured myself a glass of cold tea.

'I met Vivian outside,' said Richard, reading my mind. 'She had a few bags of food for us.'

'And know what else, Mommy?' said Ryan delighted with everything.

'What's that, hon?'

'Papa says we're having pizza for lunch.'

What I wouldn't give for a moment's dip in my son's placid pond of simple pleasures. How great life must be, I pondered, when the definition of complete happiness is pizza and cookies. I wished I could think like Ryan if only for a few hours: wished life could hold such wonder. Being here in the presence of my four year old as he plopped doughy circles onto the oven tray with painstaking precision, it almost seemed possible.

Chapter Twenty-Six

I can't decide between the hand-painted miniature tea set and the glass fruit bowl with multicoloured spiralling handles. Daddy's gift was easy to choose: a minicooler, for picnics or a few cool ones down by the river. Lori's idea but I wholeheartedly agreed.

'What do you think?' I ask her, weighing the two choices my allowance money affords me.

'I don't know. The fruit bowl is really nice but the tea set is unique,' she says. A lady in a blue hat swerves her packed cart as she approaches to avoid collision with oncoming traffic. I've never seen K-mart so busy.

Unique. I like that. The tea set it is.

We bring it to the service counter and Lori pitches in the extra two dollars it cost to have it gift-wrapped. I've never had anything gift-wrapped before. Mama will know that this is a special gift. Unique.

It occurs to me then that I will buy Lori the fruit bowl. She did say it was really nice after all. There are still two weeks left before Christmas, so with my regular allowance and if I do extra chores for Daddy I can manage. I've already bought Lucy a New Kids on the Block poster and Mrs Zingler a No.1 Teacher mug.

As we're leaving the store, Lori carrying the wrapped box, I am distracted by a row of glass balls with winter scenes inside. I reach for one on a crowded shelf, tip it upside down and make it snow.

'Come on, Bethany. Your mom is expecting us back,' coaxes Lori.

I remember Mama's words to Lori through the passenger window of Lori's Datsun as I buckled up.

Have her right back and please watch her carefully. This is prime predatory season.

Mama's at the window when we pull into the driveway. The smell of pine needles is delicious when I walk into the house.

'Oh now, what's this?' says Mama, taking the wrapped box from my hands.

'Gift-wrapped and all. Faaaancy,' she says. 'Whose idea was that?' Her tone is accusatory. I know she knows it wasn't mine. I take it back from her without answering and slide it under the tree. Maybe gift-wrapping wasn't such a good idea after all.

Since we don't have a fireplace the stockings are hung on wall hooks next to the tree on Christmas Eve. Mama says not to worry, that Santa will just walk in through the door, but I don't believe in Santa any more. Even if I did I wouldn't believe that story. Mama would never leave the door unlocked all night.

Mine is a red, stretchy, giant's sock displaying a plump, festive penguin along the leg, courtesy of Mama's knitting skills. Michael's stocking dangles next to mine. It's shorter but fatter with a green background, a red poinsettia leaf curling around its centre.

New gifts have grown steadily under the tree since its fragrant arrival on December 1st. Tonight they have exploded upwards and outwards and that's not counting the ones Santa will bring tonight (if there is a Santa that is). There is one flat circular gift at the back against the wall that is almost the same height as me. It's from Detective Adams and I know it's a sled, but knowing doesn't make it any less exciting.

No one has to get me out of bed this morning. I'm wide awake and it's only five-thirty a.m. I'll just wait here in my room until Mama wakes up. I'll just turn on my radio to keep me company. I'll just open my bedroom door a little wider, turn up the volume a little. I'll just go and jump on Mama's bed.

Mama says we have to eat breakfast before we can open presents but I'm not even hungry.

'That will give your dad time to get over here,' she says.

We have to wait for him *too*.

After an agonizing half-hour, fed, sitting on the floor at Daddy's feet, Mama hands me the first gift and says, 'OK, we can begin like civilized people.'

When the storm of flying paper has settled, I am struck by the vision of the tree. Its appearance has changed dramatically from one short hour ago. What's left are a sprinkling of unopened gifts and a single hung stocking, still stuffed to overflowing, complete with a Japanese orange and a protruding box of Toblerone.

Maybe it's that this year I am just a little bit older or that I am more aware of Daddy's presence and what he thinks, but here before me more obvious than ever lie the visible remains of my invisible brother.

Daddy says he has to go home. He is having Christmas dinner with Lori and her family. I kiss and hug him at the door. Mama yells out a goodbye from the kitchen. I join Mama once Daddy is gone. She is cutting celery sticks and onions at the counter for the turkey stuffing.

She sets me up at the kitchen table with a large pale green Tupperware bowl and a bag of green beans. I am to snap the ends off, break them in two and pile them in the bowl. I like this work, the crisp break between my fingers, the ensuing smell of freshness.

Mama hums softly to Christmas carols on the radio. After his visit to the hospital, Detective Adams will join us for dinner. I think about Detective Adams's wife lying in a deep sleep, nurses poking her with needles, a dripping machine hooked up to her arm.

'Do you think she knows it's Christmas?' I ask.

'Who? Does who know?' says Mama.

'Mrs Adams.'

'Oh, Bethany – really. I don't know. Maybe, maybe not. It's better if she doesn't.'

'Because then she'd feel sad?'

'I'm sure she would.'

'People shouldn't feel sad at Christmas,' I say.

'No, they shouldn't,' says Mama. 'But not everyone gets to be with who they want to be with at Christmas. We just have to make do with what we have.'

'Will she ever wake up?' I ask.

'Of course she'll wake up, we just don't know when. Nobody knows.'

'Not even the doctors?'

'No, not even them. Some things are just a mystery. Not for us to try to figure out.'

'Do you think Detective Adams is sad?'

'Of course he's sad,' Mama snaps. 'What do you think? Someone he loves is missing and all he has now is . . .'

But Mama can't finish her sentence because she has sliced through her finger with the cutting knife.

'Oh jeez, son of a biscuit!' Mama cries, hopping from foot to foot, squeezing a bloody index finger.

'All that's left is me,' I whisper into the beans.

I get to spend Boxing Day with Daddy and Lori. Lori and I open our presents to each other together and when we do we both spill into laughter because while she is holding the glass fruit bowl from our day at K-mart I am holding the glass water ball that snows silver flecks. We spend the afternoon drawing the winter scene inside the orb on the artist's paper Lori keeps rolled up in Daddy's closet.

'Do you want to paint it now?' she asks. Of course I do. She brings her acrylics to the kitchen table and I spot the silver immediately.

'I want to paint everything silver,' I announce.

It's harder than I think. If I paint *everything* silver then I just produce one big indiscriminate blob of silver so under Lori's deft instructions I mix the silver with various amounts of white, then purple, a speck of black to create shadow and highlight. I like it here with Lori. She teaches me nice things.

Mama waits until after New Year's Day to cart Michael's gifts upstairs to the floor of his bedroom closet, where they are stacked, Christmas upon Christmas, birthday upon birthday. I am helping her.

When I enter my brother's room I am reminded of his passion for foraging.

He was always finding things.

He was a pint-sized scavenger whenever he and Mama went for a walk. Mama told me that Michael had an acute sense of smell. That anything plucked from the ground went to his nose first for approval. It was a habit she said she didn't have the heart to coax him out of as she found it so endearing. He'd return home with smooth, nose-worthy stones, giant acorns, chewed up bouncy balls, oddly shaped sticks. Mama saved every one of his treasures. My eyes move around the room as she now packs away his gifts. His outdoor discoveries are displayed along his windowsill and on his dresser.

On the wall across from the window is where Mama hangs all of Michael's pictures. It seems funny to me how they give him a new computerized face every year yet stick him with that same old green and white striped polo shirt. I hope he liked that shirt. He might be wearing it forever.

'Bethany, can you hand me a few of the smaller gifts,' orders Mama, her butt sticking out of the closet as she bends to straighten the pile.

I squeeze in next to her with an armload of new presents. Some of the wrapping on the old gifts has ripped away along the edges of the hard plastic underneath. The faded paper brightens in upward succession. Nose-itchy dust rises as we add this Christmas's contribution to the heap. Overhead Michael's clothes are hung, price tags dangling. Pairs of new running shoes sit on shelves. I know there are pants, socks, underwear and pyjamas in his drawers. I've seen Mama buy them at K-mart.

Mama is humming 'Amazing Grace' as she spaces wire hangers along the closet's horizontal wooden post so that a colourful mix of long-sleeved dress shirts and thin summer T-shirts are suspended two-finger widths apart. As I stand behind her watching I wonder if Michael will ever get to wear any of them.

'Mama, what if—' I begin to say, but before I can continue she turns to me radiating her disapproval like some beacon warning of danger. She looks through me as though she's addressing someone directly behind me. I can see the whites of her eyes and she's stopped humming. A strong and steady index finger points at me as she speaks.

'Don't you ever think that,' she says.

I gulp.

'Ever! Do you hear?'

'Yes, Mama.' My throat dries and shrivels.

'When it's time for Michael to come home he will come.'

Chapter Twenty-Seven

I am greeted by my own face as I sip my morning coffee. The face of a tortured figure in a wax museum was on the front page of the *Helena Chronicle*, a biweekly rag that made up for its lack of daily publication by splashing sensational colour photos across its cover. Under my obscenely blown-up, reddened face caught unawares in the State Hill parking lot, the caption read *Fisher daughter mortified*.

'God, I'm sorry,' said Richard when he shuffled into the kitchen sleepily and saw what I was reading. 'I should have been up earlier to save you from this.'

Big, gentle, heroic Richard, always trying to save our family from something. Whatever sleep he was getting these days the shadowy caverns beneath his eyes told me it wasn't enough.

'It's OK,' I said.

*

Richard and I were going to visit Mama today. First we would watch Dr Ashley interview her behind a two-way mirror. Dr Ashley called yesterday to announce we'd been given approval for the viewing, a privilege I was not sure I appreciated. As usual Vivian would watch Ryan while we were out. It was as if he had two homes these days, as comfortable in one as he was in the other.

I flipped the paper over when Ryan entered the kitchen, his sleepy face assuming a special kind of pudginess reserved for early morning, his hair looping shaggily in sandy tassels. I tossed the paper into the hanging trash bag under the sink as I began to prepare his Cheerio breakfast.

Once we'd all eaten, Vivian was at the back door to collect Ryan. She came with a head of lettuce, apples and a few carrots in a bag.

'These will just go bad in my fridge,' she lied whitely, handing the bulging plastic bag to me while she bent instinctively to find Ryan's sneakers in the pile of shoes by the door. Ryan ran first to her for a routine hug then to his bedroom, from which he returned with my old stuffed penguin Genpu. It was then I remembered the books Dr Ashley had requested that I bring.

Ryan was too excited about being with Vivian for the day to put up much of a fuss about me leaving him. She had promised the making of a cherry pie and the latest *Scooby-Doo* video.

'My grandma's brain is sick,' he announced to Vivian matter-of-factly as she fitted his feet into Spiderman sneakers. 'She's in the hospital, but Mommy says I can visit someday.'

I received a mere slice of a hug before he darted through the door with Vivian, his small voice requesting exclusive rights to the rolling pin.

'I be the roller, I be the roller,' he pleaded, clasping my neighbour's hand, dragging her forwards between our homes.

I gathered my books from Ryan's bedroom shelf, twenty slim colourful hardbacks, and placed them in my backpack. Richard was ready and waiting in his leathers and boots when I emerged at the back door.

This would mark Richard's first visit to State Hill. If he was nervous or frightened he didn't show it as we walked down one long hall to the next, doors clanging shut behind us. We didn't go to Mama's ward this time but instead were led to an eastern wing where the interviewing rooms were situated. Inside two rows of chairs were placed in front of a large glass wall. Dr Ashley stood when we entered, shook first Richard's hand then mine.

'This is Dr Nancy Sloan, the assistant director here at State Hill,' he announced, holding out a hand to the smiling woman who had moved in behind him.

'Very good to meet you both,' she said, taking up our hands in greeting.

Her neat ivory suit complemented the various shades of brown in her blunt bob.

'We are doing our very best to ensure your mother's

comfort and safety here at State Hill,' she said to me. But I wasn't looking at her because just over her left shoulder was a white-coated member of staff escorting Mama into the adjoining room. Dr Sloan and Dr Ashley swivelled to follow my gaze.

'Oh, right then,' said Dr Ashley, breaking into the silent moment. 'That's my cue. Do be seated and I'll see you after the interview.'

Richard and I took the front row seats next to Dr Sloan as Dr Ashley left. Two young male interns entered, took up their post by the door like white-coated bookends. I removed writing paper and pen from my backpack. It suddenly felt like we were here to witness Mama's execution.

Mama was wearing the exact same outfit I'd seen her in days before. She probably had a whole closet full of pink State Hill smock-ware. Her hair had been smoothed back into a loose bun. She stood when Dr Ashley entered. He gently grasped her hands with both of his, then they seated themselves at a small table on the other side of the glass.

'What the dickens is that monstrosity of a thing?' she asked, referring to the leather punching bag now erect in the corner of the stark room. 'Do you also treat state boxing champions?'

Mama seemed in good spirits today.

'Well, actually that's been placed there at my request for your sake,' said Dr Ashley.

'For my sake? Goodness gracious! Whatever for?'

'Don't worry,' Dr Ashley said gently. 'We won't be

utilizing it today. It's just there as a tool we might have use for in the future.'

Mama's attention flipped to the glass wall. 'Who are we performing for today? A class of would-be psychologists?' She waved at the mirror sarcastically. 'I must be a real class case study.'

I prayed Dr Ashley wouldn't reveal our presence here.

'It's important to observe from all angles,' he said. 'There may be some experts who see things I've missed.' A diplomatic response, I thought. We all knew Mama's performance, as she called it, would be different for Richard and me.

'OK,' said Dr Ashley, 'I'd like to begin if you're ready.'

Mama shifted in her chair, straightened her back. 'Yes, I'm ready,' she said.

'Now you understand that something has happened, and yet you have no recall of the incident. Is that correct?'

'Yes,' said Mama politely, the model patient. 'That is correct.'

'I am here to draw on the memories you do have in the hopes of retrieving some or all of that forgotten memory.'

'I understand.' Mama nodded.

'OK then. I'd like to begin with your son, Michael. Would you share some of your fondest memories of him with me?'

'Anything specific?'

'No, just random memories,' said Dr Ashley gently.

Mama's eyes suddenly flickered around like an animal, trapped. The atmosphere in the room I shared with Richard, Dr Sloan and the two State Hill interns was deafening in its silence, tortuous in its tension as we awaited Mama's reply.

'Anything really,' coaxed Dr Ashley. 'Birthdays, Christmas, something that leaves you with a good feeling.'

Which of the many Michael-isms in her four-year library of memories would Mama select, I wondered.

'Christmas,' she said. 'The best present I've ever received.'

'Yes, yes, go on,' said Dr Ashley.

'Well, it was Christmas morning. Michael was three years old.' Mama's eyes were already doing that thing they did when she talked about Michael, glazing over with a kind of impenetrable film.

'He was so excited about opening his presents and I could barely get out of bed. The night before I'd been running a fever and by Christmas morning I was suffering the full effects of the flu. When Michael came into our room I told him to lay down with Mommy for a minute before we went downstairs.'

Mama always did tell a good story, built a solid background, then deftly lead her engrossed listener through a series of doorways, enticing them in before delivering the coup de grâce.

'I was hoping he'd fall back asleep for a few more hours. We were lying there and my pyjama shirt had fallen open a bit. I felt his tiny fingers on my skin and then he said, *Mommy I love a baby gofer.* I didn't know what he meant by a baby gofer. How in heaven's name he came up with that I'll never know, but when I looked down he was tracing the outline of a big mole I have. I'd always hated that mole, covered it up at all costs, but here was this sweet boy saying he loved it, naming it a gofer. It changed the way I felt about that mole but more than that it changed the way I perceived all my flaws.'

Mama had told me that story a long time ago. I hadn't realized it was Christmas morning when Michael christened Mama's mole, or maybe I'd forgotten, but it was interesting to me how my memories of Christmas were very different from Mama's. She remembered how he filled her world. I remembered how she filled his stocking.

Richard visited with Mama while I met with Dr Ashley. It wasn't his own office but one he shared with Dr Sloan here at the hospital, he told me. It was Dr Sloan's credentials on the wall, her books that crowded the shelves, her grown kids smiling from photographs.

'OK, Bethany,' he began. 'What are your thoughts or observations about today's interview?'

There was no desk between us this time, just empty space between two hard wooden chairs. I didn't have much to say to him, and had only written down a single sentence throughout the session. I decided to side-track.

'I wondered how she was doing in here. I mean, she seems to be in good spirits and I wondered how she was coping with it all, with the other patients.

'She seemed so normal in the interview,' I continued nervously. 'I'm sure you'll agree she doesn't exactly fit in here. Oh, and I wanted to ask if I could bring her some food, you know, like some baking or something. She says the food in here is terrible – no offence. And also when can her grandson come to visit? I'm sure they'd both appreciate that.'

While I spoke, Dr Ashley scribbled in hurried strokes in the pages of Mama's file.

Finally he said, 'You'll have to ask Dr Sloan about the food items and visits, and as far as I know she's doing fine. She doesn't socialize much, reads a lot apparently, but Dr Sloan is here to brief you on your mother's behaviour and activities during her stay.' Dr Ashley's wording made it sound like she was Mama's holiday coordinator at Club Med.

'What I am interested to know, Bethany, is what you observed and felt during the interview.'

I felt like I'd been told off. I looked down at my scant notes, then back up at Dr Ashley.

'All pretty standard stuff, Dr Ashley,' I said. 'Nothing new in the stories. I've been told a variety of Michael-isms over the years.'

'Michael-isms?'

'Yeah, you know, all the touching things he did and said in his short little life. I've heard them again and again over the years. At first I thought Mama kept telling them so he wouldn't be forgotten, but now I'm beginning to think she tells them so she doesn't forget him herself. With you she's got a new audience, that's all.' Michael may rest but he is strictly forbidden to die.

'How do you feel about hearing them over and over again?'

'Oh, I don't mind. If it makes Mama happy what does it hurt?'

'Doesn't it annoy you?'

'Maybe when I was younger but not now.'

'When you were younger?'

'Yeah, you know, a teenager full of angst.'

'No, I don't know.'

'Teenagers. They're all filled with anger.'

'So you were full of anger?'

How did my words get twisted so easily?

'Wait a minute. I was only saying I wasn't any different from every other teenager.'

'But we aren't talking about every other teenager. We're talking about you, Bethany. Did it make you angry when she started telling me about Michael today?'

'To be honest, Dr Ashley, listening to Mama relay a Michael-ism through a sheet of glass didn't feel much different from if I was right there in the room. Either way she doesn't see me.'

Dr Ashley's pen scratched at an unnerving pace.

'What do you do when you get angry now?' he asked.

'I don't know. Depends who I'm angry at, I guess.'

'Do you feel anger towards whoever is responsible for taking your brother?'

Of course I felt anger towards Michael's abductor, I told Dr Ashley, but it was a distant anger.

'It's difficult to work up a decent bout of anger towards a faceless perpetrator for taking someone I've never actually remembered,' I said.

'But your brother was not the only one taken from you,' said Dr Ashley.

'What do you mean?'

'Isn't it true that whoever took your brother also, in many ways, took your mother away from you?'

I pictured Mama, those vacant eyes, that place she goes.

'I hadn't really thought of it like that,' I said. 'But yes, in many ways I suppose he did.'

'Is there anything else you'd like to say about the interview?' he asked gently.

'It's hard to comment on the picture she painted, a picture I'm not in. The Christmases I remember were quite different.'

'How so?'

So I began to tell Dr Ashley about my own memories, about Michael's stuffed stocking dangling long after the festive days were gone. I told him about Michael's room and the mounting gifts in the closet, the treasures on the windowsill and the wall of pictures that Mama sometimes talked to. I told him about Michael's birthdays, the times we went shopping for him. I even told Dr Ashley about how Mama smacked me in the car for crying.

Every word that came out of my mouth felt like a deception. Mama would hate me saying these things, making her out to be a crazy woman, a bad mother, but something in me couldn't stop.

Dr Ashley finally said, 'When was the last time you had a good cry? Do you cry?'

I laughed, a sort of spit-filled cackle.

'Believe me, I cry. Haven't you seen the front page of today's *Helena Chronicle*? The whole city knows how I feel.'

'Everyone except your mother,' said Dr Ashley. 'When was the last time she knew how you felt?'

'Well, that's the last thing she needs right now, isn't it? She needs to see my haggard face plastered across the front page like a hole in the head.'

'You didn't answer my question.'

'Yes I did,' I snapped back.

'Yeeees.' Dr Ashley drew the word out until his distorted version sounded nothing like an affirmative. 'Perhaps you did.'

Richard and Mama, seated along a middle table, were almost unnoticeable amid the clamour of the visitors' room. Their chairs faced each other so they were knee-to-knee, Richard's bulky frame hunched so his eyes were level with Mama's. Her small hands disappeared in his.

I walked over to them, pulled up a chair, our bodies forming a three-leaf clover.

'Here she is,' said Richard as I sat. He released one of Mama's hands, took hold of mine. With my free hand I squeezed Mama's. A circle of hands, a touching of knees.

'How are you, Mama?' I asked. She seemed to possess a strain of strength today that had been absent the first time I'd seen her at State Hill. Richard could do that. When you were with him you felt like you could pull through anything. I often wondered what would have become of us if it weren't for Richard.

'Oh, all in all, considering where I am, not bad I suppose,' Mama replied quietly. 'Richard tells me you had a meeting with Dr Ashley.'

'Yeah, just came from there,' I said.

'How'd that go?' Richard asked, but before I could answer with a ready, noncommittal *fine* Mama was upon me with a question of her own.

'Not telling him what a horrible mother I was, I hope,' she said.

'Mama, jeez, 'course not,' I gasped with awkward urgency. It was frightening how she could do that, say things she couldn't possibly know. It seemed darkly ironic that Mama always knew what I was up to yet was in this nut-house on account of not knowing what she had done herself.

'How I was crazy right from the get-go,' she pressed.

'Stop it,' I said. I looked at Richard, who shrugged. 'Where do you get this stuff? Why would you say that?'

'These therapists have a way of making you tell them all sorts of things, you know.'

'Well, I know a little bit about psychology myself, Mama, remember? Besides, all Dr Ashley's questions were about me,' I lied.

'Oh, for pity's sake, like what?'

'He wants to read my books, see if there are any connections between me and my characters, I suppose.'

'Well, if that doesn't take the cake,' said Mama. 'What on earth does that have to do with the price of tea in China?'

'Don't worry about it,' I soothed. 'I think he's trying to go through a back door to get a clearer picture. Just trying to make sense of it all.'

'Who else have you been talking to?' asked Mama. 'The media? Nobody tells me anything around here. They won't even let me see a newspaper.'

I looked at Richard. Mama obviously didn't know anything about our interview with Lindsey Sanders or my devastated mug on today's cover page.

'There's a good reason why they don't let you read the papers, Mama. But to answer your question, Richard and I speak to the media as little as possible.'

I had to be extra careful what I divulged. I wanted

to tell Mama she'd been hailed a heroine, that the people of Helena were behind her, but it wouldn't make much sense to a woman with no memory of what she'd done to earn the martyrdom in the first place.

'This might be a good opportunity to start up again with the search for Michael,' she said. 'If the media are hungry you could feed them his photos.'

I didn't know what to say. The unending search continued. Mama had found yet another way to resurrect her son. From the bowels of a nut-house, from the deep chambers of a failing mind, he rose again with unflagging hope. Like the brush that stroked his hair, the green and white polo shirt he wore that dreaded day, Mama continued to believe in the impossible. How could I tell her that's not what the media were interested in at all? It was Richard who intervened.

'That's a good idea,' he said, nodding encouragement at my mother. She smiled in the comfort of his words. Richard was forever saying the exact right thing. Mama and I could be coming at a topic from polar opposites like a pair of warring generals and when Richard stepped in we would both walk away feeling like he was on our side.

'This obviously has something to do with Michael,' continued Mama. 'It seems that's all they ever ask me about.'

Richard and I were silent.

'Oh right, you two can't talk about it, can you?

Well then, I am going to have to trust in what you say, that I will know everything in due time.'

'And you will,' said Richard. 'I promise.'

Mama nodded. A promise from Richard was a certified cheque. Guaranteed.

Chapter Twenty-Eight

If we scrunch our legs in, both Lucy and I fit in my fantastic flying machine. With my fluorescent orange Christmas sled and her sloping back yard we can reach new cheek-pinkening, lip-chapping, wind-chilling heights.

It is March 11th and the patchy, refrozen slush we are playing on is the last of this year's snow. We are taking advantage of what Mama calls the spring-inducing cold snap, as though winter was a fever that had to be broken. She is convinced that any day now all we will see will be crocuses and daffodils amid a mixture of sunshine and light drizzle.

Everything about this day feels rare and fleeting. Mama has left me here at Lucy's with Mrs Zingler, Daniel and Benjamin on a Saturday, alone for the whole day for the first time. Ever. She and Detective Adams have some very important business with a reporter who came all the way from Helena to talk to them.

The elation of my freedom is exaggerated by the serious-injury-defying speeds at which the sled carries us to the bottom of the yard. It doesn't take long before Benjamin is on the hill with a makeshift cardboard sled of his own, attempting to race us. He soon realizes that nothing can compete with the fabulous flaming fireball.

Next Mrs Zingler appears with Daniel. He is bundled up in his chair wearing a chin-strapped bicycle helmet. When Lucy and I reach the bottom I yell out, 'Daniel, wanna go for a ride?'

Mrs Zingler lowers Daniel onto my sled and soon he is sputtering and gurgling his delight as Lucy and I pull him around the flat part of the yard.

After thirty minutes of this we are starving and Mrs Zingler announces that it's time for hotdogs and chips. We all head straight for the kitchen.

I eat three dogs, the same as Benjamin, and am too stuffed to go back outside. Lucy and I go into her room and shuffle a deck of cards in readiness for a game of Crazy Eights. Benjamin joins us for a round despite Lucy's protests.

So this is what it would be like to have an older brother, I think to myself. This is how my life would be except it would be me saying, *Michael, get out of my room. Don't touch that, dog breath* and *Shut up, you creep*. I imagine Benjamin and Michael as best friends wreaking havoc, plotting against us, driving Lucy and me to squeal for mercy.

*

Mama is here to pick me up just before dinner. She thanks Sylvie for taking care of me. In the car I ask her what the reporter from Helena wanted.

'We were just giving her an update on Michael,' says Mama.

'What's an update?' I ask.

'To tell someone what's new.'

'So what's new with Michael?'

'Well, nothing really, but a lot of things too. It's hard to explain.'

'Oh.'

'By the way, I entered your story in that contest.' Mama steers the car into our driveway. She shuts the ignition off. Silence fills the space. She turns to me.

'And you won.'

Mama was right about spring. I blinked and it was here with its crocuses and daffodils, sunshine and drizzle. Today is a particularly drizzly day. It's Sunday and I should be at Daddy's, but he has a special wedding to go to, Lori's brother's wedding, so I'm at home with Mama.

We are in the garage and she is finishing a telephone table, for us this time. I remember this table from the junk heap. It came to us last year via a spring garage sale across town, with a broken leg and four long sad gouges on its face.

Mama tells me to stay busy while I keep her company with a book or my sketchpad, but instead I have written two paragraphs in my notebook, the second Icebowland story featuring Genn and Shine. Genpu and White Sprite sit on the shelf where Mama keeps her tools and brushes, overlooking us, offering their icy, multicoloured inspiration.

Mama stirs a smelly mixture of elements as I jot down descriptions of Shine with a dull pencil, her ivory complexion, a cascade of creamy ringlets, the delicate pink of her eyes protected by lashes and brows touched by frost-fairies, the addition of vanilla glitter lipstick and fingernails of diamond-blue polish. I am pondering more similes for the colour white when I look up and find myself back in the real world gazing upon Mama's creation. Cut-out photographs of Mama, Michael and me blossom from the centre of the wooden table creating a three-dimensional rose collage.

'How do you spell *pearl*, Mama?'

'P-e-a-r-l.' She bores down hard on her stirring stick, swirling the glossy mixture with effort as I copy her dictation.

'Bethany, I need you to hold this stirring stick while I pour,' says Mama. 'If I put it down it will stick to the newspaper.'

Mama scrapes the stick against the side of the tin can full of transparent lacquer, then hands it to me. She pours the contents of the can in careful lines along the tabletop. She fills the shallow oval, covers the photographic centrepiece.

I watch in fascination, breathing in shallow puffs to guard against the enormous odour, which reeks like the gasoline Daddy puts into his lawn mower. When she's finished pouring the coagulating mixture she retrieves the stick from my hand and begins to smooth the glassy liquid gunk until it settles into a thick, even flatness and makes the centre collage appear hugely three-dimensional, like you're looking through water.

I look at the photographs of us: Mama, Michael and me. Our lives blossoming outward in the petals of a flower, each face a shining display of happiness. If you didn't know us, if you didn't know the story of our family and all you saw was this tabletop collage, you would never guess that Michael had been stolen so many years ago. You would never guess that anything was missing from this perfect family abloom with normality. You would think that Michael was right here with us, encased as securely in this family as his image in the table.

Chapter Twenty-Nine

Dr Sloan gave me the go-ahead for tuna casserole and sponge cake, and said if I had any problems with security to have them give her a call.

She had also given the go-ahead for Ryan to visit his grandmother.

He was so excited to be going to see her, stuffing his little Scooby-Doo backpack with enough bedroom paraphernalia to keep him amused for a week. Somewhere within the deep pockets of his pack were various Hot Wheels and the cloth road they often travelled on, the entire Scooby clan – plastic figures of Shaggy, Daphne, Velma, Fred and, of course, Scooby himself. He had with him, too, the three pictures he had painted for Grandma yesterday after I'd announced he could visit.

'You do *not* need your remote-control monster truck,' I now said, laying down the law to my long-lashed boy as he stood in his bedroom clutching the giant vehicle. He pulled a pout face, his mouth filling with air, returned the offending truck to a low shelf, then without hesitation replaced it with his plastic ambulance as though that had been his plan all along.

'OK, mister,' I compromised, 'but that's it.'

Richard helped us to the car with our load and Ryan and I were off to visit his grandmother in the loony bin.

The volume of reporters and photographers at the gate had lessened deceivingly. I was sure I'd got away until I heard my name shouted through the window of a white van in the parking lot of State Hill. As I made my way across the asphalt towards the side doors of the hospital, Ryan in tow, an automatic shutter began rapid fire. The bastards had followed me.

I had no security problems with the food I had brought. It was scanned through the machines with the rest of our load. The ever-serious security officers even cracked a smile at the sight of the pint-sized visitor clutching my hand. Ryan and I were led, not to the common area this time, but to Mama's room. It was a small space taken up by a single bed, a narrow child's dresser and an end table with a mushroom lamp from the Eighties. Two framed photographs had been placed under the lamp: one of me with Ryan on my knee at Mama's kitchen table in Dartmouth. The other was of Michael, his most recent electronically imagined version, a young man now. Richard must have brought them to Mama. Through the muddle and mayhem he had remembered the important things.

Up in the corner near the ceiling there was an over-seeing black lens. Poor Mama. She didn't even have privacy in her own room.

Ryan rushed to her, arms wide.

'Grandma, Grandma,' he squealed, lunged for an overdue hug and was at once unzipping his pack, unloading its contents upon the spotless linoleum floor. Mama took the casserole from me, lifted the lid to savour the aroma and said, 'Oh mercy, thank you.' We placed the food on the small end table next to the photos and I hugged her hello.

Ryan had by now created a massive traffic jam on his cotton road, the immense ambulance towering over a knot of Hot Wheels. Mama sat down there too, oohing and ahhing at his town of cars, reaching occasionally to smooth a coil of his unruly hair. I watched them at play, seemingly oblivious to my presence. Amid Ryan's rough and tumble vroooms and crashes Mama looked on with inexplicable joy.

When I announced I was going to talk to Dr Sloan for a little while, that I'd be back soon, they barely looked up.

By now I knew my way along the halls up into the stretching eastern arm which led to Dr Sloan's office. I was a bit early for our scheduled appointment, but when I knocked she seemed delighted to see me.

I took up the single remaining chair across from her, folded my legs one over the other. Dr Sloan was dressed more casually today – a flattering high-neck avocado knit, black dress pants.

'Did you bring your son?' she asked.

'Oh yes, he's in with my mother. The two of them are quite happily engrossed in a city of toy cars at the moment.'

Dr Sloan grinned widely. 'Good show,' she said. 'There's nothing quite like the relationship between a grandmother and her grandchild.' Her eyes glanced above us to the shelves where she kept her framed photos.

'You're not a grandmother, are you?' I asked. I couldn't imagine her in that role. She seemed so much younger than Mama.

'Not yet,' she said. 'But looking forward to the day. That's my son there with his new wife.' She pointed to a grinning couple. 'I keep hinting, but so far they're concentrating on their careers.'

I nodded my understanding.

'OK then, let's talk about your mother, shall we? Do you have any questions?'

I shrugged. 'Just general questions, I guess, like how is she doing in here?'

'Yes. Well, she's fine in all respects. She has a sort of neutral presence really. She keeps to herself a lot and reads anything she can get her hands on.'

'Does she socialize at all?'

'She's very polite to the other patients but she hasn't made any friends, if that's what you're asking.

'Did you bring her some food?' asked the doctor after a pause.

'Yes, a casserole. She seemed delighted.'

'Oh, I'm glad to hear that. Maybe she'll eat a bit more now.'

'What do you mean? Isn't she eating?' I champed into the sour taste of this new problem. It was so much easier than looking at the big problem, the problem of Mama's memory loss, the problem of the ever-looming court date, the problem of Mama becoming unhinged.

'She eats,' said Dr Sloan. 'Just not a lot, so maybe this will help.'

'Well, I'll keep the casseroles coming.'

'I did want to talk to you about one thing, though, Bethany. It's nothing that is cause for alarm, just an observation that perhaps you could shed some light on.'

'Of course,' I said. 'What is it?'

'We have noticed lately that every night before your mother goes to bed she holds a photograph of Michael and she talks to him. But we can't make out what she's saying; she speaks in a kind of mumbled whisper.'

Good for you, Mama, I thought. At least they can't have that, your secret moments with Michael.

'Do you have any idea what she might be saying?' asked Dr Sloan.

I remembered Mama in Michael's room, her voice wafting through the vents. 'When I was a kid it was more of a plea for him to come home. Now she almost speaks to him as a friend. I've heard her in passing on a few occasions when she's come to visit me. Sometimes she just sort of checks in with him. Tells him about her day. I guess he sort of acts as her friend, her therapist.'

'Her God?'

I smiled, looked down at the two tight fists in my lap and shrugged.

'I don't know. Maybe. She hasn't had much faith in any other God for a long time.'

'How about you, Bethany? Do you believe in God?'

'I'd like to,' I said. 'My dad does. He says the harder things get the stronger his faith becomes. I suppose by now it's pretty rock solid.'

Dr Sloan didn't acknowledge my attempt at humour.

'But it hasn't worked like that for you?'

'It hasn't been that straightforward, no. I mean I've got one parent who has discarded the possibility of His existence and the other who has embraced it. Somewhere in the middle is me. I mean I'm open. I guess I just have to find my own particular path to God.'

The numerous faces of the hospital staff were becoming as familiar as Dr Ashley and Dr Sloan. They held the softness of recognition as they buzzed and nodded me through the various doors back to Mama's ward after my meeting. Mama and Ryan were on the bed when I returned, carefully filling in the outlined spaces of a colouring book with felt tips. Sometime over the space of my absence Mama had taped Ryan's three paintings to the wall above the table. Brightening Mama's barren room were Ryan's watery sun and mountain scene, his picture of yellow and red flowers and a busy family collage, a dozen stick figures in all – Daddy and Lori in their townhouse in Dartmouth, Richard and Mama next to a motorcycle, the entire Zingler family bunched into a single unit, Will and me holding Ryan's hand and, beaming from on high behind a mountain, a face bigger than the rest. Michael. Mama had made sure he was part of Ryan's life too.

'Mommy's back,' I announced.

'Look what Grandma and I did.' Ryan held up their masterpiece for me to view, a purple and green dinosaur.

'That's wonderful. What beautiful colours, Ryan.' I took a seat on the floor beside the bed.

I watched them with a kind of reverence, their hunched bodies, intertwined limbs like a single entity. Their love was a thickness that hung in the room like a curtain, me on the other side. Mama had entered that place where she goes, Ryan the only one allowed in. I listened to her animated voice bubble and coo.

A strange and unbidden thought occurred to me then, something I'd never considered. If Ryan had been born a girl, would Mama still feel the same way?

Chapter Thirty

I'm sitting on the sofa between Detective Adams and Mama. It's nine fifty-two p.m. and there are bowls of popcorn and chips on the coffee table in front of us. It's like we are getting ready to watch a special episode of *Beverly Hills 90210*, but instead I am allowed to stay up past my bedtime to watch a show called *Newsline*. Today is Michael's stolen day and Mama is going to be on TV.

I feel both excited and horrified when the *Newsline* theme music starts. I imagine this is how I might feel if I got to eat strawberry ice-cream but had to eat it while looking at a dead cat.

The show begins with a man sitting behind a desk shuffling papers. When the theme music stops the camera has moved in close.

'Good evening and welcome to *Newsline*. I'm John Brennan.'

John Brennan shifts to the left and appearing in the

right-hand corner of the screen is the latest computer-enhanced photo of Michael.

'Tonight correspondent Maria Gray takes us back to July 16th, 1983; a day many of you will remember as the day little Michael Fisher went missing from his home town of Dartmouth, Montana.'

Following is an advertisement for pizza. Detective Adams shifts his body, a body much too large for our sofa, and stretches his arm along the back. Over my head he says to Mama, 'They've given you the lead.'

There's that word again, *a crappy lead*, *a false lead*, and I know that whatever a lead is Daddy would not approve. I wonder if he's watching. Of course he's watching and Lucy's watching and Benjamin and Mrs Zingler, even Daniel. Our neighbour Mrs Brown will be watching. Come to think of it, everyone in Dartmouth is probably watching.

'Welcome back,' says John Brennan in a forcefully sweet voice that commands you to listen and makes you want to at the same time.

'Our top story tonight comes from Montana, where Maria Gray examines the effects of abduction on small-town America *Ten Years Later*.' The last three words appear across the screen in front of Michael's photo. The camera slowly zooms in on Michael's right eye until the screen is a single magnified pupil too close to recognize as a facial feature. Cut to Maria Gray standing in Dartmouth's baseball field.

'This field behind me used to be home to the annual Dartmouth Jamboree, where the folks of Dartmouth brought their families every year for a fun-filled day of rides, contests and games.'

Maria is walking through the field. I recognize the Dartmouth curling rink behind her.

'But that all changed exactly ten years ago when Dartmouth lost one of its own: little Michael Fisher, four years old at the time. This field has remained empty since except for a single reminder of what took place so long ago.'

The camera pans out and shows a long row of Michael's face attached to sticks planted in the ground. It's the photo, the latest one that's up on his bedroom wall, duplicating itself across the field, repeating its message like real estate signs. Only here Michael is selling himself and instead of *buy me* his message echoes *find me*.

Change screen to Mama and Detective Adams. The moment we've all been waiting for. We can only hear Maria's voice now as the camera holds them in place.

'I am sitting here with Michael Fisher's mother, Doris Fisher, and Detective Richard Adams, the detective assigned to the case.'

The camera moves in slowly on Mama's tight, unmoving face.

'Can you describe that day ten years ago?' asks Maria gently. Mama's eyes begin to flicker. She looks at Detective Adams next to her, although we can't see him any more. She sighs.

'Well, you know, as you said, it was the day of the annual Dartmouth Jamboree.' Mama's words stumble out of her mouth as she recalls the day. I have never seen Mama look so shy, so scared. Tears burn behind my eyes. Mama continues the story, telling it just as she has told me so many times before, the dabs of jam in plastic bowls, me in my stroller, Michael under the table, the little dog, the big field, the terrible wind.

'And then he was gone. Vanished into thin air,' she finishes. The camera releases its tight grip on her frightened face, backs away to reveal Detective Adams at her side once again, then zooms in on him as Maria asks, 'What did the police do at that point?'

'Well, of course, a search of the area was conducted immediately. Not just the police but the whole town was out in force.' His sandpaper voice is a powerful contrast to Mama's but somehow a necessary complement. They are a team.

The screen runs silent footage of people fanning out in the field, scouring the banks of the Dart River as the detective speaks.

'With the help of the media we got the word out as soon as possible. Michael's picture was on posters and milk cartons across America within two days.'

An old picture of Michael on a milk carton appears. Then the camera pans back to the detective.

'But it all proved to be too late at that point.'

Zoom out for a shot of the two of them.

'What have the last ten years been like, first on an investigative level and then on a personal level?' Maria's question hangs a moment then the detective breaks through the silence.

'We've had an enormous amount of support from the community and hundreds upon hundreds of leads over the years, each of which we have taken very seriously and followed up to the best of our abilities, but obviously none has led us back to Michael. What is important now, and the reason we are doing this, is that people don't forget. It is not the police who will find Michael. It is the public. It is their eyes and their ears that we rely on. This town continues to mourn, this family still suffers and will not rest until Michael is home where he belongs.'

'On a personal level,' says Maria, 'tell us about the last ten years.'

The camera is back on Mama, cradling her face in its lens. The detective seems far away. Mama isn't looking into the camera. Her eyes are cast down to the left. Caught on tape, she is in that place where she goes.

'As Mr Adams said, the community has been incredibly supportive and I am so very grateful to them. The detective himself has been a great source of hope to our family. But what has primarily kept me going, made me get out of bed every morning and put one foot in front of the other and carry on, is Michael, knowing he's out there, knowing that I will be here when he returns.'

Then Mama comes back to us, peers deep into the camera.

'We just want you to come home, Michael. Just come home, baby. Just come home.'

Mama's last word breaks up. Her agony is TV-screen magnified, her eyes fill, her bottom lip trembles and so does mine. She spills her grief out for everyone to see. I am crying and can't stop. Detective Adams gives me a squeeze with his bear-hairy arm. I am sobbing into his chest in deep gasping wails but I am not crying for Mama. I'm not crying for Mama's pain, Mama's grief. I'm not even crying for Michael, for the evils he's seen or because I miss him. How can you miss someone you've never known?

I'm crying because I've just remembered something. I'm crying because tomorrow when I stand up to receive my story award people won't think of me as Bethany Fisher, the girl who can write good stories. Everyone will think of me as Michael Fisher's sister, that poor girl from that poor family.

I watch as Maria finishes her report with a phone number for people to call if they have any information and I feel something for Michael that I've never felt before.

I feel intense hatred.

Chapter Thirty-One

Daddy took a week off work in early December to be with us. He didn't bring his wife this time but instead my best friend Lucy. Richard took the opportunity to return to Dartmouth for a few days, tend to some unfinished business. He was retired now from detective work but had been toying with the idea of buying into a motorcycle business with the existing owner on the outskirts of Dartmouth. It should have been an exciting time for him, the thought of being surrounded by his passion after a lifetime of hard work, but it came to him almost as an afterthought now, a loose end that required temporary knotting.

Before Richard left he bought us a Christmas tree. Knowing I didn't have much in the way of ornaments, he also bought a bag of decorations: shiny gold and red baubles, ropes of silver tinsel, miniature lights that blinked on and off.

We hadn't planned on spending Christmas in Helena. It was a given that Ryan, Will and I would be in Dartmouth for the holidays. Ryan would sleep with me up in my old room, tear into Mama and Richard's room early on Christmas morning to announce the day's arrival and we would spend the morning snapping photos and delighting in Ryan's animated excitement. Later Will, Daddy, Lori and the Zinglers would join us and we would crowd around Mama's kitchen table for a Christmas feast, admire the large bird that Richard would carve.

All that was a given, an absolute. That was how Christmas was done in my family these days. Except for this year. This year Will would go to be with his family in Dartmouth and we would remain to mould a Christmas around our bizarre set of circumstances, make do, as Mama would say. Try to convince Ryan that it was perfectly normal to spend the morning around our small tree and the afternoon with Grandma, that Christmas came in two parts this year. Nothing says Christmas like a visit to the nuthouse.

I tried to convince myself that Ryan wouldn't care one way or the other. As long as the vital elements were in place – a path of cookie crumbs from the tray we'd left for Santa in the living room to the front door, gifts from Santa under the tree and family surrounding him with festive enthusiasm – he wouldn't mind.

So Daddy and Lucy moved in while Richard moved out, a changing of the guard. It was good to see Daddy again, a bit steadier this time. But I was thrilled to have Lucy by my side for a whole week.

The first thing we did once she unpacked in Ryan's room where she would be sleeping, Daddy and Ryan in the living room twisting and climbing their way through a game of Snakes and Ladders, was plonk ourselves on my son's bed and begin the riveting process of catching up. I told her how Mama was doing and how I'd been listening to her tell the story of our lives from behind glass. I told her how I'd been meeting with Dr Ashley after the sessions with Mama, revealing my own memories, and I told her how Mama wasn't any closer to remembering those bloody moments in TRF's kitchen. Then I asked her about her own mother, Sylvie.

'Yeah, Ma'ma's great. She met someone.'

'That is so cool,' I said.

'I know. He's a physiotherapist where she takes Daniel. Her other physio got pregnant and he replaced her. He's like German or something. They are now in the process of completely demolishing our back yard. They've gone on some kind of gardening frenzy and are putting in a new pond, building archways, planting exotic trees that Ma'ma keeps chattering on about like I know the difference between a Japanese maple and a bonsai. She's gone happily insane and the place is an utter disaster.'

I laughed and snorted but felt like crying. How I had missed my friend.

'How's Ben?' I asked nervously.

'Ben got that job he wanted, apprenticing for Doug Sanburg down at the garage. He won't make much money until his third year or so but he seems happy enough.'

'Oh, that's perfect. He's always wanted to be a mechanic. And the gang, how's everyone?'

'Well, the best is that Nicole is doing community service work at the Dartmouth Care Facility because she and Dave Matthews got pissed up on tequila, which she stole from her parents' liquor cabinet, and then tried to rip off the N out of the Bixbie 'N Son's auto supply store sign so she could hang it on her bedroom wall. When the cops high-beamed the two in action Dave took off running and left Nicole on the roof. She was charged with attempting to destroy public property and has to do six months.'

'Ohmygod, trust bloody Matthews to leave her hanging.'

'I know, but it was all Nicole's idea. She didn't even rat on him. But enough about them. Who cares? Listen to this, I think I'm in love, his name's Andrew and he works at the video store but he's studying to be a chef just like me. That's where we met and he's sooooo cute, has curly black hair and those eyes would melt Icebowland.'

Oh yes, yes, tell me more, don't stop, don't ever stop. This is exactly what I need, something as manual as digging in earth, as ridiculous as stealing a giant N, as airy as a new romance. Yes, take me away, take me back, take me forwards, let me be nineteen again for

*this one blessed moment. Let me be normal, perfectly
normal for a few minutes before my reality descends
upon me again . . .*

'You cancelled two appointments last week,' said Dr
Ashley accusingly. I sat across from him in my usual
chair in his shared office. There was no trace of the
beacon that was Dr Ashley's smile.

'Yes, sorry about that,' I said, 'but my Dad and my
girlfriend were up for the week and, to be honest, I
needed a break.' It sounded perfectly reasonable to me.

'Well, the courts don't take a break, Bethany. Quite
frankly, your mother and I need you right now. There
will be plenty of time for visits once this is over.'

I'd never seen Dr Ashley in any mood other than
courteous and gracious so this no-tolerance, *quite-
frankly* straightforwardness came as a bit of a shock.

'We've still got three months,' I protested weakly.

'We have just *under* three months and there's
Christmas fast approaching and we are no further
ahead than when I saw you last and that wasn't very
far.' His hound dog eyes took on an acute and scrupu-
lous glare.

'I said I was sorry.' I slouched in the chair like the
chastised twelve year old I felt I was.

'I've read your books, by the way,' said Dr Ashley.

'Oh, good,' I said, happy to discuss a new topic.

'Found them very interesting.'

'How so?'

'The characters.'

'There are a lot of characters. Any in particular?'

'The main ones, the children who go to Icebow-land.'

'Yeah, what did you find interesting about them?'

'They all seem to have something wrong with them,' he said.

'That's one way to put it, I guess.'

'How would you put it?'

'I'd say they were different. That's the point of the stories. When they go to Icebowland they aren't treated any differently. Everything and everyone is different there, so it's like going home.'

'Is that how you felt when you wrote them? Like you were going home?'

'I don't know. It relaxed me to write. I liked writing them and they started as an assignment, remember.'

'You could have written anything for an English assignment. You could have done a book report or written a poem. Why did you decide to write these stories?' Dr Ashley's questions sizzled with purpose. It felt as though he'd rehearsed his part and I'd come to the stage unprepared.

'I don't know. They just came to me.'

'Who was the girl with the broken legs, Raine?'

'Nobody. I made her up.' It felt like I was shooting my words through the small spaces he left me between his list of questions.

'In her real world she couldn't walk or run, couldn't

get to where she was going. Do you think, metaphor-
ically speaking, maybe you couldn't go where *you*
wanted?'

'I don't know what you mean. My legs weren't
broken. I could go anywhere I wanted. I just made her
up.'

'Perhaps you wanted to go to school. Perhaps like
Raine you were stuck at home. Perhaps instead of
telling your mother that you wanted to go to school
and thereby disappointing her you simply made up
Raine and in doing so you could in fact go wherever
you wanted.'

'I don't know, Dr Ashley, sounds like you're reading a bit much into all this, a bit psychobabbly for me.
I think I had an English assignment to do and I made
up a story.'

'And how about the albino girl? Same thing? You
just made her up?'

'Yes,' I said.

'She goes from being a bit of a freak to a princess
before her status is significantly reduced.'

'So?'

'So are you saying you don't see any connections
with your own life?'

'I was never a freak and I'm certainly no princess.'
I remained adamant.

'I'm not suggesting you take literal reference. Surely
you understand metaphor.'

'Of course.'

'Can you then entertain the possibility that because

it was you who invented these characters that it could be possible a little of your subconscious also made it into their appearance and behaviour? That perhaps you did feel like a freak at one point, that you were suddenly treated like a princess and then somehow all that disappeared when the attention shifted onto someone else?'

'Like Michael?'

'Yes, quite specifically, like Michael.'

'I suppose there is that possibility, yes.'

'I would like to suggest to you that it is more than just a possibility. Do you mind if I read you something from the Shine and Genn story?'

He lifted the book from the heap on his desk as though this moment was the climax of the performance, my book an important prop. He fingered the thick pages to a place pre-marked by a yellow Post-it and read my sentences into the room like breathing memory. In an instant I was both a million miles away in a distant galaxy and child-cradling safe.

'Shine is the winner,' he reads. 'A shimmering crystal tiara is placed upon her head by last year's snow queen. As Shine finishes her victory walk the MC announces the arrival of the King of Silver City, here to say a few words.'

I know what's coming and I want to stop Dr Ashley from reading it aloud, snatch the book from his fingers and tell the old limey to mind his own business. It is all becoming so obvious, like a purple lump on a forehead that everyone can see but you.

'There the great King stands at the end of the runway, a thing of splendour, the thing the people will remember today at the Whitest of the White beauty contest.'

Dr Ashley reads the last sentence from memory, no longer looking at the book but directly at me, his eyes like tiny, indisputable mirrors that reflect my life.

'To Shine's utter amazement the Royal King of Silver City is made of pure gold.'

There wasn't much to say in the ensuing pause. I'd been clobbered by my own words, printed, published and on display for all to examine. Somewhere along the line I had buried this confession of rage and jealousy in a safe place and here it was now undeniable like an old bloodied rag dug up by the family pet.

'OK, I admit there is probably a connection,' I finally said sheepishly.

Dr Ashley nodded gracefully and left it at that. He was the epitome of tact and kindness, something I was busy resenting at the moment.

Changing tack slightly he asked, 'Did writing the stories give you a sense of freedom?'

'Yes, I suppose they did.'

'It's interesting,' said Dr Ashley, looking into his notes.

'What is?'

'That your mother was both overprotective of you, which of course is rational behaviour considering what happened to your brother, but also very neglectful.'

'Neglectful? She was never neglectful, Dr Ashley.

She was anything but that. Haven't you been listening to me? She home-schooled me for goodness sake. She did everything with me. We were inseparable.'

'There are different types of neglect, Bethany.'

Dr Ashley was turning up the heat again. Making up for lost time.

'How do you get that?'

'From what you've said so far, your mother rarely cried, she denied her own feelings of sadness and grief, hid them under the flurry of action she created searching for Michael. Then when you showed your emotions she denied them too, talked you out of them, distracted you. You're right, you *were* inseparable, but that's the issue here. She couldn't separate her own emotional denial from yours. No wonder you felt freedom in Icebowland. As I recall in Icebowland there are over seventy thousand colours, each representing different emotions.'

I smiled, impressed by his memory of the details in my stories. I tried to absorb his words, tried to shift my thinking, but my mind would snap back to what I knew like a stubborn crease resisting the heat of an iron. 'I'm not sure, Dr Ashley,' I said, shaking my head. 'There were plenty of times I was sad with Mama.'

'Yes, but what would she tell you to do or show by example?'

'I don't know. It was different every time.'

'But the message was the same. Earn your tears. You don't deserve to cry. This is small. What I've endured is big and what you're upset about is nothing.

If I can face every day and carry on, you have nothing to complain about. She even downplayed your achievements. Don't get too excited. Don't forget what's important. Your mother played the martyr, did she not?'

I hated this, hated him saying these things about Mama. It was like he had taken everything I'd ever said about Mama and moulded it into the self-serving shape of a crazy woman. Who was he to talk? He didn't have his kid stolen. He didn't know what it was like for her. What did he want her to do, I asked him, have a nervous breakdown every other day, fall apart when she had me to raise?

'Might have done her some good to have a breakdown. It would have been a respite for her.'

'Well, she kind of did, for your information. I have seen my mother come apart at the seams, split open, spill her guts out. Does that make you happy?'

'This isn't about making me happy, Bethany. This is about trying to figure out why your mother followed Thomas Freeman home and killed him with a fire poker and still has no recall two months later.'

'My mother was not neglectful,' I told him. 'She did the best she could.'

'She can't hear you in here, Bethany. You don't have to protect her. You can entertain the possibility that your mother made mistakes, that she's human, that her coping method may have done both you and her more harm than good. It's not betrayal.'

It felt like the floor was sliding out from under me.

I couldn't tolerate much more of this. I felt dizzy, overheated. Dr Ashley's shared office suddenly felt closet-small. I wanted out. Why was he doing this, trying to show me my own mother in a bad light, expose Mama for the monster she really was? I wouldn't listen to it for another second. How could this help her remember? Wasn't that the point?

'I gotta go.'

'You're free to go, Bethany, but that won't make it any easier. Not in the long run. Eventually you'll have to face things.'

I stood up. 'What things?' I spat the words out. My hands were shaking.

'What you need is to tell your mother how you feel.'

'Mama knows how I feel.'

'Does she?'

'What do you want?' I repeated.

'I want someone to start telling me something. Between you bailing out on appointments and your mother talking about the weather we are fast approaching our court date with nothing to offer. You say you want her out of here, say she doesn't belong in a place like this, that besides the little incident she's perfectly normal. Well, guess what? Your perfectly normal mother might be in here for years at this rate unless you decide this is important enough to look inside for, do a bit of work.'

'What kind of work? What can I do?' I shouted the last question almost beseechingly. Dr Ashley cleared his throat, allowed the echo of my screeching words to settle. Then he spoke with unnerving calm.

'Start asking questions.'

'What questions?' My eyes were on fire. I wanted to go. I needed movement, air. I was on the verge of disintegration. I dragged my stone feet towards the door.

'I can't stop you from leaving, Bethany.'

My hand was on the doorknob.

'But for starters please think about this. If there was one question you could ask your mother and be guaranteed an honest, straightforward answer, what would it be?'

I couldn't respond, my throat a clenched, aching fist. I opened the door and walked out.

PART 3

PART 3

Chapter Thirty-Two

1997

In a family there are times when a great tempest is necessary to manufacture calm. Things must be ripped apart, blown away down to their bony foundation so that construction can begin afresh, the process of rebuilding a new history. All history begins somewhere and it's never easy.

I get my period before Lucy and race to the phone to report. Not before Mama *fixes me up*, though, gives me a box of removable-strip maxi-pads with both hands as though it is a sacred object.

I'm not afraid when I see blood in my panties. I know exactly what it is as Mama and I have spoken at length on the topic. She says it is a natural progression into womanhood, something wonderful, something to be proud of, and I am.

What Mama forgot to mention was how I would suddenly start crying while listening to a love song or become overly sensitive to the slightest criticism. How it feels like I'm carrying a brick around in the pit of my stomach. And she most certainly didn't mention how I would start to look at Benjamin Zingler. But I don't mind all that because I'm a woman now.

'What colour are the Snowballites?' asks Lucy.

'What colour are the snow-mountains they come from?' I return.

'Oh, yeah, right,' says Lucy and searches among the pots of poster paints for orange.

Thanks to Mrs Zingler's brainstorm and Lori's artistic abilities (we'd like to thank all the big people) we have constructed a mural the size of Lucy's bedroom wall featuring scenes of Icebowland. The white construction paper, six pieces glued together and cut in a floor-to-ceiling semi-circle, is filled with pencil and charcoal drawings. It has taken three months to complete and tonight Lucy and I begin to spread our first drops of paint.

Featured are Silver City, the Lustre Valley, Mount Echo, Pastel Mountain, the Pinecicle Fields, Soda Springs, Spiral Forest, Yellow River and Lake Violet. All the penguins and their children are represented, plus the snow princesses, the ice queen, and my latest addition, Snow Boulder and her Snowballites. The extras are here as well, all the flightless creatures amid groves and lines of leafless trees.

Our mural has a definite *Where's Waldo?* appeal. Lucy and I have spent a good many hours examining our work, discovering forgotten details. At first glance it may appear to be a land of utter snow-filled chaos but upon closer, more meditative inspection one soon comes to see a series of scenes, each a visual representation of their particular story.

Drawing is one thing. Though it took a long time, it was more a matter of consistent mindless doodle. As I put my brush to paper I am aware that paint has a feel of finality that charcoal lacks. I wonder how long the painting will take us. It suddenly seems a daunting affair.

'Maybe Jenny can come on Saturday and help us,' offers Lucy, as though she too has been pondering the overwhelming intricacies of our project.

'Think about that for a second,' I say with a knowing smirk.

'Oh yeah, right. How could I forget?' she says. 'The big game.'

Lucy has acquired a lot of new friends. I don't mind, though, because they are my friends too. In the beginning I minded. I minded a lot. I minded when Jenny Jacobs came over to Lucy's and talked about nothing but boys. I minded when Kelley James came over and played her Boyz II Men tapes on Lucy's ghetto. I minded when Nicole Wilkinson came and bragged about how she smoked behind the school and stole alcohol out of her parents' cupboard at Christmas. I minded how Lucy laughed at their stupid jokes and how when Benjamin came into Lucy's room to tell his sister the phone was for her they all invented high-pitched squeals and tugged their shirts a little snugger.

But I don't mind any more because I like talking about boys now and my breasts are as big as any of theirs, but mostly I don't mind because when they go home it's just Lucy and me and we are the same as we ever were.

Yes, some things have changed and some things haven't. The ones that haven't are the things I rely on, that keep me going, as Mama would say. For example, I still come to Mrs Zingler twice a week for French lessons. I still stay until Lucy gets home from school and we still go to her room to hang out. What's changed is that Mama no longer sits in the living room during all of this and I am allowed to stay until nine-thirty p.m. because these days in exchange for French lessons I help Lucy with her math homework.

I don't like math the same way I like English but I find it easy enough and maintain good grades. Lucy's Grade Eight math is twice as easy as my Grade Eleven math so I don't mind helping her a bit.

When it's *tutor time*, as Mrs Zingler has dubbed it, we have to go into the kitchen and sit at the table under Mrs Zingler's watchful eye because both she and Mama know if Lucy and I tried to do homework in her bedroom while listening to Nicki French belt out 'Total Eclipse of the Heart' it just wouldn't happen.

During tutor time Lucy is not allowed to accept phone calls and neither Benjamin nor Daniel is allowed to bother us. I am under strict orders and supervision not to *do* Lucy's homework but to help her figure out how to do it herself.

Lucy hates math.

Luckily she loves art but there are times I wish the same rules of segregation applied to our mural moments, like now, as the door bursts open and Benjamin leans between the doorknob and the wall, his thick hair hanging in his eyes.

'Erg! Get lost,' says Lucy without looking up, eyeing the peach smudge this sudden interruption has caused.

'OK then, I won't tell you,' says Benjamin.

'What?' Lucy and I say together.

'Oh nothing, just some *boy* on the phone.'

'Whatever,' says Lucy unflinching.

'OK, I'll tell him you're busy.'

'Who is it then, Mr Knowitall?'

'Ooooh, I don't know, maybe it's Nick or Howie or A.J.,' teases Benjamin indicating Lucy's latest Backstreet Boys poster, which has been moved above her bed since our mural took over.

Mrs Zingler's impatient voice calls down the hall.

'Lucy, this phone has been sitting here waiting for you to answer it.'

'Told ya,' says Benjamin pulling a face.

Lucy spears the brush into a jar of coloured water, shoulder butts her brother as she passes and Benjamin enters the room, stands behind me with his arms folded, studying our masterpiece.

'Don't say it.' I'm trying to deflect his criticism before it shoots out of his mouth.

'Say what? I'm not going to say anything. 'S awesome,' he says.

I let my guard down just in time to hear his laughter. 'What?'

'What's that?' He's pointing at Snow Boulder. 'That's hilarious,' he says. 'I love the expression as it rolls down the hill.'

Snow Boulder rages forwards down Mount Echo, Egu and Daw swaddled inside her immense bulk like twin sausages in a snowy bun.

'It's a *she* and she's just been woken up,' I say but realize he wouldn't know what I was talking about. 'Never mind. It's part of the story,' I quickly add.

'So where is this story?'

'There are loads, but I'm just working on this one at the moment.'

'I'd like to read it when you finish,' he says, but I can't tell if this is a set-up for his next joke.

'Really?' But I hate the way I say it. I sound small and desperate.

'Yeah, really. I'd love to know what that giant snow-ball is all about.'

I can feel my ears heating up. Lucy rushes back in and bundles Benjamin out of the room.

'You will *never* guess what! *That* was Kyle Peterson,'

she says in a mouse's voice. 'I think he just asked me to the dance.'

Ah yes, the dance. The dance that I won't be going to as there is no convincing Mama to let me.

Two things have happened this week. The first is that Lucy got her period. She could have at least waited six months, given me that.

The second is that no matter how many times I remind Mama, Mrs Zingler, Lucy, anyone who will listen, that now that I am a woman I would rather be called Beth, it just doesn't seem to stick. Lucy, bless her magnanimous spirit, tries at least and might even get two Beths out in the space of fifteen minutes but unwittingly reverts back to Bethany every time. Mama just says, 'Bethany, don't be ridiculous.'

It only stands to reason then that the week should end on a humiliating note. Mama is not only driving Lucy, Nicole, Kelley and me to the big basketball game (Dartmouth Dolphins vs the Warmish Wombats, or Warmish Wimps to us) when we would much rather walk, but she's staying with us for the match.

'I don't have to sit with you,' she says as I attempt one last time to grovel, argue, reason my way into changing her preposterous decision.

But Mama is Mama and no is no. I drag my defeated self to the Volvo.

'Can you not walk in with us, either?' I say, resigned to my fate.

'Watch your mouth, young lady, or you won't be going at all.'

I don't say another word about it. First we pick Lucy up, then Nicole and finally Kelley around the streets of Dartmouth, then inch closer to the school. For the seven minutes it takes to get to Dartmouth Junior High with the car full of us I breathe shallow breaths and pray nobody says anything incriminating. I pray Lucy doesn't say anything about Kyle Peterson asking her to the dance or the fact that he will be at the game today. I pray Kelley doesn't say anything about me thinking Benjamin is cute and I pray Nicole just doesn't say anything at all. In a single second Mama's greatest worries could be confirmed (that I *am* in fact a teenager, that I *do* think about boys) and the few privileges of freedom Mama does allow thus thwarted forever.

But the girls stick to the topic of basketball, past wins and losses. My sigh is give-away audible when we park in the busy school lot and I unlatch the passenger door the moment Mama raises the gearshift to P. We group outside the car then walk towards the gym entrance, cruelly ignoring Mama lagging behind.

Kelley leads us inside and we follow her up the Dartmouth side of the bleachers, lunging forwards in awkward giant steps and clearly annoying everyone sitting in our path. Mama has thankfully kept her word and is nowhere to be seen. I know, however, that wherever she is in this explosion of young fans, she can see me.

We take seats three bleachers from the top, adjust

our hair and clothing, pretend to talk to each other in a sort of we-are-so-interesting-and-hilariously-funny-and-everyone-else-is-a-bore conversation while looking around to see who's looking.

'There he is,' says Lucy. 'Don't look!'

'Is he looking this way?'

'I don't know, I'm not looking.'

'Well, look!'

'No way, I'm not looking. You look.'

'You told me not to look.'

We are saved by the sudden roar of the crowd as Dartmouth's cheerleaders and roadrunner mascot incite the masses to hysteria. We join in.

'Dartmouth, Dartmouth, here we go, Dartmouth, Dartmouth, it's your show,' rave a line of eight emblazoned cheerleaders. Flashes of silver and red pompoms streak the air below us like the wildly dancing heads of punk rockers and there she is, our friend Jenny, smiling, kicking, chanting, twirling with the best of them. I can't help but feel a spark of pride.

By the time the players enter, silver and red uniforms versus blue and gold running laps in opposing directions, the entire gymnasium is pounding, thumping, thundering with frenzied excitement. I wonder if Mama knew what she was getting into.

The Dolphins plough into the Wimps from the onset and by half time my voice is hoarse and we are ahead 52–36. The girls and I follow the crowd to the cafeteria for a soda. The drink's queue snakes into the hallway, the perfect opportunity to be seen without looking obvious. Jenny catches up with us, her cheeks flush, make-up sweat-smudged, her sparkling uniform even more dazzling at close range. We inch along, talking, giggling and before we know it we are at the counter. Lucy is ordering lemon cider when a hand dangles over her shoulder with a five-dollar bill between its fingers and the owner's voice says, 'Make that two.'

Another voice behind us orders Kyle Peterson to the back of the line but Lucy's got the money now and is paying for both drinks with it.

Once we all have drinks we form a cluster. It's us and them, us and Kyle Peterson's three-boy entourage. They all have the same dark hair, cut short around the back and sides, left long in front, except for one boy whose hair is a white-blond mass of curls.

Kyle is talking to Lucy. Two boys handle Jenny's pompoms in fascination. Nicole, Kelley and I slurp our sodas. I am looking down at some invisible object at my feet when I hear, 'I know you.'

I look up. Blondie seems to be talking to me.

'Huh?'

He's looking right at me but I don't know him.

'You came to my house,' he says.

Now I'm sure he's not talking to me. I look at Nicole and Kelley who are holding back giggles.

'No, I didn't,' I say.

'Yeah, it was you. Does your mother make furniture?'

Who turned the heat up on my face?

'What are you talking about?'

'I think your mother fixed one of our chairs or something and you came along. You were watching us outside.'

There are a swarm of bees inside my head.

'You mean the man . . . um, up the mountain.'

'Yeah, I live on the mountain.'

'Ohmygod, that was sooo long ago, that was like . . . how do you remember that?'

'Dunno, y'look the same, I guess.'

'Gee thanks, I look seven.'

Laughter all around.

'No, I didn't mean . . . whatever, I just remember that's all.'

We make our way back for the second half, only it isn't just us now on the third row from the top of the bleachers. It's all of us with Blondie sitting right next to me. I can't see Mama, but I can feel her eyes.

I try to recall the day I was at this boy's house but I can't.

'What's your name, then?' I ask with hopes of jogging my memory.

'Will. Will Cooper.'

The Coopers. Of course.

'You have a twin brother and a sister. You were bouncing on the trampoline.' It's all coming back to me.

'Yeah, guess so,' he says, then adds, 'Sorry about what I said earlier. I didn't mean you look seven.

I remember you mostly because we didn't have many kids our age visit.'

The game thunders on, our girls so far ahead now the outcome is rather predictable.

'You going to the dance tonight?' Will asks shyly.

'No, I'm going to another party,' I lie, ready to invent whose and where but he doesn't ask.

'I'm not going, either,' he says. 'My mother doesn't want me out late. She's a little paranoid.'

Wow, the truth, and it didn't even seem that hard. We watch as the game winds down. Will is nothing like Benjamin, I think to myself, a curly mass of honesty and apologies, searching his way through the conversation. Maybe it's that he's my age or maybe it's the edge of melancholy he holds in his blue eyes but I feel at ease sitting here with him. Considering where he comes from I feel an ironic sense of equality.

Kyle announces to his gang that they are leaving.

'You can come visit me again if you want,' says Will. 'My parents wouldn't mind. Come up for a swim.'

We all say goodbye and the boys make their way down, then out of sight.

'What was Will Cooper talking to you about?' It is Nicole who asks but three sets of anxious eyes await the answer.

'Nothing.' I'm answered by a chorus of groans.

'No, really. It's just that he remembers me from a long time ago when I was like seven. It's so weird.'

I don't know why I don't say anything about the

invitation. Oh wait. Yes I do. Because it will never happen. Because Mama would never allow it.

'Open mine first,' I demand, handing Lucy the rect-angular box I wrapped this afternoon.

'What could it be?' Lucy shakes it, smells it, drags the moment out an excruciatingly long time. She knows exactly what it is. What she doesn't know is that my gift is part of a theme that will set her birthday party into motion. The girls and I move into a tight circle on Lucy's living-room floor as she begins to slowly rip the bright paper.

'Hurry up,' groan the gang. Even Daniel watching in his chair and Mrs Zingler on the sofa seem restless.

In a rare fluke of events I am allowed to sleep over on Lucy's birthday. The first fluke was that it was Mrs Zingler who asked Mama if I could stay. She said it would mean the world to Lucy on her special day. The second fluke was that Mrs Zingler omitted vital infor-mation that would have ensured an unequivocal no on Mama's behalf. She didn't mention that Nicole, Jenny and Kelley would also be spending the night making it not just a sleepover but a sleepover party, an absolute taboo.

Mama even let Richard drive me over because he wanted to treat Mama to a video, which he said he would pick up on the way home. Mama didn't even drill me with the usual artillery of questions before I left. It's nice having Richard around.

'Ohmygod.' Lucy's surprise is feigned but her

delight is sincere at the sight of the Ouija board she specifically told me (on several occasions) she wanted. From Kelley she receives a set of tarot cards with an instruction booklet. Jenny gives her a Wicca kit for beginners and Nicole a palm-reading book. Mrs Zingler completes the party's motif with incense, candles, gypsy headwear, bangles and a crystal necklace which we unanimously insist Lucy wear for the evening.

If Mama could see me now. I am practically frothing at the mouth in the deliciousness of forbidden pagan worship. I can't wait to get started as we cart Lucy's haul to her bedroom along with enough pop, chips, popcorn, and chocolate to last us three nights.

Once inside, on go the Backstreet Boys, the candles and incense. Out come the tarot cards, Madam Lucy presiding. It takes two-and-a-half hours to learn Nicole will become confused and led astray from her rightful path. Jenny will discover the revelation of a painful truth. Kelley will seek outside help in intellectual endeavours, creativity turns to gold for me, and Lucy will be a guide to the self-defeated.

'OK, let's make a spell.' Nicole, our High Priestess, is already reading up on the possibilities.

'How to make someone say yes,' she reads from the Wicca handbook as she lays the contents of the kit out in an orderly line along Lucy's bed. I imagine asking Mama to drive up to the Mansions, drop me off for the afternoon at Will's house for a swim in his pool. Mama doesn't argue or ask questions. She just says *yes*, then collects the car keys.

'How to make someone say no,' Nicole continues. I can't think of how this would be beneficially applied to any of us.

'Oh, here we go. The order of love.' Nicole drags out the word love and directs it at Lucy.

'You can't make someone love you, but Wicca can help you manipulate the elements and circumstances that will ensure success. The forces of nature, intuition, foresight and spiritual revelation of the most mysterious sort are at work here,' reads Nicole. 'OK, we need a bowl or a pot or something.'

Lucy goes into her closet and yanks a wicker basket down from the top shelf. She dumps the two half-finished embroidered pillowcases and the twisted silky bunches of coloured yarn that are inside onto her closet floor. She places it in the middle of our circle of knees on the floor. Meanwhile Nicole has separated the necessary ingredients for the love spell.

'OK, you lay this silk patch on the bottom.' Nicole gives the shiny white square to Kelley, like a nurse handing a doctor some important instrument. 'Then you drip exactly three drops of red candle wax on it.'

It's Jenny who finds the red candle amid the array Mrs Zingler bought. We watch with open-mouthed awe as she lights it, then expertly splatters exactly three bright drops onto the material. It's eerily blood-like.

'Good,' says Nicole. There is a hush in the room.

'Now, Lucy, write your name and Kyle's name on these strips of paper with this red pen.'

Lucy follows orders, but not without sighs and eye rolls. She lays them one on top of the other in our growing cauldron.

'OK, we take our sweetener.' Nicole unscrews the cap to reveal an eye-dropper doused in thick golden liquid. She sniffs.

'Hmm, honey,' she says and hands it to me. 'Put enough sweetener on the names so that the ink runs. Make sure the ink of one runs into the other.'

I do my best, careful with the sticky substance.

'Now, we take these rose petals.' She gives Kelley a small zip-locked bag.

'How many?' asks Kelley.

'Doesn't say, better use them all.'

Kelley scatters the dried petals over the mass.

'Now, a little orris, better known to us witches as love root.' Nicole sprinkles this herself.

'Lay the feather over the petals.' It is a single white feather sealed between two layers of plastic, which Nicole peels back before doing the honours.

'Now it says to hold hands in a circle and say the name of the person three times, but every time you say his name you have to also say, "Moon, moon, bring unto me my one true love for all to see." This is the spell to bring all elements together for the moment of love to present itself.'

We hold hands.

'Ready?' asks Nicole. 'On three. One, two, three.'

We inhale simultaneously and chant 'Kyle' and promptly split a gut laughing.

'OK you guys, come on,' says Nicole in a lame attempt at order. We try it again, but by the time Nicole reaches number two we are already rolling in teary giggles.

We laugh ourselves out and try again. Nicole has become deathly serious. Hand holding is resumed, a few practice chants are uttered then, 'On one, two, three,' inhale, 'Kyle, moon, moon, bring unto me my one true love for all to see,' only I'm saying a different name in my head.

'Louder,' says Nicole.

'Kyle, moon, moon, bring unto me my one true love for all to see.'

Last one.

'Kyle, moon, moo—' But we don't get it out because Lucy's door flies open in a terrible erratic flickering of candlelight and a series of horror-movie screams as we all jump and shriek.

'Oh, my God, what the . . .' Benjamin is examining our sticky concoction of petals and wax drippings. 'What are you doing?'

'Voodoo doll that looks just like you is next,' says Lucy.

'That's not a very nice thing to say to your dear brother who just came to give you your present.'

He shuts the door behind him and pulls out a bottle of Blue Nun from his backpack. Nicole says, 'Oh, my God, I totally love you.'

'How the hell did you get that?' says Lucy.

'I have connections.' He places the white wine

above his sister's outstretched hands. 'If you get caught I don't have anything to do with it, get it?'

'Got it, give it here.' He lowers the bottle and Lucy pulls it to her.

'You can stay and drink it with us,' Kelley whispers.

Benjamin laughs. 'I think I'll leave you to it,' he says. 'But you might want to hide it in case Mom comes in.'

Lucy removes the pillowcase from her pillow and places the bottle inside. She passes it to Nicole, who gulps back a mouthful before passing it on to Kelley. When it's my turn I try not to let my face tell everyone this is my first sip of alcohol. The bottle is drained after it has circulated four times at lightning speed and we are soon laughing at everything.

I have a sudden urge to eat an entire bowl of popcorn and once I do I have an urge to visit the toilet, head first.

I know I won't look at popcorn quite the same way again once I see its regurgitated version afloat in the toilet. I check out my blood-drained face in the mirror and hope Mrs Zingler continues to stay away. When I get back to the room the girls are once again in their circle, this time with Ouija set up in the middle, a conspicuous empty spot in the human chain.

'Come on, hurry up,' says Lucy, thumping the floor next to her.

The moment we've been waiting for. I wriggle in, filling the gap between Lucy and Nicole.

'OK, who should we call?' says Jenny, as though she's done this a thousand times.

'How about Kurt Cobain?' says Nicole.

'Ew!' says Lucy. 'We can't call anyone who's killed themselves. That's just wrong.'

Ouija etiquette.

'I know,' says Nicole. 'How about your brother?'

My stomach drops. The word brother hangs in front of me like a detached limb. Nicole is looking at me awaiting an answer but I can't speak. Lucy to the rescue.

'Her brother's not dead!'

'Well, he might be,' says Nicole. 'This is one way to find out.'

'Shut up Nicole,' says Jenny.

Am I in the room?

'Yeah, Nicole, it's a stupid idea,' backs Lucy.

I must be here.

'Well, at least I *have* an idea,' says Nicole.

I can see them all.

'They never found his body, you know,' says Kelley.

I can hear every word.

'That doesn't prove anything,' counters Nicole.

I can smell the candle wax and salt and vinegar chips.

'We're not doing it, so shut the fuck up,' says Lucy.

I can taste remnants of popcorn puke.

'You shut the fuck up, Miss High-and-Mighty. Some people prefer to live in the real world.'

I can feel a tingling that begins at the base of my spine and climbs upwards. Then I pass out.

Chapter Thirty-Three

The day after Christmas I bundled Ryan up in his red parka, the navy knitted hat with matching scarf and mittens that Vivian had given him, the new winter boots from Daddy. My child could barely move; he resembled the Michelin Man.

I was taking my son to the park behind our townhouse. It was too cold for slides and swings, but I didn't care. I didn't care that we were the only ones there, that an early morning snowfall had left an inch of dry snow on the metal slide and the plastic swings. I had to get outside, breathe air that was crisp enough to hurt, feel something raw and cruel.

Christmas Day had arrived with a kind of subdued anticipation. Even Ryan seemed to open his gifts with tentative delight, as though he wasn't sure how happy he should be without Grandma present. Richard had saved a large bag of gifts for Ryan to open in front of his grandmother at State Hill. When we arrived at the facility that afternoon, Ryan decked out in the smart green cords and dress shirt I bought him for the occasion, we first went to Mama's room, where we shared our private gift-opening moments in full view of the overseeing glass eye. More Scooby paraphernalia, vehicles of every size and shape, colouring books, play dough, necessary socks and underwear. Mama received slippers and toiletries, two safe bets in her current housing situation. Richard gave me perfume. I gave him motorcycle books. After we tidied the trail of crunched wrapping paper, we made our way to a place in the hospital I'd never been to before, a large open cafeteria where you queued between a metal railing and a stretching counter for turkey and all the trimmings.

It was difficult to be there, to line up behind the crazies for a meal that Mama lovingly slaved over every year, and planned for weeks in advance.

But we did it. We weathered the line-up. We collected our pre-made plates from the fat, weary arms of cooking staff. We plucked our buns from a heaped basket of brown and white crusty bakery items with a pair of salad tongs. We found our utensils in a row of deep stainless-steel tubes loaded with white plastic knives, forks and spoons. We ate the offerings without complaint. It didn't matter that the potatoes were whipped from a box, the cranberry sauce a blob of canned jelly or that the gravy resembled split pea soup. Christmas was a day for family and we were at least together.

*

Richard had left early this morning in search of a bookstore that carried a good selection of small business manuals. His trip home had been fruitful. He told me his potential partner was keen to hand over half the responsibilities of his motorcycle shop. Now Richard had to make the big decision. Would he go ahead with the deal?

'Mommy, I'm cold,' Ryan complained as I absentmindedly pushed the back of his puffy coat.

Dr Ashley had been right. I did have a question for Mama, a single question that had haunted me for as long as I could remember.

'OK, let's try the monkey bars,' I said, untangling his feet from their plastic slots. Ryan ran red-cheeked to the frosty bars, climbed up the three-rung ladder then dangled.

The thing about being the sister of an abducted boy, the unstolen one, was the questions you started to ask yourself very early on.

Ryan jumped down and started packing the snow into balls.

I never really pondered over why the abductor (or maybe there was more than one) took Michael instead of me. I guess I always saw that as a question of logic. I was in my stroller near my mother while Michael had toddled away unseen, unprotected, towards danger. I often pictured him following that little brown dog. Creeping up to it quietly, almost having it within petting reach before it darted off again deeper into the baseball field, repeating the game again and again, the way a toddler follows a bouncing ball onto a highway.

I stood watching Ryan making his snowman. He was the same age as Michael had been when he was abducted, stolen from us, ripped away from Mama's heart. A boy in a field following a dog: a boy fixed in his mission, snatched unawares.

I understood why Michael was taken instead of me. No, the question I asked myself on the nights when wind dreams woke me was a question I knew I'd never know the answer to, but couldn't stop asking anyway. *Does Mama wish it was me who had been stolen?* That's what Dr Ashley wanted me to ask her.

'My snowman fell down,' said Ryan, peering disappointedly at its flaky, crumbling head.

Growing up, I had misunderstood the tragedy of Michael's disappearance. I always thought of it as loss, as injustice, as a wrong to be righted. I knew what loss was, I saw it in my mother's face every day, felt it as the leftover child, but now looking at Ryan, happily absorbed in rebuilding his snowy creation, lost in a world of his own, the family loss I had understood seemed hard edged, defined. The thought of losing my own child felt nothing like that. It felt like an endless sea of grief, a hole in the sky. What if I had a baby girl? Would I rather it was her? How could I answer a question like that? How could anyone?

I looked at him there, the same age as my brother, so full of the wonder of life. The thought of losing

Ryan, of someone snatching him when I looked away for a second, of me never seeing him again, never being able to smell his baby fine hair, hear his contagious giggles, feel the solid bulk of his body, kiss his pudgy morning face, not know his whereabouts, his fate, was utterly unbearable.

God, Mama. Dear God. I didn't know. I'm so sorry. I didn't know.

I remembered my heart racing, my skin heating up to a sweat, then the blackness. When I opened my eyes, a woman's long, cold fingers were tapping my cheek. Her round, black face hovered above me, suspended like a dark balloon.

Where's Ryan?

How long have I been out?

The hot rush of panic streamed through me.

'Ryan,' I yelled but my voice was a hollow whisper.

'Ryan!' I struggled. I tried to sit up, but this woman kept me down in a single firm motion. Her mouth was moving, but I couldn't make out what she was saying. I could only hear my heart race, my own raspy words, a distant police car siren.

I looked away and he was gone. This was how Mama had felt.

'Ryan. Ryan.'

I tried to fight her. Why wouldn't she let me up? Why couldn't I hear anything? I was thirty thousand feet up and my eardrums had caved in. I was plunging to my death.

I attempted one more thrust upwards but she pinned me, secured my arms to something. I couldn't move. I was gasping. The woman cupped a plastic triangle to my face. Air streamed into my body. I gave in to it and sucked it in and out of my lungs until I fell as limp as a mop. She removed the cup. The back of my head throbbed. She held one strong hand just below my neck in a steady hold, the other brushing away the hair from my face.

Who was this woman, straddling and comforting me both? I heard her words now. 'It's OK, it's OK.'

The police siren grew louder. The black-faced angel smiled, an oxygen mask dangled, the ground beneath me vibrated.

'Ryan,' I said again. An angel of mercy released my arms from their straps, lifted me upright, tilted my head. There was Ryan strapped into the front seat, riding shotgun in his favourite vehicle next to a monster truck.

Chapter Thirty-Four

Every year the students of Dartmouth Junior High School are allocated two months off for summer vacation. Mama affords me exactly two weeks.

How else will you get ahead? is her reasoning.

This year, however, I receive a three-and-a-half week vacation and get to stay with Daddy the whole time on account of Mama and Richard's cross-country talk-show circuit journey. Today's social studies class involves Mama explaining her twenty-five-day itinerary.

'From here we will hit all the major cities.' She fingers the map as she talks. 'We go from Helena to Boise, Seattle and LA. From there we head east to Phoenix, Denver, Des Moines, Madison and finally Chicago, where we will be on *The Oprah Winfrey Show*.' She taps Chicago extra hard with her index finger when she says Oprah Winfrey, like it's really important.

'You're going to Los Angeles! Lucky!' I say. 'Are you going to go to Disneyland?'

'No, Bethany. There won't be enough time, but we will be going to Hollywood to do a number of TV and radio shows. We'll bring you something back.'

I'm not sure when Mama and Richard became a *we*. Not long after his wife passed away, I suppose. She stayed in that coma for what seemed like forever until one day Mama hung up the phone in our hallway and announced it was finally over.

'Phoenix,' says Mama, tapping the red star in the state of Arizona. 'Now that's somewhere I've always wanted to go. Maybe we can sneak away to see the Grand Canyon.' Mama seems to be talking more to herself than to me. 'We'll see how it goes,' she continues. 'This is a business trip.'

'I know,' I say. The business of resurrecting Michael.

But it's good to see Mama excited about something. Even if it is a business trip I can tell she's looking forward to it.

'OK, let's get back on track. Are you ready for next week's exams?'

'Yes, Mama.'

'How's the English paper coming?'

'Almost finished.'

'Let's go through what you've got so far.'

'OK.'

I go upstairs to my room. In the drawer of my bedside table I find several paper-clipped pages entitled Egu and Daw. I bring them down.

'OK, read me what you've written, then we'll go through the grammar,' says Mama. She is sitting upright in the kitchen chair, her arms crossed over her chest. I clear my throat and begin. I am nervous reading to Mama. My throat tightens like a hand is squeezing it and breathing becomes something I must think about. I inhale sharply.

'Go on,' she urges, but there is impatience lurking behind those eyes.

My voice wavers and I lose my place. Finally I fall into a kind of sketchy, jerking, reading-voice rhythm. As long as I don't look up into those eyes I'll be OK. I feel a sort of helplessness like I'm being forced to throw something away that I desperately need, like I'm watching it drive away from me in the back of a garbage truck or catch fire after being flung onto a heap of burning coals.

I look up at Mama, who hasn't moved since I began. She is wearing her thinking face, the one where her lips bunch at the side of her face in a rosebud as she nibbles contemplatively on cheek flesh.

'That's it,' I say. 'That's all I've got.'

'OK, well, let's get to the grammar and spelling and I want you to finish it by the end of the week and I don't mean Sunday night.'

I want to ask her if she liked it, if she thought the characters were interesting, if there was enough action, enough description, but I don't. Instead I just say, 'Yes, Mama.'

It's easier.

Chapter Thirty-Five

'Well, look at you,' said Dr Ashley, taking a seat at the end of my bed. I attempted a smile but managed only a pain-filled wince. Somewhere under the bandage swaddling my head existed a morbidly musical throb.

'Leave you alone for five minutes and what happens!' He reached for my hand, gave it a squeeze. 'Quite a bonk you've got there.'

'Yeah, couldn't just faint gracefully like a Jane Austen heroine. I had to smash myself up on the way down,' I said. It hurt to speak.

Dr Ashley was the first to turn up at the hospital. When no one could get hold of Richard or Vivian I gave the hospital staff Dr Ashley's number. With my two reliables unavailable and Will at school I didn't know where else to turn. Ryan had been taken to the hospital day-care centre.

'Are you in much pain?' he asked.

'Only when I breathe,' I joked. 'Listen, I'm so sorry about the other day in your office,' I said.

'Don't be silly.' I looked at Dr Ashley sitting there at the end of my bed, his face full of tenderness and concern.

'I behaved badly. I never should have . . .'

'Shhhh,' he said, a finger to his lips. 'So what happened? What's your story, young lady?'

'I think I had a glimpse of Mama's grief.'

'How's that?'

I told Dr Ashley what had happened before I passed out and banged the back of my head against the monkey bars. I explained my insight: told him I'd never before thought about Michael's abduction from Mama's viewpoint as a mother.

'I was wondering when it would hit you.'

'Oh, it hit me alright.' I blinked and winced with pain. 'You mean to say you saw this coming? You could have warned me, saved me a split head.'

'I'm afraid that was something you had to see for yourself.'

'How did you know?'

'Because, every time we talk about Ryan, every reference to your son has been in relation to your mother, as though Ryan is an extension of you. It's like you're saying, here's more of me so now you have to love me more, as much as Michael. Until now I don't think you've seen Ryan so much as your son as your sacrifice. The ultimate sacrifice: part of you, in exchange for her love and acceptance.'

'How did you know I'd get there?'

'Because nothing else was working. Everything you tried was bigger, better than the last thing. It was a predictable momentum that, if followed to the extreme, would amount to you giving your mother a replacement for Michael in one way or another.'

Dr Ashley made it sound so simple, the thoughts and actions of my entire life wrapped up in a few wise sentences.

'What now, Dr Ashley?' I asked.

'When you're ready I think it's time for you and your mother to have a wee chat.'

A new kind of pain entered me then.

Chapter Thirty-Six

You'd think Mama was moving out by the size of the heap of luggage blocking the front door. When Richard arrives he doesn't attempt to come inside but starts hauling bags to his truck. I help.

'So, squirt, you think you'll survive without us?' he asks, taking a bag from me, fitting it into the space of the cab.

'I'll manage,' I say.

'Looking forward to spending some time with your dad?'

'Guess so.' I shrug. More like looking forward to no schoolwork. No Mama.

When there are no more suitcases and no more room inside the truck we return to the house. Richard and I take a seat on the sofa, wait for Mama. We can hear noises coming from upstairs, the rattling of drawers, footsteps, shuffling.

'What *is* she doing?' asks Richard.

'Beats me,' I say.

Whatever it is she's doing, Mama has been doing it all morning. She's been in her bedroom moving things around, mumbling to herself.

Finally she appears in the living room looking flustered, slightly out of breath. In one hand she clutches one more black bag, purse slung over her shoulder. She looks overdressed for travelling in tan dress slacks with a perfect crease running their length, and a matching blazer. She's even made up her face, a smear of peach lipstick, a dusting of rosy blush. Mama doesn't say anything, doesn't seem to notice we are here. Her restless eyes tell me her brain is hard at work. The conspicuous scent of some flowery perfume wafts between us like a fragrant shield.

'Got the tickets and your passport?' Richard's rough, jocular voice intervenes.

Mama snaps back to us. 'Of course I do.' She finds no humour in Richard's attempt to lighten her mood. He goes to her, removes the bag from her hand.

'Well, that's all you need then. Shall we?' he says gently.

Mama rushes to me almost panicked. I reach in for a hug but she's got something to say.

'No sleepovers.'

'Yes, Mama.'

'No dances.'

'Yes, Mama.'

'And absolutely no parties.'

'Yes, Mama.'

'If you visit Lucy, you are to be home by nine-thirty at the latest.'

'Yes, Mama.'

I move in to her.

'Oh and, Bethany.' She smooths my hair. 'Make sure you brush your hair two or three times a day, you know how it gets.' She's grasping now, making stuff up. I always brush my hair. Hair has never been an issue before.

'Have a good time, Mama, and don't worry about me.'

'I'll call every day.'

'OK, have fun.'

'I'm not going away to have fun.'

'No, Mama.'

Daddy receives the same barrage of orders when we arrive at his house, but I scoot by them and go straight to my room to unpack. By the time Daddy has closed the front door and Mama and Richard are pulling out of the driveway my clothes are hanging in the closet, socks and underwear in the drawer.

Lori surfaces from Daddy's bedroom, which is really hers and Daddy's bedroom. Her timing is perfect.

'Wow, moved in already,' she says when she sees my clothes. 'Wanna help me make brunch?'

I am in charge of designing the pancakes into various shapes on the electric frying pan – hearts, clovers, moons, a special happy face for Daddy, which turns out to be more of a leering one. Lori is in charge of frying sausages on the stove and Daddy sets the table outside on the new deck he has built.

Pancakes and maple syrup, sausages and eggs, orange juice and coffee, plastic furniture and an umbrella. Mama is probably just pulling into Warmish by now, but she already seems very far away.

'Anything you want to do today?' asks Lori.

'Not really,' I reply.

'I thought we might go down to the pond,' says Daddy. 'What'd ya think, sweetie?'

'Yeah, sounds good,' I say, my mouth full of grease and flavour.

No sooner do we finish cleaning up the brunch dishes than we begin another mess of picnic making – tuna-salad sandwiches, apples and lemonade. The day is already hot and the inside of Daddy's truck feels like the heater has been on. We roll down all the windows and let the wind whip our hair around. Daddy pushes his favourite Tom Petty tape into the slot and we all sing 'Free Falling' as loudly as we can.

Families have already set up blankets and umbrellas at the Dart River pond when we arrive. Children splash and squeal in the clear water. We find a shady spot under a huge maple and unravel our three straw mats out along the grass. Lori peels away her outer wear immediately and announces she's going for a swim.

'I'll join you later,' says Daddy, leaning back on the mat. Lori looks to me for a swim mate, but I am comfortable now in the subtle breeze. She shrugs and heads for the water in her flowery one-piece.

'Another glorious summer day in Dartmouth,' Daddy says, smacking his lips like he's actually tasting the early afternoon.

'Daddy, do you think Michael's dead?' I blurt out.

There is a pause while he fixes his gaze on me, his brow crinkling in wonder. 'Well, just say what's on your mind, sweets. Don't hold back.'

I ignore this.

'I mean we know Mama thinks he's alive, out there somewhere waiting to be found, but what do you think?'

'Well, hon.' He shifts his body, rests his head on his elbow. 'I would really like to believe he's out there too. Sometimes when I see your mother working so hard to find him I almost do.'

Daddy looks towards the pond. Lori waves up to us.

'But . . .' I urge.

'Yeah, there's always a *but*, isn't there. My *but* is that there's a time to look, to work, to hope and there's a time to let go. That was the problem with your mom and me. I let go and she didn't. She couldn't.'

'She still can't,' I say.

Daddy sweeps a strand of hair from my face. 'Finally I had to let go of her,' he says. There is sadness in his voice or maybe it's disappointment. 'It's not what I had planned for my life but Michael's disappearance wasn't what anyone had planned for their lives.'

'So do you think he's dead?' I press.

'I don't know, Bethany. I wish I had an answer for you. Nobody knows for sure. That's the trouble with all of this. There are no answers.'

'Come on, you guys,' beckons Lori. 'The water's great.'

'But I'll tell you this, honey,' says Daddy, lifting my chin until our eyes meet. 'If he *is* out there I have no doubt that your mother will find him.'

Daddy has to work overtime at the mill today so Lori drives me to my final exams. My completed English composition is in a manila envelope on my lap. I finished the Egu and Daw story when we came back from the pond. Afterwards, Lori helped me with the illustrations.

'Are you nervous?' she asks as she grinds the gear into second from the stop sign.

'A little.' I nod. 'I always am.'

'But your marks are incredible and, my goodness, it won't be long before you're done. Finished high school, at your age. You must be so proud of yourself.'

I'd never really thought about it much. I guess the end wasn't that far off, a matter of months now. To me my school grades were as much to do with Mama's teaching as they were to do with my studying. The stories, though, they were all mine.

'I guess,' I shrug.

'Hey, I want you to think about something,' says Lori.

We are almost at the school and Lori's hardly left me alone to look over my notes (Mama would not be pleased).

'What's that?' I ask.

'When you've finished your exams we should celebrate.'

'And do what?'

'That's what I want you to think about. Think about something you really want to do or somewhere you really want to go. It doesn't have to be with your Dad and me, it can be with a friend or anything, just think about it.'

'Don't you want to wait until my results come back?'

'I think we both know you'll kick ass, excuse my French. Besides, who wants to wait a few weeks?'

'Good point.' I chuckle.

We pull into the school parking lot. Lori swings in close to the side doors.

'I'll be back in a few hours to get you. Good luck and think about what I said, OK?'

As I walk towards the doors, about to write five major final exams, I can think of little else. I know exactly where I really want to go and I recognize my one chance in hell when it's being presented.

*

Mrs Cooper approves my visit when Lori calls, but she isn't even home when we arrive. Neither is Mr Cooper anywhere in sight. It seems to be only Will and his sister Victoria taking care of things. I can't imagine Mama ever leaving me without supervision.

People say things appear smaller when you're grown, but the Cooper residence remains as vast and impressive as I remember. The bigness of everything up here in the Mansions has somehow swollen in my memory. It surprises me how well I recall the details, the panoramic view of our town along the stretching, winding ascent and the gently embracing snake of water that both defines its borders and cradles its occupants. Vivid are my recollections of the smooth, wide streets leading to the rambling Cooper front lawn and the massive Douglas fir to the left of their stone walkway.

The sound of the doorbell, too, is magnified both in my memory and now as Lori and I stand dwarfed by a set of imposing double doors. Its ring is like a thousand chimes: we wait for a long time before we hear the sliding and settling of a series of metal locks. Unlike the ping and tick of door locks down below, these lofty security measures hold the solid tone of impenetrability, the reinforcements of castles, the fortification of fortresses. Then Will appears, sprite-like, with a halo of feathery curls, looking fragile and precious against these substantial measures of protection. I say goodbye to Lori and cross the threshold into a world both familiar and utterly incomprehensible.

'See you at three,' she shouts from the roller-rink-smooth driveway, reminding me of our deal: the deal to be home before Daddy's back from work. Not that Daddy would mind, but if he knew Mama would surely find out somehow and then both Daddy and I would be in trouble.

I remove my sandals in the lobby and follow Will over cool marble floors in my bare feet to a polished wooden staircase so wide that four people could walk side by side to the top. I am aware of my dull finger smudges on the mirror-shiny finish of the wooden handrail. It gleams as though the thick twisted branch of oak has been tumbled for eons in a giant rock polisher.

The steps aren't the standard height or length apart. They are shorter and wider. As I watch Will ahead of me, he doesn't seem to be walking up the stairs at all but gliding. They are stairs constructed for a princess, a prom queen. It seems a sacrilege to be traipsing up them in bare feet and cut-off jeans.

We pass several doors in a long hallway before we get to Will's room.

Finally there is carpet under my feet but it is not the gritty pile green of my living room or the tangled blue shag of Lucy's. It is something plush, as deep and soft as packed powder, the grey of moody clouds.

'Do you like Hootie and the Blowfish?' Will asks, but before I can answer he is switching dials at his stereo unit and 'I Only Want to Be With You' is pounding out of flush wall speakers. His fingers are dancing down two towering CD racks stacked with music in preparation for his next selection. I sit on a sofa that seems completely at home in this room, though I've never seen a sofa in a bedroom before. Next to me is a desk with a computer and printer on it. Above me rest shelves filled with books and magazines. Is that a small refrigerator in the corner?

'Or would you rather watch TV?' My mouth falls open as a flat screen descends from the ceiling.

'Ohmygod,' I say. 'You are so . . .' I almost say *rich* but sputter out *lucky*. Will smiles like he knows my thoughts.

'I thought we were going swimming,' I say.

'Don't worry, we are,' he says. 'I just wanted to show you my room.'

The tour begins with the inside of Will's walk-in closet, which looks like the sporting goods section at Dartmouth Hardware Store. I stare up at shelves which hold ice hockey skates, roller blades, a skate board, a snow board, boxing gloves, scuba gear, two tennis rackets, a squash racket, various sized balls and a variety of footwear from hiking boots to smooth-bottomed trainers.

'Do you do all this stuff?' I ask in disbelief.

'Well, not every day, obviously, but I know how to use it all if that's what you mean,' says Will.

'Wow,' I say, truly impressed. 'I can skate.' I sound like the seven year old Will remembers me as.

'Can you snowboard?'

'As if,' I reply. 'That takes money. Is it fun?'

'It's loads of fun. It's the best sport of all. You feel like you're flying,' he says. 'Maybe we can take you sometime.'

I laugh out loud. 'I doubt my mother would let me go.'

'Oh, I don't know. My parents can be pretty persuasive sometimes. My father's a lawyer. If they talked to her she might acquiesce.'

'Acquiesce?'

'You know, agree.'

'Why do you talk like that?'

'Like what?'

'You know, like a grown up.'

'I don't know,' he shrugs. 'It's how I was brought up, I guess.'

I nod sympathetically.

We leave the closet and sit on the edge of Will's bed. My feet dangle inches from the floor.

'I want to show you one more thing,' says Will. He goes to a wide sturdy chest and removes a sketchpad from the bottom drawer. He shows me charcoal drawing after charcoal drawing: racing cars, snowboarders, hang-gliders, boxers, hockey players.

'I copied these from magazines,' he says.

'They're incredible,' I say and I mean it. His lines are bold and deliberate.

Then he turns the pages pointing out delicate pencil sketches of his mother, his father and his friends.

'I can draw you sometime if you like.'

'I would love that,' I say, forgetting myself.

'OK, hang on,' says Will. He gets up and rummages through one of his many drawers, pulls out an automatic camera, aims it at me.

'Smile!' He clicks the shutter. I am blinded by a flash of white light.

'What'd you do that for?' I protest, squinting up at him.

'I usually draw from photographs,' he says.

He sits down next to me again and I continue to flip through his sketches. 'These are so good. I draw too,' I add. It almost sounds like I'm making it up to impress him.

'I know,' he says.

I look at him strangely. 'How? Did Lucy tell you?'

'No,' he says. 'I've seen your drawings.'

'Huh?'

We are having another one of those *I know you* moments that leaves me speechless. How could he possibly have seen my drawings?

'My mother grades your papers.' He says it so matter of factly that I want to say, oh right, of course she does, but instead I just stare blankly into his face.

'You're home-schooled, right?' he says.

'Yeah.' My voice is tentative.

'Well, when you write your exams where do you think they go for marking?'

'I never thought about it. I assumed the school assigned a teacher.'

'That's right, but the home-schooling programme contracts its own teacher to mark papers and that's my mother. She's been doing it for years for all the kids up here who are home-schooled.'

'So you've seen my drawings?'

'And read your stories, which are great, by the way.'

'Ohmygod. I feel . . . That's so weird.'

'I guess it is a bit. My mother used to read your stories to us at bedtime when we were growing up. We used to look forward to the next adventure. I loved Icebowland.'

'You did?'

'Oh yeah, we all did. Sometimes mother would even read to my friends if she was looking after them for the afternoon. You've got quite a little following up here. One year she bought me a penguin for Christmas. I still have it.'

Will goes to the same chest his sketchbook came from and takes out a stuffed penguin, a little smaller than Genpu, from the top drawer. 'See,' he says, dangling it in front of me. I take the fuzzy creature from him. 'This is Gup,' he says.

'You even named him?'

'Of course. How else could I go to Icebowland in my dreams? Maybe one day you'll write him into a story for me,' says Will. He's smiling widely, teeth like carved pearls.

'So, are you ready to go swimming?' he asks suddenly. 'We should get going if you have to leave by three.'

*

We make our way back down the princess staircase. I really do feel like a princess, bare feet and all, descending from on high where miracles are bestowed upon the unsuspecting. The miracle is not so much that my stories should end up here high in the Mansions amid the people of influence and power. That part almost makes sense considering what Will's mother does and how many children are home-schooled. The miracle here, the one I wear like a silk shawl that makes my skin tingle as I descend the stairs, is that Will likes my stories. No, he loves them.

I loved Icebowland. I hear his voice in my head and I am floating.

We follow a long, narrow, grass-tamped trail, swishing thin branches and leaves away from our faces as we go.

'We're not going to the pool,' he announces.

'We're not?'

My skin is already hot and sticky from the heat of the day. Will, who is ahead of me carrying his backpack, seems unaffected.

'Almost there,' he calls out.

'There'd better be cool water at the end of all this,' I say and as I look up it's as though I have wished it into existence. Ahead the sun reflects white light on turquoise water as if thousands of lit sparklers float just above the surface. As we approach, the trees seem to part and the lake expand until we are standing on the rocky shoreline of a mountain-fringed jewel. The colour of the water turns from teal to emerald depending where you look. It is in the shape of a perfect oval gem. The water at our feet is table-lacquer clear. How many miracles can be bestowed upon a girl in a single day?

Will directs me left of the trail, where the stones at our feet give way to a small sandy patch. He removes the towels from his backpack and spreads them in two colourful strips across the smooth ground. He hands me a can of lemon cider, which has gone from the icy cold of his refrigerator to room-temperature cool. We open them simultaneously. Crack. Pssst.

'Listen to this,' says Will. He brings his hands to his mouth and shouts *hello*, to which the echo replies in kind. We laugh, our merriment returning to us faintly from a distance.

We slurp our lemony drinks in unison. I gaze across the lake, try to absorb its dangerous beauty and hold it in me.

'This is the lake,' I say, realizing I've said it out loud.

'What lake?' asks Will. 'Have you been here before?'

'The lake Mama told me about, the one the authorities dragged when they were searching for my brother. The one with the mysterious depth and undertow that made it impossible to continue.'

'I heard about that,' says Will. 'Your brother, I mean.'

'Everyone knows about him,' I say. 'My mother makes sure of that.'

'He's still missing, isn't he? I mean ... they never ...' Will stutters.

'Found a body?' I finish. 'No, they never have.'

'Well, we have something in common then, Bethany.'

'We do?'

'Yeah, big time. Six years ago my twin brother drowned in this lake and they couldn't find his body either.'

I feel a chill run up my back.

'I watched him fall off the back of my uncle's speedboat. He was wearing a lifejacket but he just slipped right out of it. He had disappeared by the time my uncle got the boat turned around.'

'Oh my God, Will, that's awful. I never knew anything about it.'

'No, you wouldn't have, because while your mother makes sure everyone knows about your brother, my family makes sure nobody knows about mine.'

'Why?'

'It's not a secret, I suppose, but we pretty much keep things to ourselves up here.'

'God, Will, that's just terrible. I mean he was your twin. You grew up together. I was only a baby when mine disappeared.'

I paused, then asked, 'Why do you come back here?'

'I love this place now,' Will says. 'I know it might sound weird but I feel closer to him here. It's where he lives. Sometimes when I come here alone it's like I can feel him near me.'

I look out onto the lake's perfect beauty and as I do a fish breaks through the surface in a silver flash, spanks the emerald on its return. I feel a bizarre comfort in the idea that if Michael is here in this lake that he at least has company, an eight-year-old companion spirit to dance on water with when no one is looking.

It's hard to concentrate down here after my trip to the clouds.

Lucy and I brush the final strokes of our masterpiece. I am highlighting mountains in light violet. Lucy is defining the lines in the rainbow with bright yellow, red and orange. Our mural jumps off the wall and turns her bedroom into an icy rainbow fortress.

Daddy is letting me stay over at Lucy's tonight because she is going to camp tomorrow and I won't see her for two weeks. She goes to Camp Thunderbird every summer, where kids learn archery, canoeing and water-skiing. The timing couldn't be worse. My yearly allotted time off is even more precious this year without Mama and I will be best-friendless.

'I wish you could come with me,' Lucy says without missing a stroke.

'Me too.'

'Hey, maybe your dad will let you,' she says like she's just thought of something brilliant.

'Yeah, whatever, and what if Mama finds out? Besides, you had to register a long time ago.' The voice of reluctant wisdom.

I step back to admire my work, check for weak spots. I find a peak in need of a snow-cap and resume painting.

'So tell me more about Cooper,' Lucy says. 'Do you like him or what?'

'Who's Cooper?' A deep voice interrupts me before I can answer. Benjamin is standing at the door we have carelessly left ajar.

'Beat it,' says Lucy.

'That wouldn't be Will Cooper by any chance now, would it?' Benjamin asks.

'Maybe,' I say.

'Ooh, Prince Charming has lured the peasant girl up to his castle in the sky, has he?' Benjamin approaches as he speaks; his fingers are crawling up my back like small crabs and I am squirming.

'Looks like Cinderella is a bit ticklish.'

'Bugger off or I'll call Mom,' Lucy snaps.

I accidentally on purpose swipe my paint brush across Benjamin's face and Lucy and I burst into fits of laughter at the white-violet streak across his cheek. He grabs me under my arms and carries me to the full-length mirror on the back of Lucy's door.

'There'd better not be . . .' He catches sight of himself then turns my own brush-wielding hand against me until my nose is snow-capped.

'OK, OK. I give. Surrender!' I shout.

Lucy backs away from the mural. 'Voilà! C'est fini,' she announces.

Benjamin and I stop goofing around to share in the

moment of glory. It really is finished. The three of us stand and look at the completed world of Icebowland, the pastel mountains illuminated by the multicoloured rainbow. I don't realize Benjamin hasn't taken his arm out from around my waist until he squeezes his congratulations.

'Nice work, guys. Well, hate to stop a paint fight and run but got people to see,' he says, opening Lucy's door wide so the mirror bangs against the wall. 'Oh and, Bethany, I still want to hear that story.'

After Benjamin leaves Lucy and I clean up the paints, then I clean up my nose. Mrs Zingler calls us for dinner, chicken strips and homemade French fries, which we're allowed to eat on trays in the living room during an episode of *Cheers*. Mrs Zingler stays in the kitchen to eat with Daniel.

I love Lucy's house. There seems to be order without many rules. People come and go and yet things get done. The landscape of this family is a perfect balance. There is privacy, yet also the comfort of others.

After dinner Lucy and I do the dishes. She washes, I dry. We can hear Mrs Zingler reading to Daniel in his room.

'So are you going to see him again?' Lucy asks, placing a plate in the plastic dish rack.

'See who?' I play stupid.

'Cooper, who do you think?'

'I don't know.' I can see rising frustration on Lucy's

crinkled forehead. 'He's just a friend, you know. It's not like you and Kyle.'

Lucy and Kyle are now an item. It all came together at the dance, where I am told they talked all night, slow danced to the last song, after which he kissed her in front of everyone. I wonder if our spell had anything to do with it.

'Are you sure you don't like Cooper in that way?'

'Nah, he's too . . . I don't know, different I guess.'

'What do you mean different?'

'I don't know. I don't think of him as someone who could be my boyfriend. It's just not that way, but I really like talking to him. It's weird. It's like we're so different and yet we have this connection.'

I know I am disappointing Lucy. She wants juice. She wants passion. She wants me to have a boyfriend so we can double date. She hands me a clean wet pot.

'I bet you'll see him again and fall madly in love.'

At about nine p.m. Lucy and I are hard into a game of Yahtzee when Mrs Zingler knocks softly on Lucy's door.

'Come in,' Lucy yells.

Mrs Zingler peeks her head shyly into the room, as if it's not her house at all.

'I hate to be the bearer of bad news, girls, but, Lucy, if you are to be up by five for camp and if I'm the one who's driving, then we should both get to bed soon.'

Mutual groans.

'You don't have to go to bed so early, Bethany. You could stay up a while and watch TV if you want,' she says.

Mrs Zingler is standing over us and the game we have spread out along the floor.

'Actually that's probably a good idea now that I think of it,' she continues, 'otherwise you girls will be up till all hours giggling. You could join Benjamin in the pit if you like. He's brought a couple of movies home with him.'

Mrs Zingler doesn't call it the *pit* for nothing. Benjamin lives underground in a world apart from the bright, boisterous business of the house. In the windowless basement there are a washer and dryer and a folding board along a far wall. Two bikes hang from the ceiling above a tangle of boxes and sporting equipment: a vast contrast to Will's neat closet shelves.

On the other side of the room is a makeshift den with an L-shaped sofa, a shoe-scuffed powder-blue carpet, a coffee table and a TV on a wooden cable spool. Decorations Benjamin has added include a sagging American flag, a poster of a silver Porsche and, overseeing it all, is Mariah Carey in patriotic tank top and cut-offs.

I am careful as I descend the wood-plank steps in utter darkness. This staircase was constructed for pirate's prey. I follow the TV glow around the corner and there is Benjamin, his body sunken into the overstuffed rectangular cushions, his blue-jeaned legs sprawled on the coffee table. His hair glistens blue then purple then red in the TV light. He is holding an open beer bottle between his legs. He is absorbed in *Pulp Fiction* and barely notices me until I am practically standing in front of him.

'Whoa, what are you doing down here?'

'Nice to see you, too,' I say. I plop myself down in the opposite corner of the L. 'Everyone else is going to bed early for camp tomorrow. Your mom said you had movies.'

'Yeah, no worries. You seen this one?'

'No.' I don't say Mama would never let me watch such a violent film.

I watch a bit of it nervously until Benjamin breaks in.

'Wanna beer?'

'Sure, I love beer,' I lie. I've never actually had one. Benjamin reaches into the case at his feet. 'So what's up with you and Will Cooper?' he asks, holding out the bottle.

'Nothing,' I say reaching, grasping air.

'Yeah, whatever,' Benjamin says and shoves the bottle into my hand.

'Nothing, we're just friends. How do you know him?'

'I've seen him around. I hear he's a bit of a girl.' Benjamin chuckles.

'Well, I like him.' I take a long swallow of beer followed immediately by a loud hiccup.

'Oh, you *do* like him then?'

'Not like that,' I exclaim, feeling trapped in my own words.

'Well, who do you like, like that?' asks Benjamin.

'As if I'd tell you.'

Benjamin makes a *psss* sound like he's deflating. It is the last sound made until the video and my beer are finished. Benjamin is on his fourth.

'Do you want to watch *Ace Ventura*?' he asks.

'Nah, think I'll go to bed,' I say. The darkness and the beer are making me drowsy.

'Hey, wait a second. You said I could read something later.'

'Oh yeah, how about tomorrow? My backpack is upstairs.'

'No way. Go get your backpack. I want to read it now.'

'It's really not a big deal, you know.'

'Go!' he commands.

Luckily my backpack is by the back door and I don't have to wake Lucy shuffling around in her room. When I return to the pit Benjamin has switched on a floor lamp, which makes the den slightly more inviting.

I hand him four sheets of scribbles and explain that it's a very rough copy. I remove the video from the machine as he begins to read to himself. I feel nervous. Jay Leno is presenting his monologue when I switch the machine over to TV mode. I take my seat back on the sofa and watch Jay but I can't concentrate on his jokes.

I remind myself that Will likes my stories, that they

always bring in good marks from up the mountain. It's no use, though. What Benjamin thinks is important. I can hear my blood coursing. I am beginning to wish I had just handed him the story and headed right back up those dungeon stairs. He's taking a painfully long time to get through the first page.

'Who is the boy?' he finally says.

'What do you mean?'

'I mean did you write this about someone you know?'

'No,' I say. 'I just made it up.'

He reads on then starts to read aloud in confusion. 'And with a final effort suing . . .'

'Give me that.' I snatch the papers from him, find the spot he left off on. 'And with a final effort *swung* the pickaxe up and over.' I breeze through my own writing. 'Tell you what,' I say, scrunching in beside him. 'I'll read the rest, OK?'

'Go for it.' He moves himself closer and I clear my throat.

'OK,' I say and start to read.

I can feel the rhythm of his heart beating along the back of my ribcage, his warmth at the back of my shoulder. His body is perfectly still.

Up they went, higher and higher. Daw felt his legs weakening, his arms become heavy as sledgehammers.

Benjamin's breathing is barely audible, but I am acutely aware we share the same oxygen.

Daw shivered with a kind of fear he'd never felt, a fear with both excitement and doom in it. But he

*trusted Egu. He trusted him with all his heart. He
jumped. Falling, falling, falling.*

Benjamin's eyes are staring at an unknown spot on
the filthy carpet. When he realizes I'm finished he turns
to me. His face is so close I can feel his warm breath. I
can smell the beer he's been drinking and the musty
stench of the sofa. He stares at me for what seems like
a long time but doesn't speak. *Say something, say
something*, my mind reels. Ohmygod, he's kissing me,
short kisses at first like he's testing the terrain. I can't
move. The words of the story float back to me.

'*I've been waiting for you.*'

I can feel his tongue in my mouth.

'*I knew you'd come.*'

His hand is on my face, stroking my hair.

Falling, falling, falling.

I am kissing him back, afraid he'll stop. *Don't stop.
Don't ever stop.* His hand moves under my T-shirt,
grasping, squeezing.

. . . trusted him with all . . .

He's pulling my shorts and panties off in one
motion as though they are sewn together. His jeans are
at his knees.

I feel something hard and I know it's his penis and
it hurts as he pushes, but I don't care because he's so
close to me and I feel like I've wanted him this close
my whole life.

Chapter Thirty-Seven

Dr Ashley assigned me homework. I was to write down all the things I wanted to discuss with Mama. It was hard enough to put pen to paper. I could barely imagine saying these things to her face.

I didn't want to do this. I wanted to call Dr Ashley and cancel the whole thing. Who was I to bring up old hurts after all Mama had been through? But that was the point, according to Dr Ashley. I did have the right and things had to be said, cast out from murky, festering depths into the open air where only there could they begin to shrivel and heal.

If it wasn't me he was talking about, I would tend to agree. But it was me going in to see Mama with the full knowledge that she would not like what I had to say. Knowing I was going to cause her yet more pain.

My head still hurt, but not the way it did a few days ago in the hospital. Now it was only tender when touched or when I accidentally rolled over onto my right side in the middle of the night.

Ryan loved to look at my scar.

'I see a scar, Mommy? I see a scar?'

'Yes, Ryan, no touching now.'

But he couldn't not touch; a shiny and red patch, seven stitches as tempting as candy. He would tentatively reach his tiny fingers to my scar, then snatch them back when I cringed with gross exaggeration.

'I'm sorry, Mommy, I was gentle.'

'Yes, Ryan, you were gentle, but it's very sore.'

Leaning on my left side now against my bedroom pillow, making out my list of worm-filled cans to be opened, it was my guts not my head that ached. Who was it who said childhood was a thing that ruined everyone's life? Why was it, I wondered, that the human species spent their entire lives trying to figure themselves out?

I was in the fish tank this time with Dr Ashley and Mama. Richard and Dr Sloan observed from the other side, two ever-ready interns by the door. Mama and I sat at either ends of the small table, Dr Ashley between us, scanning an exploding file of notes. I was armed with my own notes, three neatly crammed, single-spaced pages. The only one defenceless was Mama. All she had to protect herself was that stern look on her face and two folded arms across her chest. I could tell she already felt ganged up on and no one had yet said a word.

Dr Ashley began. 'Now, Doris, I've given Bethany a bit of an assignment. I've instructed her to write down some long-unspoken comments and questions she would like to share with you.'

'This should be good.' Mama tightened her arms around herself, holding herself together.

'Just so you know,' Dr Ashley continued. 'This was not easy for Bethany to do. In fact I don't think she wanted to do it at all. Let me preface by asking you not to react until Bethany has taken the time to say what she needs to say.'

My eyes were already burning and I hadn't spoken a word, my mouth a cotton-dry, thick-tongued pothole. How was I ever going to get through this? Even knowing Richard was behind the glass did nothing to help.

'Go ahead, Bethany.' Dr Ashley nodded his encouragement.

I scanned my notes, found point number one. I reached for a cup of water, sipped life into my parched mouth, my weapon.

'Mama, I want to start by telling you that I love you and that I am so very sorry for your loss. To lose a child . . .' I had to pause. I felt tears sting, my throat fight to close. 'Well, it's the worst thing that could happen to someone and I commend you for your bravery and dedication over the years in your efforts to find your son.'

Mama's face was deadpan. She seemed to be waiting for the other shoe to drop. I dropped it.

'That said, I need you to recognize that somewhere in all of that was me.'

'I was always there for you.' Mama's voice was low and without emotion.

Dr Ashley stopped her with a raised finger. This was how I would get through, with the encouragement and interception of an unbiased referee.

'You were, Mama, in so many ways. I don't deny that, but in other ways you weren't there at all. You must know that.'

'I did the best I cou—' Again Dr Ashley brooked no interference.

'The purpose of this meeting, Doris, is not to prove who was right or wrong, but to explore feelings and thoughts that haven't ever been expressed before.'

'Go ahead,' Mama huffed. 'Say what you have to say, then. I'm listening.'

'I just want to tell you that there were times when I felt left out, invisible. Like the times you went on about how smart Michael was when it was me who needed the praise. There were a hundred small incidents like that where you tacitly admitted he was more important than me and it hurt, Mama, it hurt.' I was unable to hold back the dam of tears then. I'd got it out, but I didn't feel any better for it.

'Well, poor you,' said Mama, her tone sarcastic and cruel. Didn't she know how hard this was for me? 'I knew it would come to this,' she said. 'I knew you would say bad things about me in front of Dr Ashley and whoever else is nosing around out there. I just knew it. Well, you can say anything you want but I don't have to sit here and listen to it.' Suddenly Mama bolted from her chair and rattled the locked door in frustration.

'I'm afraid you do, Doris,' said Dr Ashley calmly. 'It's important for both of you to discuss these issues.'

Mama moved to the other side of the room, stood with her back to us.

'Mama, please stop worrying about what other people think,' I pleaded. 'It's too late for all that. It doesn't matter. What matters is what you and I think.'

She turned around sharply, her eyes fierce.

'I'll tell you what I think,' she spat. She stood, pointing a finger at me, accusing me. 'I was there for you in every respect and don't you tell me I wasn't. How dare you try to make me out to be a terrible mother in front of everyone? I protected you in every way I knew how . . .' She paused. 'So that what happened to your brother would never happen to you.'

'No, Mama, you protected yourself.' It was so hard to say these things. Each word felt like a stab. 'You protected yourself from everyone on the outside. Daddy left, but I couldn't. You shut me in then you shut me out. No matter how well I did in school, no matter how many stories I wrote, how many awards I won, it was never enough to compete with Michael. It was always him you needed. I joined the police force to help find missing children. I even had a baby, Mama, but nothing I did was good enough. Mama, for God's sake, the focus is always on Michael. Even now you've managed it.'

'I protected you, I fed you, I educated you. I made your dreams come true.'

'Those were *your* dreams, Mama. They weren't mine. I don't even know what my dreams are. There's never been enough room for me to discover them. I am a grown woman now, Mama, and I am still fighting for some attention and acceptance from my own mother. Only now, as well as Michael, I have to fight the media and the psychologists, even Ryan, and I lose every time.' I hesitated. 'Sometimes, just sometimes, I wonder if you wish it was me who was stolen.'

There. I'd said it.

'*I don't want to talk about this any more.*' There were tears in Mama's eyes now.

'You never do,' I pressed. 'You never want to talk about the real reason you have hidden away all these years. Why you have spent your whole life preparing for his return.'

'That's enough.' Mama raised her voice, brushed away the tears.

'You do it because you can't allow yourself to believe that I might be all that's left.'

I got the last words out before finally cracking into sobs. I saw Mama come towards me and I braced myself for the hug I was about to receive. But what came instead was one pointing finger in my face and eyes like spikes.

'Don't you *dare* attempt to tell me what I do and don't feel or how I should or shouldn't deal with any of this. If I want to stay in *my* house and look for *my* son my whole life then I will do exactly that. When I want to talk about Michael I will talk. If I don't want to talk about Michael I won't. Don't you *ever* presume to know how any of this feels for me or have the audacity to think you know how I should behave.'

I was clenching and unclenching my fists, digging my nails into my pockets.

'How can I possibly know how you feel when you don't even talk to me?' I said, my voice wavering like distorted radio waves. 'I don't know how you feel about anything I do. Are you proud of me? Do you think my stories are any good? I don't know anything any more because you never tell me.'

Mama backed away, hugged her arms tight. She began to speak in her best teacher's voice.

'Your imagination is your gift, Bethany. It frees you. It takes you places and shows you beautiful things. My imagination is my curse. It bounds me. It shows me only perverted images, takes me to horrid places. It is where hell is, where eternal suffering resides. I escape it by keeping busy, keeping ahead of it, because the moment I slow down it is there, waiting to devour me.'

I had underestimated Mama, something I should have known by now never to do. Her poignant words tumbled down on me as solid as the well-built furniture of past decades. Mama ruled again.

'OK Mama, but what about me?' I withered at the weight of the painful disclosure I had provoked. For the first time I felt I needed Dr Ashley's support to go on. A kind, smiling nod from him and I persevered.

'I'm asking you to let me in,' I said. 'I'm asking you to love me. Michael might come back, but in the meantime, Mama, I am here.'

'Someone had to look for him,' she said quietly, suddenly defeated, her eyes straying. She was drifting.

'He was taken from me, too, you know.' I tried to bring her back, reel her into the room. 'He's not just your son. He's my brother too. You weren't the only one affected by Michael's abduction. You don't own all the grief. But you have a choice now. You don't have to let the abductor take you away from me, too.'

The three of us fell silent, let the duelling words settle. Dr Ashley reached out, touched my knee, nodded his approval. What jolted us back to Mama was a loud thwack. She had picked up the plastic bat and taken a swing at the leather punch bag.

'I did everything I knew how to do,' she said, her knuckles white around the bottle neck of the plastic tube. Thwack.

'I took care of you the best I could.' Thwack.

'My dreams did not come true.' Her voice rose with each word, her face that of a crazed woman.

Dr Ashley and I looked at each other, then back at Mama. We heard the outside latch release on the door. Dr Ashley held back two interns with a raised hand. Then Mama was no longer whacking the bag the way a batter hits a ball. Her strikes were not the frenzied blows of a moment ago but were now eerie rhythmical thumps. With each exacting pound a word.

'Give.' Thwack.

'Him.' Thwack.

'Back.' Thwack.

Then she screamed and threw the plastic tube away from her as though it had grown red hot in her hands. Mama dropped to her knees in slow motion like she was melting, her wide, terrified eyes focused on some unseen image. We rushed to her, Dr Ashley on one side, me on the other, carefully cradling her stiffened frame.

'What have I done?' she murmured over and over.

'It's alright,' said Dr Ashley. 'It's over now.'

'Shhh now, we're right here, Mama.'

Tears flowed out of her, thin streams that raced down her frozen face, streaked her smock. Whatever was inside her was gone now. She made no sound.

PART 4

PART 4

Chapter Thirty-Eight

Mama's back along with her luggage and two additional heaving shopping bags in which I'm expecting to find something for me. Richard is here too, but leaves once the bags are inside the house.

It has only been three weeks but Mama looks different somehow. I want to say happier or younger but that isn't quite it. I search for the word as I observe her unpack the open suitcases on her bed. She has come home with clean clothes thanks to the wonderful laundry service at the fantastic Omni Hotel she and Richard stayed in on their last night, compliments of *The Oprah Winfrey Show*.

Sophisticated. That's what's different about Mama. She looks sophisticated. There is an air of confidence in her purposeful movements that I've not witnessed before and it scares me a little. I'm not sure what to expect.

'I want to hear all about your holiday. How was your dad?' It's more an order than a question.

'Yeah, fine,' I say. I suddenly can't think of a single thing I did at Dad's.

'And what did you do all this time?'

'I don't know. Hung out, I guess. Dad worked a lot.'

'Then what'd you do when he was working?'

'Hung out with Lori, watched movies,' I say.

'Nothing R-rated I hope,' says Mama by rote.

'No, Mama.' My standard reply. 'Hey, guess what?'

'Bethany, hang these up for me, will you?' She hands me two hangers with suits on them, an airy film of plastic over each.

'Look at what a wonderful job they did,' she says, stroking the plastic. 'Just wonderful.'

I nod and veer towards the closet.

'I got an A-plus on my story,' I announce.

'No, not there, Bethany. The suits go with the other suits. Oh, never mind,' she says, taking them back from me as I fumble to slot them in correctly. 'I'll do it.' Mama slides them effortlessly into their proper place.

'Why don't you empty my make-up bag. Put things on my dresser.' She points at a small, hard suitcase on the end of the bed. I start to unpack it.

'And what about your tests? Did you study for them like I asked you to?'

'Yeah, my marks are—'

'Shampoo!' says Mama, grabbing the bottle I've just placed on the dresser, holding it up for me to read the label. 'Is that where we keep the shampoo?'

'No, sorry. What about your trip, Mama? How was it?'

'Grand,' says Mama. 'Just grand.'

Grand? Who is this woman? What can I say to her?

'That's great,' I reply.

'Yes, everywhere we went we were welcomed with open arms. But the day before yesterday was the best of all. Everyone on the Oprah show was so kind, and her guests, well, let's just say that I was finally surrounded by people who understand me. They're all in the same boat. If I ever had a doubt in my mind as to what I was doing, that one day made up for everything.'

Mama had found her people.

When Oprah comes on Mama's in her chair and Richard and I are on the sofa. Mama's not the feature story like she was years ago on that *Newsline* programme. Instead we watch an hour filled with others. Other mothers, other fathers with missing children. So many others.

Mama's story is last, but in this case Richard says that's a good thing because people will remember. Mama's segment opens after a commercial break with Oprah sitting in a roomy, soft chair. 'Some of you may remember this next story,' she begins.

We watch a re-enactment of the incident, blurred images of people running in all directions at the jamboree, wind-whipped papers and bags, a long shot of an empty field and a tiny dog in the distance. Next is old footage of various newscasters reporting the breaking news and finally the townspeople searching the area. Back to Oprah, only now Mama and Richard are on the stage with her.

Oprah introduces them, then says, 'This is a picture of Michael Fisher when he went missing.' She turns to a theatre-sized screen behind her. 'And thanks to the wonders of technology we are able to see what he looks like now.'

Michael's eighteen-year-old face fills the screen. The audience releases an overall gasp. Back to Oprah. Her first question is directed to Richard.

'Tell us what the chances are of finding someone so long after an abduction takes place?'

Richard moves forward in his chair.

'Well, of course, the sooner after the actual abduction the better the chances of finding someone. Seventy-four per cent of abducted children who are murdered are dead within three hours of the abduction.' Oprah repeats the number.

'Seventy-four per cent.'

'But in Michael's case the body was never found and that made us hopeful that this was an abduction for purposes other than homicide. One out of six missing children are found because someone recognizes their photo.'

Oprah's next question is for Mama. She leans a little closer to her.

'What makes you think after all this time that your son is still out there?'

The television talk-show host has just asked the very question that I've never been able to articulate.

'Well, as the detective said, there's no proof to the contrary,' Mama begins. 'But on a much more personal level it is something I feel, something a mother knows. I've always felt it, like an invisible connection from me to Michael.'

And that's it.

Mama had done it, the thing she'd set out to do. She'd shown them. Shown them all. No one could accuse her of mindless obsession. Not with Oprah and America on her side.

The endless calls over the next three days seem to give Mama buoyancy. As she bobs from room to room, her movements like a fine juggling act, I see something in her resembling happiness. But I see through it, too. Just beyond Mama's quick smiles and flighty movements, beyond her purpose and hope, I see something truer and darker lurking and it frightens me. I see someone ready to throw one too many balls in the air.

Mama resumes her seat next to mine and I barely get the first sentence of my paper on Freud out before we are, yet again, interrupted by the ring. Normally during school hours Mama would turn the ringer volume down low and let the answering machine pick up the call, but these calls are too important and Mama makes no apologies. Any one of these calls could be *the one*.

Mama leaves the table like a butterfly on its journey from flower to flower. It must be obvious to her from the sly delight expressed in my smiling eyes that I don't mind one bit. My joyful respite lasts as long as it takes for Mama to answer, then to utter my name. Who is calling to talk about me? Is it Mrs Zingler? Is she calling to say she's just remembered the morning she found Benjamin and me curled up on the basement sofa? Is it Lori, guilt-ridden, ready to expose *our little secret*? I eavesdrop on a series of unhelpful clues as Mama speaks.

'Yes, she has. I'm sure she would. Well, that's very kind of you to say. We'll think about this very generous suggestion.'

I am aware that I'm breathing in quick bursts when Mama returns. She sits down and looks at me for what seems like a long time. Finally she speaks. 'That was Mrs Cooper.'

God, I knew it. How could I think I could keep anything from Mama? I nod like a dog caught stealing the steak off the barbecue and brace myself for a flurry of questions.

'As you may or may not know,' Mama begins.

It's going to be a long philosophical lecture.

'Mrs Cooper marks your papers.'

How do I play this? I wonder. 'I heard that,' I say, teetering on the tightrope between truth and lie.

'Anyway,' Mama continues, 'she seems to think that your stories are really good.'

'Icebowland?'

'Yes. She has offered an assignment for your final mark in English.'

'What assignment?'

I can't believe I'm off the hook.

'She wants to know if you are interested in handing in an overall collection using previous stories and a few new ones complete with illustrations.'

Speechless, I manage a quick nod.

'It's a big task. You'll need a computer. I could ask Sylvie if you could use hers.'

'Yeah, OK,' I say.

'If you're sure.'

'I'm sure, I'm sure,' I blurt.

'OK, back to our friend Freud,' says Mama.

I pick up my neglected paper, but can't concentrate on the words.

'Oh, and one more thing,' says Mama. 'If the collection is adequate, Mrs Cooper wanted to know if you'd be interested in having her submit it for publication. Apparently she knows someone who is an agent for children's books. She says her own children have enjoyed your stories over the years at bedtime, but you probably already knew that due to your visit while I was away.'

Before I can speak the phone rings again and saves me.

Will's story emerges like a birth, a hairline crack around a warm egg, pecking and chipping away at me from the inside. Gup and Liw are born at six forty-five p.m. I am in my room, pen to paper. It is a watery place, emerald liquid velvet, where I imagine Will goes in his dreams.

'Bethany!'

'What?'

'Phone.' I get up, leave my pen and paper on the bed.

'I'll get it in your room,' I yell down the stairs to Mama.

'Got it,' I say into the phone when I pick it up. I wait for Mama's click, but before she hangs up she takes the opportunity to remind me not to talk all night because she is expecting . . .

'Yes, Mama.'

'Don't be cheeky.' Click.

'Hello.'

'Hi, what's going on over there?' says Lucy.

'Oh, you wouldn't believe it. I have so much to tell you. I'm sooo glad you're back.'

'Yeah, I've heard what you've been up to and I have to tell you I'm not exactly impressed.'

'What are you talking about?'

'I'm talking about something I shouldn't be talking about over the phone. Come over.' She says it as if my life depends on it.

'I can't believe you did it.' Lucy is pacing like a nervous father outside a delivery room.

'Did what?' I am truly confounded.

'It!'

'Oh *it*,' I say, hanging my head in shame. 'What did Benjamin say to you?' I asked.

'He came to me all freaked out,' says Lucy.

'What'd he tell you?'

'Well, to quote him he said you kind of did *it*. I mean, come on, my fucking brother or should I say fucking my brother. Ewwww! How could you?'

I ignore her disgust. 'What else did he say?'

'Are you listening to me? Of all the people in the world why did you have to pick *him*?'

'Well, all the other people in the world weren't available,' I say.

'This isn't funny, you know. It's so gross. I can't stand to even think about it.'

'Then don't,' I say.

'Ewwww!' says Lucy, squirming. 'What were you thinking?'

'I was thinking about how good it all—'

'Don't tell me. Don't say another—'

'You asked.'

'He's my brother!'

'Well, we've established that. God! Take a pill. Relax, will ya?' I say. 'And tell him to do the same. It's not like I'm expecting marriage.'

Lucy sighs. She tries a new approach, attempts concern.

'Were you at least protected?'

'God, now you sound like my mother.'

'Well, were you?'

'Not exactly.'

'What does that mean, not *exactly*. This is a simple yes or no question.'

'OK, no.'

'God! How stupid can you be! What if, ohmygod, what if . . .' Lucy has gone into some kind of trance-like state where I'm not even in the room any more.

'Just chill, OK?' I grab her arm, try to shake her out of it, but she snaps her limb away. 'Take a chill pill and re-fucking-lax,' I say in the angriest voice I can muster. She stops fretting a moment and stares at me blankly.

'Well, what do you fucking expect me to say?' she asks.

'How about asking me how I feel about it all instead of being so self-absorbed and trying to figure out how it affects you?'

She thinks about this a moment. 'OK, how the fuck do you feel about it?'

I concentrate on her bare feet on the floor. 'I don't know,' I say in a low voice.

'Oh well, that's just fucking great, isn't it? You don't know! You don't know! What the fuck do you mean you don't know?' Once the word fuck is out it seems to be a fuck-fest free-for-all.

'I just mean I don't know. I mean you know I've had a crush on Benjamin forever and it just happened and . . .'

Lucy is right. My lame answer to how I feel about it really isn't an acceptable explanation, but when I try to think about how I really do feel about it, 'I don't know' is all I can come up with. I don't know how much the alcohol influenced my decision. I don't know if I feel taken advantage of. I don't know if I love

Benjamin. What I do know is that I don't want to see him at the moment and I know that the *what if* that Lucy so delicately mentioned scares the hell out of me.

'Can we talk about something else?' I call a truce. I want to tell her about Will and my story and how the phone's been ringing since Mama's been back.

'So my idea is that I'll cut up the mural and use our work for illustrations. It's so weird. It's like all the work is already done. I just have to put it together and English is finished forever.'

'Wicked.' Lucy feigns excitement. But I know she's thinking about her brother and me. I know she feels betrayed.

'Tell me about camp,' I say.

Instead Lucy reaches into a pocket of her backpack and pulls out a bulky handmade envelope. She hands it to me. The thick paper looks like compressed confetti and feels like rough material. I picture Lucy bent over a mortar with pestle in hand crushing bits of tree until her hands are raw. I open it. Inside there is a beaded wristband and a card. The computerized inlay reads: *Best friends are God's gift. Thank God for Bethany. Love, Lucy.*

I don't want to cry but I can feel the tears welling.

Chapter Thirty-Nine

'I'm very proud of you,' said Dr Ashley, leaning over his desk. 'I know how hard it was for you to confront your mother, but you'll be happy to know she has made great progress since.'

We were in Dr Ashley's downtown office, the roomy space with his rugby trophies and the photograph of his wife. He had asked me to discontinue my visits to State Hill until Mama's memories were under control. He said her thought process was too fragile at the moment. She needed to stay focused.

'What does she remember?' I asked.

'Bits and bobs,' said Dr Ashley. 'But the images are very disturbing for her. We've had to sedate her every night since the first memory presented itself.'

'Are we able to tell her what the police found, that Aaron Wetherall is alive?'

'Not yet. In due time. This is a process that must not be rushed. First we need her to gain control over the memories. They're coming at a frightening speed and it's all a bit overwhelming for her. One thing at a time.'

'Does she at least know who Thomas Freeman was? Why she did it?'

Dr Ashley nodded. 'She knows.'

Over the following weeks Dr Ashley kept me informed as to Mama's progress either by phone or in person as I made weekly treks to his office. Mama's memories began backwards starting with bloody flashes. She saw blood-splattered walls and floor. She saw TRF's white wall phone, her trembling hand reaching . . .

When it came time to write his report for the courts Dr Ashley had all the ammunition he needed. Mama's court-appointed lawyer, a woman in her late fifties named Margaret Reager whom I met only once during her court appearance, worked closely with Dr Ashley and Mama in the weeks leading up to the court date. Dr Ashley told me Mama's story was a classic case of temporary insanity. He said they'd invented the plea with her in mind. He stated in his affidavit to the courts that she couldn't have predicted any of it as it was an ironic coincidence that she'd run into him after seeing a sketch for the first time the night before. Her amnesia of the incident, then her later full recovery of the memory, suggested she had undoubtedly experienced temporary insanity.

Dr Ashley went on to write that Mama saved Aaron

Wetherall by placing her own life in grave danger. More importantly, however, was his declaration that on a gut-churning unconscious level Mama was protecting her grandson, ensuring with each blow to TRF's head that what had happened to Michael would never happen to Ryan. The realization that this child-murderer lived in close proximity to her beloved grandson, a grandson she could no longer watch over and protect on a daily basis, was the defining factor in Mama's actions.

In closing, Dr Ashley wrote that he would continue to work closely with Mama to help her cope with the reality and consequences of her actions. He stated that it was his professional opinion that Mama would eventually leave State Hill with one hundred per cent mental health, that she would pose no further danger, either to herself or to others. He said what had occurred on the early evening of October 15th was the result of a terrible and unresolved past meeting an unusual and ironically similar set of circumstances. He mentioned, too, that Mama hadn't had any therapy whatsoever after the disappearance of her own child.

Dr Ashley's judgement, along with police reports and photographs of the gruesome findings at the victim's home were enough for the judge to make a quick decision. The courts were merciful and Mama was sentenced to stay at State Hill for the amount of time it would take Dr Ashley to determine her complete recovery. Mama's freedom depended on herself now.

Chapter Forty

Richard is setting up the new fax machine he bought Mama so now the police and the Child Find Organization can send documentation directly.

Richard also bought doughnuts, jelly filled, rainbow sprinkled, chocolate covered, and I am waiting patiently at the kitchen table while Mama makes coffee. When the last drop has seeped through the filter and when Richard has connected all the right electrical cords between the phone, fax machine and wall outlet, I will be able to choose.

It's only been a few minutes and I'm not even halfway through my doughnut when the machine beeps and springs into action. I am hoping its non-intrusive hum will take the place of the interminable telephone ring. I take another bite, a light dusting of icing sugar tickling my lips. Mama appears with the silky pages of fax Number One.

'Dear Mrs Fisher,' she reads aloud.

'Thank you for forwarding us your fax number. We would be happy to oblige with any relevant information concerning your case. There is currently nothing new to report. We have occasionally received false leads and therefore you will understand that unless we feel we have something substantial we won't bother you. Signed Chief Harrison Wathy of the Helena Police Department.'

Mama looks at Richard like he's a naughty boy.

'Did you pass the number on?'

'Of course,' he says.

'Well, thank you.'

I recall the look on Mama's face the day she first met Benjamin. I wonder if Mama sees Michael wherever she goes. How many daily cruelties must Mama face? Does she even notice them any more? As I chew the last bit of my doughnut I understand something about Mama I haven't thought about before. I think about how she has lived with agony all my life. That I've never known her to be different. But she must have been some other way before Michael's stolen day, a way that was filled with lightness and contentment.

I feel a certain detachment from her as I think of these things. It's as though I've made a slight shift and have moved outside her realm. For a moment, I think of her not as Mama but as a woman who lives each day in search of treasure. She lost more than her son that day. Much more. Maybe Mama isn't looking for Michael at all. Maybe she's trying to find a way back to herself.

*

The calls do lessen over the next few days, but now Mama has a new hobby. She is building a paper trail from coast to coast. On her bedroom floor is a patch-work quilt of shiny faxes from east to west, most of them with the Child Find logo stamped in the left-hand corner. When she's not adding to this geographical wonder or answering the phone she is helping me prepare for the college entrance exam or my Grade Twelve finals, which basically amount to the same thing. If all goes well, I will have finished high school before Christmas.

Today is Saturday, my day off, and I've been in my room all morning putting together Icebowland stories in readiness for next week when I will type them on Mrs Zingler's computer. She agreed to it, no problem, when Mama asked her. She said she was very excited for me.

Mama sprouts an odd smile when I come down to the kitchen for lunch. Her face radiates secret knowl-edge. I follow her shrewd eyes to the table where a letter-sized manila envelope lies in the centre addressed to me. It has been opened. I hate it when Mama does that even though I don't normally get mail, just birth-day cards from Grandma and Grandpa, but still . . .

I look from the envelope to Mama then back at the envelope. She seems to be waiting for me to say some-thing.

'Is it from a university?' I ask.

'Not quite,' says Mama. She seems to be loving all this.

'Grandma?'

'Why don't you just have a look.' Now there's an idea.

I lift the envelope and peek inside. I can see a charcoal drawing. Maybe Lori sent it, but why wouldn't she just give it to me tomorrow when I spend the day with her and Dad? I pull it out and am face to face with a black and white smudged version of myself.

'Will,' I whisper, remembering our deal.

It is an extremely sensitive depiction – even I can tell that – and I instantly love it. It feels so personal that I'm almost embarrassed to look at it in front of Mama.

'Did you see the note?' asks Mama.

It's a folded bit of paper at the bottom of the envelope. I read it to myself.

Hi, Bethany.

A promise is a promise, so here you are. Hope you like it. Please come back and visit sometime soon. You and your mother are welcome here any time.

Regards, Will.

I no sooner finish reading the note than Mama suggests we go and deliver my English project in person once it's finished.

'Sure, yeah, sounds good,' I say but I can't believe she's acting so cool. She hasn't asked a single question about my visit or why Will drew my portrait. She really is in her own little world these days. And I'm not sure if I like it.

'We still going shopping today?' I ask. It seems to take her several seconds to astral plane herself back into the room.

'Yes, yes, of course. After the dishes are done.'

Mama washes and I dry, then we are on our way to K-mart in the Volvo in pursuit of new shoes. My feet seem to have gone through a growth spurt to match the three-and-a-half inches I've grown over the last six months. The proof is there in the lead pencil mark on the wall outside my bedroom where Mama occasionally measures me if I request it. I'm five foot two now, shoe size six, and Mama believes I've still got plenty of growing to do.

We pull into a packed K-mart parking lot and when we're in the store Mama and I head straight for the shoe department. I want a pair of name-brand trainers, but I know Mama's going to tell me they are too expensive and that the nerdy generic brand will do just fine. I'm thinking about this when we approach the shelves lined with shoes but Mama doesn't stop in the girls' section. She keeps moving forwards until we are in the boys'.

'These are boys' shoes, Mama.' I point out her mistake.

'I know.' She says it as though it's obvious. 'I have to pick up some trainers for Michael. I can't remember the last time I bought him shoes. I imagine if you've outgrown yours then he's bound to have . . .'

Mama's still talking, babbling on, picking up shoes, checking the size, the price, but I've stopped listening because a deafening thought overtakes me. It seems to have come out of nowhere, this sudden shopping spree for my invisible brother, but then I realize Oprah is to blame. She has recharged my mother's hope. I look at Mama's face. There isn't a hint of embarrassment or hesitation in it and I know that she truly believes Michael is coming home any time now. This is why we've come to K-mart today. I mean, I can't remember the last time Mama bought Michael shoes either, but I am sure it was a very long time ago and I can't believe it because not only is she buying him shoes but dangling from her left hand are the very brand of trainers that are much too expensive for her to buy me.

No matter how many times I make the trip up the mountain, the view always takes me by surprise. Dartmouth shrinks away to insignificance and the river gleams and twinkles through the trees. The surrounding mountains lend me a feeling of power like I am part of them. It all leads to the surreal moment when the streets widen and the Mansions appear, some as old as the huge evergreens which grace their front yards.

Mama is visibly nervous at Will's front door as we wait for the four-part-harmony doorbell to be answered. She is biting her lower lip. The legs of her mint dress pants swish together. Will answers, smiling widely.

We remove our shoes in the lobby and follow Will through the house to the sliding glass doors on the other side. We enter the pool area, where Mrs Cooper sits under a large, forest-green umbrella at a wicker table and chair set. I see where Will gets his head of blond curls. I recognize her triangular face, her large smile from Will's drawings. A small-boned woman with long, delicate arms, she looks too fragile to be the lady of a house this size. I expect servants to come rushing to our aid, but after Mrs Cooper greets us she asks if we'd like coffee, tea or a cold drink, then disappears to fix our orders herself.

It's a nice day, not too hot. It might be stifling if the clouds didn't continually move in to smother the sun. There is a refreshing breeze up here in the mountains. Just when it begins to cool down the clouds separate and the sun warms us again like some perfect cooling system that is an extension of the house.

Mrs Cooper returns with colas for Will and me and tea for her and Mama on a round, mother-of-pearl laminated tray. Mama never drinks tea.

'Congratulations, Bethany, on the completion of your stories. You must have worked very hard on them,' she says. She says it sincerely, but this meeting suddenly feels like a formal interview for some better life. I retrieve my stories from my pack and place the green binder they're in before Mrs Cooper on the table.

'That's splendid, Bethany. I can't wait to have a look,' she says. Mama would never say a word like splendid. It sounds gracious and natural coming from Mrs Cooper.

'Thanks,' I say quietly. I don't want to gush. Just because she's rich doesn't mean I'm supposed to be thrilled she's given me a compliment, does it? I'm starting to resent this visit. It feels too much like a set-up. A trap.

'I thought these stories would be perfect to show my good friend, Diane Pent,' Mrs Cooper continues. 'Her agency has been finding publishers for quality children's books for years. I think she will adore Ice-bowland.' She draws out the word adore and I feel like I'm in the movie *Steel Magnolias*. 'Actually, to tell you the truth.' Mrs Cooper pauses. 'The whole idea was Will's.'

I look at Will. Mama and Mrs Cooper sip their tea.

My stomach is doing some kind of flip-flop dance. As though he can feel my pain and discomfort at this table of dragged out words and continuous compliments, Will says to me, 'Would you like to come upstairs and see my latest drawings, Bethany?'

I instinctively look to Mama for approval.

'Go on then,' she says, as though allowing me to go up to a boy's bedroom is standard behaviour.

I collect my backpack and follow Will up the Cinderella staircase, but this time I don't feel like a princess. I feel like an escaped fugitive. It's one thing to watch Mama be a phoney but another to support her doing it.

*

I plonk myself down on Will's bed with the informality of someone who comes by every day. Will climbs up next to me.

'So?' says Will.

'So what?' I return.

'Do you have something for me?'

'Oh gosh, yes,' I say. 'I almost forgot.' I reach for my pack next to me on the bed, unzip it and reveal the thin folder I've kept separate from the others.

'Liw and Gup,' I announce. 'Your story.' I pass it to him with both hands.

'Can I read it now?' he asks but he's already flipped the cover page open and is scanning the words.

'Is there any stopping you?' I laugh. As he reads I announce I am going to visit the bathroom.

The upstairs washroom is intimidating in its cleanliness and size. Not a splash of water in the golden shell of a sink, not a finger dent in the crisp, cream towels folded with precision over a polished brass bar. Even the creamy, soft, flower-printed toilet paper suspended importantly on an independent, floor-mounted brass holder has never been used. At first I tread softly, grasp gently, use sparingly, but finally I give up trying to cover my trail of shame and wash my hands generously with the untouched, mint bar of soap and demolish the symmetry of the towels with my vigorous drying.

When I return to the bedroom Will is cross-legged on top of his fluffy comforter, embracing my story against his chest. I resume my seat on the bed.

'Well?' I say. His silence is painful.

'I loved it,' he says, his voice sweet and sincere.

'I'm glad,' I say. 'And I loved the picture you drew of me.'

Will gets up, drags a sketchbook out from under the bed. It's a different one this time with larger, thick, rectangular pages. We scrunch together. Both our laps are required to support its pages once he begins to flip through. We come to the lake, the mountains, the trees and finally his latest. A drawing that looks suspiciously like me from behind watching a single fish curling out of the water in the distance. A small gasp escapes my mouth.

'You like it?' he asks.

'No,' I say. 'I love it. It's beautiful.'

I am looking at the drawing but I can feel Will's eyes on me.

Slowly I raise my eyes to meet his. My face is burning, but he seems as calm as the lake. 'I think you're beautiful,' he says.

No one has ever told me that before; not Mama, not Dad. Nobody.

Will is smiling at me. If his smile had a texture it would be the inside of a down pillow.

Chapter Forty-One

Mama's Child Find mountains are growing and spreading. She doesn't let me in her room now. She's afraid I'll step on a pile and mix up the pages. I don't want to go in there anyway. Aside from the floor space allotted for the door to swing open there isn't a square inch to spare.

Today is a regular day. I study math all morning in my room while listening to the Celine Dion CD Richard brought back from the mission holiday for me. I think he just didn't know what to buy me. At first I thought I wouldn't like it, but now after listening to it a few times it's grown on me. There's something oddly angular to Celine's voice while I calculate equations. I wonder if I could figure out the exact range of notes.

It's not quite eleven a.m. and my stomach is churning. I think of Benjamin and me on the sofa in the pit, Lucy's words, *what if . . . what if . . .*, how Benjamin hasn't given me the time of day since that night. I decide I'm just being paranoid. I must be hungry, that's all, yet the thought of food makes my stomach roll in waves of nausea. When I can't concentrate on numbers any more, five past eleven, I go downstairs to see if Mama has prepared anything for lunch yet. I want to ask her to prepare something light.

But there are no smells of steaming soup, frying eggs, browning toast. There is no food and there is no Mama. I open the fridge and take a good, long look, letting all the cold air out into the room the way Mama hates. I decide I'll try to force down some leftover spaghetti when I hear an odd distant sound like a muffled giggle. I shut the fridge to stifle its hum and listen. It's not long before it comes again, clearer this time. I follow the noise into the hall and what I see there stops me cold, twists my already uneasy stomach into a series of tight knots.

I can't move my legs because it's Mama crouched over on the floor next to the fax machine, which is spitting out pages. Mama's face is hidden by her hand and the paper she's clutching. I can tell she's crying because her body is convulsing and I can hear her short rapid breaths.

'Mama?' I finally say and my own tears instantly fall like someone's pulled a switch. She doesn't look up. The paper in her hand rattles and jerks. It could be the cause of all this. I go to her and kneel in front of her, force her hand down, see her red, streaming eyes.

'Mama, what is it? What happened?' I try to keep the panic I'm feeling out of my voice. My words come out strained and overly friendly. Mama cries harder until she throws her head back and I can only watch in morbid fascination this display of keening lament. I can't recall ever seeing Mama cry like this. Every line in her face is magnified in its twisted strain. I feel detached from my own tears.

I can't think of what to say, what to do. Mama folds into herself, holding her stomach as though her guts may spill out. She rocks like a baby. What's coming out of her mouth are a bunch of *ohohoh*s and quick, deep breaths like she's just run two miles.

I feel the bitter stab of anger. She's scaring me and she had better tell me what's going on. I don't want to begin guessing but I can't help imagining a number of horrid scenarios. Michael's remains have been discovered, Richard has been killed in a motorcycle crash on the highway, someone has sent Mama a horribly cruel letter saying she'll never get Michael back and if she keeps looking they'll kill her. Whatever is in that letter she's vice-gripping I am convinced is the cause of it all. I try to remove it from her hand and to my surprise she releases it. I unravel the crunched wad slowly, immediately recognizing the Child Find logo. Then I read the crumpled, blurry words to myself.

As a result of the highly visible broadcast of The Oprah Winfrey Show *we have received a great many calls, and Child Find would like to inform its members that as of Sunday, September 16th Joey Adams has*

been found and happily reunited with his family.
Thank you all for your support.
    Executive Director, W. Waddel.

    I don't get it. This is good news, isn't it? Yet here's
Mama absolutely heart-wrenchingly bereft.
    I rub Mama's arms. Her sobs slowly diminish. Her
eyes are fixed on the ceiling like she's having a staring
contest with God.
    'It's OK,' I say. 'It's OK, Mama. This is good news.
Good news.'
    More of Mama's tears follow my words but with-
out the whimpers. They just stream silently down her
face and onto her T-shirt, leaving dark-blue spots.
    'I know,' she whispers. 'I know. That's the thing.
That's the whole thing. It *is* good news and yet I don't
feel a scrap of happiness for Joey or his parents
because . . .' The short, quick sobs are back. 'Because
I'm so full of envy I can't feel anything else. I have
become this pathetic, selfish old woman obsessed with
her missing son who hasn't got a shred of love left
in her heart for anyone else.' She takes a deep breath,
releases it loudly.
    'I hate that they found Joey and not Michael. I hate
that he's home right this minute having dinner with his
family, being tucked into bed and Michael's not. But
mostly. . .' Mama looks into my eyes, 'I hate that I
hate it.' She turns away from me.
    'Why not Michael?' She's sobbing again now. 'It's
my turn. Joey's only been missing a few years;

Michael's been gone fourteen. It's my turn. It's my turn.'

'You are not pathetic,' I say gently, trying to bring her back. I'm holding her limp hand. She's looking at the floor but I know she isn't seeing anything any more.

'When are they going to find him? When is he coming home?'

I help Mama stand. She says she wants to lie down, so I help her to her bedroom. She doesn't seem to realize I am struggling to support her weight as we lurch up the stairs. She ploughs through her paper mountains despite my best efforts to guide her around them. She collapses into bed with her clothes on, assumes the foetal position. I shut the door behind me as I leave.

I try to continue with my homework. I think it might take my mind off things but I can't concentrate on the numbers. My stomach continues to churn and all I can see is Mama's face streaming with tears, hear her final words, tinged with doubt.

'When is he coming home?'

They are the saddest words I've ever heard.

Mama is eating listlessly while Richard potters around the kitchen wiping various surfaces and I sit at the table pretending to read my biology text. I can't help but steal glances at her. She seems shrunken, swimming in her white terry-cloth bathrobe. She takes ridiculously small bites of her toast, shuffles bits of hash browns around her plate as though she is setting up a strategic battle between potato and egg. She catches me staring above my book and I smile dumbly.

'I'm OK,' she says, as if that's all there is to say about everything.

I'm OK? What the hell does that mean?

It means, I soon realize, that all the paper floor-mountains have disappeared the next time I look into her bedroom. It means Richard is removing the fax machine from our house. It means Mama begins to refurbish everything in the garage for no particular reason. It means Richard moves in. It means I am hardly ever alone with Mama and when I am she is so far away I can't reach her. It means I can hear her soft sobs curling up the air vent in the middle of the night like a secret, sad poison.

You might be OK, Mama, but I'm not, in more ways than one.

Our living room is ridiculously over-crowded with furniture. Instead of getting rid of Mama's old arm-chair or our beat-up sofa, for some reason they've just crammed Richard's sofa in along the wall where the TV used to be. His matching love seat blocks the entrance to the front door so you have to run an obstacle course just to get to it.

Richard has built a shelf that juts out from the corner of the two walls opposite the window in a triangular shape. The TV sits on it so now we have to strain our necks to watch it. Then there's Mama's refurbished furniture. Pieces have been magically appearing in our house as though they turn into cartoon tables and chairs at night and walk in themselves.

I am not surprised when I smash my toe into the leg of an old-fashioned Singer sewing machine, which as of this morning resides in the upstairs hallway. The worst part is that nobody is talking around here. The things themselves have become the voice. Mama doesn't sit me down and explain that Richard and she are in love and she wants him to move in with us so she can share her life with him. No! The sofa and love seat tell me instead. They say, 'Hello. We're here. Deal with it!'

But I don't want to deal with it. I'm getting tired of dealing with it. I want to deal with my own life. I want to deal with school and impending exams. I want to deal with Benjamin's indifference, Will's tenderness. I need Mama to be Mama again.

When I enter the garage I am struck by the violent smell of Mama's two-part adhesive. I breathe into the sleeve of my sweatshirt and watch as she expertly brushes the glue onto a rectangular wooden frame. She is wearing a surgical mask and a pair of eye goggles. She is oblivious to me standing less than three feet away.

I am so nervous I can feel the pulse in my sleeve. The whole world pounds a native drum and my ears vibrate. I am dizzy with glue and thunder.

I finally blurt a muffled 'Hi,' and she jumps. I didn't mean to scare her.

'Goodness, Bethany. You shouldn't sneak in here like that,' says Mama, talking to my feet.

'Sorry, Mama,' I say. 'Need any help?'

'No, thanks. I'm almost done. I just have to . . .'

'That's what you said last night and you stayed in here until one in the morning.'

Mama stops what she's doing and looks at me for the first time. The paintbrush dangles in her right hand. She lowers her mask with a baby finger. Her goggled eyes make her look like she's just jumped out of an old air bomber.

'I came upon an unexpected problem that couldn't be left,' she explains. I can see her eyelashes flipping nervously behind the plastic lenses.

'Well, what if I had an unexpected problem?' I say. The defiance in my voice surprises even me but I can't stop it.

'I'm growing impatient with you, Bethany. What are you getting at?'

'I'm just wondering when it's all going to end,' I say.

'What are you talking about?'

'I'm talking about you in here every night.'

Mama releases a hearty sigh. 'This is my hobby, Bethany. It also happens to be the way I make a living. I don't hear you complain when we are heading to the checkout counter to pay for a new pair of jeans.'

'So how many orders have you filled lately?'

'That is quite enough, young lady. I can come in this garage all I want.'

'You mean hide in here.' It feels good to speak my mind and scary as hell.

'How are you speaking to me?'

I fiddle sheepishly with some loose screws Mama has left on the plywood counter. 'Better than not speaking at all,' I say under my breath but not low enough.

'I beg your pardon?' Mama lays the gluey paint-brush down on a tin lid, lifts her goggles then places her hands strategically on her hips, her feet planted as firmly as a tree. The battle stance.

I try a diversion tactic. 'I just miss you,' I say.

'Oh, Bethany, don't be ridiculous. I'm right here.'

There is so much I want to say. I want to tell her I love her. I want to tell her I hate her. I want to tell her to look at me, to see me, to stop hiding, to come out of this garage. I want her to abandon her secret and closed world, but I can't say any of it because she turns from me, slams the door of communication between us and picks up her paintbrush. I begin to make my way back to the door but stop just before I get there. She has already refitted the goggles and mask, her face bug-like. She resumes brushing. From this distance I have to yell.

'I need you right now!'

Mama looks up. All I can see are two searching eyes behind small, round windows. Two eyes awaiting an explanation. I give it.

'I'm pregnant,' I say.

Chapter Forty-Two

Finally Mama and I had time to be alone together. So much had happened since that day in the observation room when the first flicker of horror crossed Mama's mind. There was something different about Mama now. She still wore the same pink State Hill smock, still tied her hair in a loose bun the way she always did, but this woman on the edge of the bed had a different flavour about her. She had changed in a good way.

I didn't know what to say. My last words to her had been stinging and hurtful and I didn't know where to begin. Thankfully I didn't have to. It was Mama who spoke first.

'Thank you for helping me through this,' she said. 'I couldn't have come through it without you.'

It was the last thing I had expected her to say. I started to apologize for the day in the observation room, for bringing up old wounds, but she hushed me with an unexpected embrace. She held me for what seemed a long time and when she released me her face was oddly serene.

'I never wanted it to be you,' she said. Her hands held my face as reverently as God might hold the world. 'You are my daughter. And I am so very proud of you.' Then she leaned in and kissed my forehead, a kind of christening.

There was a gentle rap at the door. Mama and I turned. Dr Ashley had signed in a surprise visitor for Mama. Sharon Wetherall and her two children, Amy and Aaron, timidly entered Mama's small room.

I couldn't take my eyes off Aaron, this beautiful fragile boy peering out from under creamy, white lashes at the woman who had saved him.

Some missing children turn up dead, others are never found and a few are saved. Mama had saved one, that much was certain and it seemed more than enough for her to go on with. A rush of pride raced through me as potent as a drug. And as I watched Mama reach for this little boy's hand I knew that she would now be forever free of her demons.

This is a work of fiction inspired by the abduction of Michael Dunahee from a school playground in Victoria, BC, Canada, in 1991. All characters and place names, with the exception of major cities, are fictional.

For thoughts on amnesia and buried anger, I am grateful to Willard Gaylin MD, *The Rage Within: Anger in Modern Life* (New York: Simon & Schuster, 1984).